"I want you." Mia's smile was candy-sweet, but the light in her eyes was pure challenge. "Do you want me?"

Spence would rather take a bullet than hurt her, but he knew a trap when he teetered on the edge of one. Truth or lie, either way he'd be in trouble.

The upside? She didn't wait for his response.

"What do you say? Want to see if we're any good together?"

The downside? Her words were tempting enough to destroy his resistance.

He stared at that gorgeous face, with her full lips tilted in a bold smile and those fairy eyes glowing. Refusal was on the tip of his tongue, then he looked closer. There was just a hint of nerves lurking there, just beneath the desire.

That vulnerability hit him even harder than the desire, melting the rest of his resistance like fire melted wax.

Where was a sniper when he needed one?

* * *

Don't miss *Navy SEAL to the Rescue*, book one in Tawny Weber's thrilling Aegis Security miniseries

* * *

D0019852

Dear Reader,

Woot! I'm so excited to share the second book in the Aegis Security series with you. *Navy SEAL Bodyguard* features Spence Lloyd, a SEAL building a new life after leaving the team, and his first assignment: going undercover to protect the daughter of his commanding officer.

And while Spence is skilled at all things under the covers, working undercover means lying to a woman he's seriously attracted to. This was a fun conflict to write, as was one of the main challenges that Spence and Mia have in common: parental meddling. Aah, parental meddling... Her father, his mother and all those behind-the-scenes attempts to interfere in their adult children's lives. Not that I have any personal experience with that, of course. I enjoyed combining that family vibe while writing these intense characters. As much fun was weaving in the luxurious locations, the fancy charity events and, one of my personal favorite topics, obsessive planning, along with the twisted turns of suspense and betrayal.

I really hope that you enjoy the story and all of these elements. And after *Navy SEAL Bodyguard*, I hope that you'll check out the rest of the Aegis Security series, as well as my other books. I'm looking forward to sharing many more stories with you and can't wait to hear what you think. Feel free to stop by my website, tawnyweber.com, where you can check out my books, subscribe to my newsletter and enjoy lots of romance-addicting fun.

All my best,

Tawny

NAVY SEAL
BODYGUARD

Tawny Weber

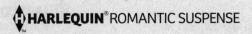

HARLEQUIN® ROMANTIC SUSPENSE

Recycling programs
for this product may
not exist in your area.

ISBN-13: 978-1-335-66203-3

Navy SEAL Bodyguard

Copyright © 2019 by Tawny Weber

This edition published by arrangement with Harlequin Books S.A.

For questions and comments about the quality of this book, please contact us at CustomerService@Harlequin.com.

® and TM are trademarks of Harlequin Enterprises Limited or its corporate affiliates. Trademarks indicated with ® are registered in the United States Patent and Trademark Office, the Canadian Intellectual Property Office and in other countries.

Printed in U.S.A.

TM www.Harlequin.com

Tawny Weber is the *New York Times* and *USA TODAY* bestselling author of more than forty books. She writes sassy, emotional romances with a dash of humor and believes that it all comes down to heroes. In fact, she's made her career writing about heroes, most notably her popular navy SEALs series. Tawny credits her ex-military alpha husband for inspiration in her writing, and in her life. The recipient of numerous writing accolades, including the RT Reviewers' Choice Award, she has also hit number one on the Amazon and Barnes & Noble bestseller lists. A homeschooling mom, Tawny enjoys scrapbooking, gardening and spending time with her family and dogs in her Northern California home.

Visit Tawny on the web at www.tawnyweber.com. You can also find her on Facebook, Twitter, Pinterest and Goodreads.

Facebook.com/TawnyWeber.RomanceAuthor

Twitter.com/TawnyWeber

Pinterest.com/TawnyWeber

Goodreads.com/Author/Show/513828.Tawny_Weber

Books by Tawny Weber

Harlequin Romantic Suspense

Aegis Security

Navy SEAL to the Rescue
Navy SEAL Bodyguard

Harlequin Blaze

Nice & Naughty
Midnight Special
Naughty Christmas Nights

Uniformly Hot!

A SEAL's Seduction
A SEAL's Surrender
A SEAL's Salvation
A SEAL's Kiss
A SEAL's Fantasy
Christmas with a SEAL

A SEAL's Secret
A SEAL's Pleasure
A SEAL's Temptation
A SEAL's Touch
A SEAL's Desire
One Night with a SEAL

HQN Books

Team Poseidon

Night Maneuvers
Call to Honor
Call to Engage
Call to Redemption

In memory of Ismael Ramirez, whose love, support and son I will always treasure.

Prologue

"*Is everything in place?*"

"*It will be. I've got Mia Cade just where I want her. A few more days at the most and she'll be our conduit to Senator Penz.*"

"*Perfect. Penz has no idea what's going to hit him.*"

"*And Mia? When you murder the senator? What'll happen to her?*"

"*Señorita Cade is our—what's the term? Fall guy? First we use her to lure in Penz. Then we eliminate her in a simple murder-suicide. Loose ends are tidied, our enemies are dead and we are avenged.*"

"*Poor Mia won't know what hit her. It just goes to show that it never pays to be a do-gooder.*" *Laughter rang through the phone line, cold and vicious.*

And just a little insane.

Chapter 1

Mia Cade had two goals in life. One, to put as much distance as possible between herself and the manipulation, irritation and, most of all, interference of her family. Two, to help raise millions of dollars for charity.

She figured both goals were a direct product of her upbringing.

She'd spent her formative years as a Navy brat, her family packing up every couple of years to relocate to a new place in the world. With every move, Mia's older sister, Megan, threw another fit about leaving her friends, and her younger sister developed some new ailment that ensured their mother's full attention. Leaving Mia to organize and handle the details of unpacking and getting the family settled in their new home.

Their mother toured them through every new city or country, ensuring that they saw the good and the bad.

The rich and the poor. Her purpose was to instill appreciation in her children, along with as much culture as possible.

In London, they'd visited Buckingham Palace, watched *Macbeth* onstage at the Royal Opera House and organized a Fill Your Boots charity campaign, collecting money on base for the Royal National Lifeboat Institute.

In Shanghai, they'd prayed in the Jade Buddha Temple, toured the Shanghai Museum and spent a few hours a week reading to disabled orphans.

Megan had gotten in trouble for shoplifting in London, had a screaming match with their mother in the Louvre and had tried to run away in Tibet. Marley, on the other hand, developed migraines in Virginia, violent allergies in Tokyo and pneumonia in Alaska. And so it went in Honolulu, Bahrain, Venice and New York. Every new station was a sea of unfamiliar faces, cultural education and charitable works, combined with high drama, hospital visits and Mia desperately trying to organize her life into some semblance of sanity.

By the time she'd finished college, she'd seen enough of the world to know she wanted to stay as far away from travel and her family as possible.

She'd chosen San Francisco.

All the way across the country from them.

Too far away for drop-in visits. Yet no distance was too far from nagging phone calls.

"Mia, you should listen to your sister. She warned you about that girl."

"Jessica is my roommate and she's twenty-six, Mother. A year older than me. It's okay to call us women now."

"Girl. Woman." Her mother pshawed. "You'll always be my baby."

God help her.

"But that isn't the point. Your sister's concerns are the point. I told you, she thinks this Jessica girl is mean and nasty and vindictive. She's a bad influence, a backstabber and someone who surely has it in for you."

"Because I was crowned homecoming queen instead of her? Mom, that's ridiculous."

"Don't forget that you were valedictorian, too. Marley said this girl holds grudges. There's no way she forgot that you swept into that school and knocked her right off the pedestal."

And off she went, in the style only Anne Cade could. Ranting with half facts, high drama and a heaping helping of guilt. Mia let the words roll over her while she went back to searching for a way to fit an extra fifty seats into a dining room for the upcoming charity ball. She'd managed to squeeze in thirty by the time her mother wound down.

"Look, Jessica is fine. She's nice. She's safe. She has a good job. She pays rent, helps with the bills. She's not luring me into bars or doing drugs. No wild parties, no illicit affairs, no disreputable men."

And just like that, her mother turned on a dime.

"You could do with meeting some men, Mia. You're a good-looking girl, smart and fun, and your table manners are exquisite."

"Can't forget those table manners."

"Speaking of, I know the perfect man for you. He's good-looking, six foot six and very clever with languages. He fixed my computer last week. Remember the trouble I was having with it? It's so handy to have a man around who can fix things, don't you think? And didn't you say you needed a new computer?"

Not enough to want a man to go with it.

"What's his rank?"

"Petty officer," her mother replied, biting off the last word in obvious frustration. "Now don't be silly, Mia. Your bias against military men is ridiculous. Are you going to throw away the opportunity to meet the perfect man just because he serves his country?"

In a heartbeat.

"I don't have time for dating, Mother," Mia side-stepped, knowing her perfectly justified arguments always fell on deaf ears. "I'm super busy with work. And speaking of—"

"Fine, fine. If you want to refuse to meet the perfect man, that's your choice. That's not why I called, any-way," her mother said dismissively. "Your uncle will be in town later this month, meeting with donors and at-tending a climate change event. I can count on you to be a proper hostess, can't I? Show him around, keep him company?"

Of course she'd take care of her uncle, US Senator Luis Penz, who'd spent as many years in California as she'd been alive, show him around and keep the poor, bored-with-nothing-to-do man company.

A part of her wanted to offer that sarcastic thought aloud. To point out that she was an independent adult, a professional with a good head on her shoulders, solid social skills and a strong sense of responsibility.

But that wouldn't stop the nagging interference. It'd only irritate her mother into bringing in backups, usu-ally in the form of Mia's siblings. Or worse, her father.

So she kept her thoughts to herself, settling for a roll of her eyes and an innocuous, "Of course, Mother."

"As you can see, it's poor timing for you to have that woman living with you."

"It's not like Uncle Luis would stay in my apartment, Mom. There's not enough room for his suits." To say nothing of his security detail.

"I don't want him meeting this woman, Mia. She's bad news."

"Because she lost the homecoming crown?"

"No," her mother snapped. "Because she works for a criminal."

Mia grimaced. "Actually, she works for a businessman. Santiago Alcosta is totally on the up-and-up, Mom." Not an idiot, Mia had researched the man as soon as she heard who Jessica worked for. "He's built his business in real estate, and Alcosta International is above reproach. Sure, he has a few family members who got in trouble, but who doesn't? Your own sister was arrested last month."

"A few family members? His father was considered a drug lord. His brother was arrested for smuggling. Mia, your Aunt Phoebe shoplifts cat toys to donate to the local shelters."

But Alcosta wasn't his father or brother, Mia wanted to point out. And being a smart businesswoman, she had done her due diligence. Not only had she done a standard background check on the man, she'd asked around. She'd used her resources, she'd checked with other event coordinators, with her social contacts and best of all, she'd grilled her roommate. As the man's personal assistant, Jessica was a font of information. She'd not only filled Mia in on Alcosta's preferences and tastes as it applied to possible events, she'd discussed his work habits, his feelings about his criminal relatives and his hopes for helping others.

But Mia knew, just like any protests she made pointing out her own independence and maturity, the words would fall on deaf ears.

So before her mother could launch into one of her lectures on the depth of family roots, Mia changed the subject. "I have to go now. I've got a lot of work to do. Why don't you call Megan? I heard she's having the twins tested for ADD."

"ADD?" Anne snapped. "They're not even a year old yet."

"I know, right." And with that, Mia sicced her mother on her sister and ended the call with a grin.

The key to winning a battle, her father always said, was knowing the enemy's weakness. In her mother's case, that weakness was a chance to boss people around.

Yet another reason for putting a country between them. A great choice, she decided yet again, resting her elbow on the table to support her chin as she stared out the wide plate-glass window of her apartment at the misty view of the Golden Gate Bridge.

She loved it here—the weather, the people, the variety of things to do and, most of all, the generous altruism of the charitable community. It was an event coordinator's dream. The Bay Area—and Northern California, in general—was home to some of the wealthiest people in the country, many of whom loved to give back. To their community. To the needy. To research, to civil servants, to causes, and to people and charities.

That's where Mia came in.

All those years with her family made her especially

aware of how much need there was in the world and how impossible it would be for her to fix it all by herself.

So she'd turned her organizational skills, people savvy and gift for smoothing the waters, combined with her bent for out-of-the-box thinking, into a career as a premier freelance event coordinator, serving some of the top international charities in the country.

And she was kicking butt.

Okay, she thought, looking at the files stacked like walls around her laptop, which was sitting on the kitchen table, maybe she wasn't quite kicking butt *yet*. But after three years, she was definitely getting closer. Was there any such thing as nudging butt?

But a little more time building her reputation and event portfolio, a few more big clients on retainer, and a handful of successful, high-dollar fund-raisers, and she'd be there, dues paid, success in hand.

Before she could pay those dues, she had to pay the bills. Mia sighed, looking at the tallest stack on her desk. So, so many bills.

Okay. So maybe she was struggling a little financially, but she hadn't chosen this career to get rich. And sure, she'd had to give up her tiny office and take in a roommate to help make ends meet, but that made her resourceful. And yes, she'd chosen to settle in one of the most expensive cities in the country, but she knew if she could make it here, she could make it anywhere.

So she focused on that.

She had a few other events coming up this month to handle, as well: a local ladies' club holding a tea party to raise funds for a veterans' memorial, a high school jamboree focused on building a new football field and an author event raising money for literacy.

She'd just lifted her cell phone to start those calls when it chimed in her hand.

Forever Families, the readout said. Mia's biggest client to date, and her biggest challenge. Not in terms of her ability to handle things—she knew the organization so well, she could plan its events with her eyes closed—but because the director was incredibly determined to hire. And as appealing as regular hours, reliable paychecks and health care sounded, Mia was determined to make it on her own.

To prove that she could.

But Lorraine Perkins didn't like to hear the word *no*.

The wife of one of the biggest real estate developers in the state of California, Lorraine was a social maven and one of the best-connected women Mia had ever met.

"Mia, darling, I'm just checking on the progress of our gala," Lorraine said in those rounded tones only the wealthy seemed to pull off. "Not that I doubt for a second that you have it all well in hand."

Of course she didn't. Four phone calls a day was a sign of absolute faith. Mia silently waited for Lorraine to continue.

"As you know," and she did know because Lorraine had insisted on mentioning it in each of those four daily calls, "if this weekend's fund-raising goals are met, there's a good chance that I'd put you in charge of our Winter Ball."

The Winter Ball. Mia's holy grail. A luxurious, complicated, multifaceted event spanning ten days, necessitating clever and innovative fund-raising techniques, savvy organizational skills, and, if rumor was true, the ability to juggle fire, water and ice all at the same time.

She knew this weekend's event was the last in a series of what were essentially interviews testing her abilities. She knew, too, that Lorraine would rather handle the event in-house than bring in an outside coordinator.

But if Mia impressed her enough, she'd get the contract, she'd continue to freelance and she'd be able to bill herself as one of the top charitable-event coordinators in the country.

Best of all, she'd have done it all on her own.

"We'll meet that goal," Mia vowed. "Actually, things will be so amazing that I'll bet we surpass it."

"Oh, Mia, you're such an optimist. But if anyone can do it, I'm starting to think you could." Before Mia could revel in that compliment, Lorraine's friendly tone turned pure business. "Now, you got my note about adding another fifty seats to the dinner, yes? Where are you at with that?"

"I've already spoken with catering and the location staff. The florist will add two more bouquets to the table," Mia said, running her finger down her list as she recited check-marked items. "Because we're losing square footage, the string trio will set up on the balcony just outside the ballroom."

As she continued to recite her progress, she made a quick mental note to add extra space heaters to that balcony. Even though it was summer, evenings in San Francisco could get chilly.

"Perfect. It sounds as if you have a solid handle on it all. You're one of the best planners in the Bay Area. And speaking of, I heard a rumor," Lorraine said, her voice dropping with hushed excitement. "A wonderful, too-good-to-be-true rumor."

"What'd you hear?" Mia scooted into a more comfy position in her chair and smiled, ready for some fun.

She'd discovered the only thing the wealthy loved more than seeing their names written next to the word *altruistic* and the promise of tax deductions was gossip.

"It's come to my attention that a certain young lady we both know and love has hidden connections."

Oh, no. Mia cringed. Lorraine had been nagging her to convince her uncle to one of her events, claiming he'd be a huge draw. But before Mia could think of the right excuse, Lorraine continued in an giddy rush, "International real-estate connections, ones with very deep pockets."

Mia frowned. It didn't sound like Lorraine was describing Senator Penz. Thankfully the woman kept dropping those juicy hints.

"This connection is, as I hear it, very distinguished, cosmopolitan and charming. A man who rose above his juicy, scandalous family. In other words, just the kind of guest to add such a delicious panache to my ball."

Ahhh.

Not her uncle. Mia was torn between relief and frustration as she realized whom Lorraine meant.

"Santiago Acosta?" Why was everyone bringing up Alcosta today? "I'm not sure he'd be available at such short notice. I do know a number of other people we could invite, though. Dignitaries, celebrities, even politicians."

"No, no, no. It has to be Alcosta. Everybody has been talking about him at the club, but he's not taking invitations. He even turned down the Grangers."

He did? The Grangers counted a congressman, a US diplomat and a Tony winner among their numbers. They were a group high on Mia's event-organizing wish list.

"But if I could put word out that Alcosta is attending

the gala, attendance will go through the roof. And by attendance, I mean donations, of course."

"Of course." Mia blew out a breath. "Let me see what I can do."

"I knew I could count on you, Mia. You are so efficient and dependable. Your association with influential people like Alcosta does carry a lot of weight in considering you for my biggest events," Lorraine declared before saying goodbye.

Mia hung up with a sigh.

To pull off getting a man like Alcosta on board—to say nothing of getting the man's business—meant doing something Mia abhorred. Something she'd vowed to avoid at all costs.

Using a friend.

Her family was big on offering help and opinions, and thanks to years of military service all over the world, it had tons of connections. All of which she'd availed herself of when she'd started out.

But her brother-in-law's bookkeeper pal had garnered her penalties by forgetting to file quarterly taxes. Her sister's BFF snuck a strip show into a simple fund-raiser for firefighters. And her parents' start-up loan offer had come with so many strings, Mia would have owed them 50 percent of her profits, along with her firstborn, before she'd have been able to untangle the mess.

Half the setbacks and problems she'd had with her business were thanks to her family's "help." Which was just one of the reasons why Mia now insisted on doing it all on her own. She'd even refused her uncle's offer to bring her onto his senatorial staff for a year so she could garner government creds, something that might have gone a long way toward making her job easier.

For Mia, asking for favors for charity was simple. But asking for personal ones was akin to being poked in the eye with a burning stick, since no personal favor came without a few sticky strings.

The trick was going to be asking Jessica for help without making it obvious that she needed it.

"Why the long face?"

Speak of the devil.

Jessica Alexander posed in the doorway. The petite, curvaceous blonde looked like a cross between a china doll and a centerfold.

Mia shot a fast glance at the clock in the corner of her computer screen to make sure she hadn't lost a few hours. Nope, only one o'clock in the afternoon.

But like Mia, Jessica didn't have normal work hours. As an administrative assistant to Señor Alcosta, some days her roommate was home at five o'clock, some she waltzed in at two o'clock in the afternoon and others still she swept out at nine o'clock at night, wearing evening wear.

Their work schedules—or lack thereof—was pretty much the end of the similarity between the two women.

Despite measuring in at a lean five foot ten, Mia knew her sharp features gave her the look of a fairy. She wore her ebony hair in a pixie cut, the long bangs sweeping in a curve over eyes the color of bittersweet chocolate. She leaned toward textured fabrics, rich colors and avant-garde jewelry.

Jessica, on the other hand, was petite and built with enviously lush curves. She accented her fluff of blond curls, cornflower-blue eyes and a Cupid's bow mouth with delicate fabrics in pastels and lace, skyscraper heels, and—in her only departure from her baby-doll style—flashy diamonds.

They were complete opposites in every other way, too. Mia was quiet. Jessica was flirtatious. Mia had cut her teeth on diplomacy. Jessica thrived on excitement. Mia was an introvert who loved nothing better than peace and quiet; Jessica was an extrovert who needed crowds and noise and attention. Jessica reveled in a secret love affair, sharing every detail—*every* detail—but the man's name, while Mia had no more interest in a relationship than she had in dancing naked over hot coals.

And yet somehow they'd become friends. And despite Mia's family's concerns, she thought Jessica was good for her. The other woman brought spice and energy and excitement into her life, something she hadn't realized was missing until she and Jessica had run into each other on the street two months ago.

It'd been the first the women had seen of each other since they'd attended the same boarding school. She'd been surprised Jessica even remembered, let alone recognized, her. But Jessica had swept her into a hug, taken her to lunch and—as soon as she'd found out Mia had a two-bedroom apartment—begged to move in for a few months.

"I thought you were working today," she said as Jessica leaned one arm against the doorframe and propped the other on her tiny waist.

"I decide to take a half day," Jessica said in a husky voice that made men melt. "Fridays should always be half days, don't you think? Besides, I have a date tonight."

Jessica hadn't lived here long, but Mia knew from experience that a date night meant spa time, a Victoria's

Secret binge and a juicy morning-after story hot enough to singe Mia's imagination.

What must it be like to have that kind of love life? Mia wondered. Incendiary passion, breathtaking excitement. Heck, she'd take enduring interest, something she'd yet to have with a man, much to her mother's disgust.

"You didn't answer my question." At Mia's frown, Jessica added, "Why the long face?"

Mia thought of Lorraine's mandate that she get Santiago Alcosta to attend the gala. The best way to get something done was straight out, her father always said. Just do it, find it or ask for it.

She opened her mouth to do just that.

"Just thinking about the business of, well, my business," Mia heard herself saying instead. "I have three smaller events this week to deal with, plus the gala next weekend, and I still need to find an assistant."

Preferably an assistant who thought raising funds for charity itself was an ample paycheck.

"I can help you out," Jessica offered, crossing the kitchen to start pulling out ingredients. "I've got a little extra time on my hands after tonight. My hottie is heading out of town for a week, so I'd love a project to keep me busy."

A week of free help?

"What about your job?"

"I'm sure I can work it out," Jessica said, flashing her most engaging smile. "Ready for your favorite matcha mocha latte?"

Mia hesitated.

Not over the latte. That, she wanted.

It was a favor she wasn't so sure of.

"I appreciate the offer…"

"I'll take care of any research, handle vendors, pay the bills and organize your database," Jessica assured her, starting to work on her caffeine creations.

As the scent of coffee filled the air, Mia pictured Jessica's room, with clothes thrown over furniture, a vanity table splotched with spilled makeup and shoes dumped in piles in the closet. And the papers. Papers were stacked, piled, spread and wadded everywhere.

Mia placed a protective hand on the files next to her.

"I appreciate the offer. I really do. But that's not really—"

"I'll even handle finding someone to help you at events to replace that gal. What was her name? The one who kept breaking things? Your computer, that case of glassware, her leg."

"Bree was my coordination assistant," Mia murmured. "And she was just a little accident-prone."

"Right. Coordination assistant. I'll find you one." Jessica began pouring ingredients into the blender. "You won't have to worry about anything."

"But—"

"I know how you are about taking help with the business end of things, but I promise, I know what I'm doing," Jessica said, setting two tall glass mugs on the table, each frothed high with whipped cream and a delicate layer of almond dust. "It's not like I'd screw things up for you."

"Of course I don't think that," Mia denied half-heartedly, wrapping both hands around the mug to inhale the rich blend of scents to buy a few seconds. "But I've already put a call into Karen Lawson. She coordinates volunteers for a number of charities. I've worked with her before and am sure she'll be sending someone my way soon."

"Maybe she will, maybe she won't. You don't want to depend on a maybe," Jessica said, reaching into a slender pocket in her silk suit to pull out a business card. She set it on the table amidst Mia's piles of folders and stacks of files, and using one pink nail, pushed it forward. "Not when you're going to be really busy since I just snagged you a dream event."

"A dream event?" Curious, Mia lifted the card.

Unsurprised, she read the name Santiago Alcosta, embossed in glossy black ink on heavy white card stock, with the entire card framed by a slender gold line. Elegant, understated decadence, she decided. That'd be the theme she'd pitch to go with these cards.

"Tell me more about this dream event," she invited, wondering how to parlay what was probably a corporate luncheon into a chance to personally invite Alcosta to the Forever Families gala.

"I showed one of your fund-raiser pitches to my boss this morning, and Señor Alcosta is not only excited—he's ready to rock and roll. There are some conditions," Jessica continued before Mia could ask how she'd gotten her hands on one of Mia's fund-raiser pitches. "You know, I told you how picky he can be. Lunch at twelve-twelve every day. At every meeting, people have to be seated in alphabetical order. The scent of the flowers can never overpower the scent of the food. That kind of thing. I'm not kidding when I say that Alcosta is seriously particular."

Mia flipped the page of her notebook to write that all down.

"What are you doing?"

Mia glanced up.

"Making notes for the event. A luncheon?"

"Luncheon?" Jessica laughed. "Oh, no. Bigger than that. He wants to build a new children's hospital in Mexico City and he wants you to handle a series of events to raise the funds."

"A series of…"

"Yeah, a whole bunch of events. Like a half dozen whatever it takes to raise twenty million. I think that's what he's estimating it'll take to get started."

Twenty-million worth of events? Holy bananas.

So many thoughts bounced through Mia's brain. Images of all the children who'd be helped by a new hospital. The thought of the benefits of health care for thousands. And, hoo baby, multiple events, wow, the benefits to her business. If Mia had a contract like that, after Lorraine Perkins was done doing backflips, she'd hand over the Winter Ball on a golden platter. Carte blanche. No nagging, no micromanaging, no peering over Mia's shoulder, no deep sighs over preferring to keep the job in-house.

"What does he need? I should meet with him. Do I call him directly, or is that something I set up with you?" Mia flipped to a fresh page in her notebook. "Do you know if he has preferences already in place? Is he open to suggestions? Will you handle carrying through the arrangements once the plans are made, or will that be my responsibility? Knowing that ahead of time will help with my bid."

"Bid?" Jessica waved that away with a flick of her baby-doll-pink fingernails. "You don't have to bid, Mia. The job is already yours."

"Mine? Just like that?"

"Oh, but he's not looking at any other event planners. The job's yours if you want it. I mean, you'll have to create an outline of your plans for Alcosta's approval, of course, and adhere to his wishes and rules. And there is a wee little time crunch involved. But after the way I've talked you up, I'm sure you'll get the contract."

Oh. My.

Mia bit back the urge to get up and dance.

Twenty million. A children's hospital. A half dozen events. All hers.

While Jessica organized her files.

Mia's urge to dance froze.

Before she could voice her concerns, Jessica made a show of grimacing.

"Um, look. It's no big deal," Jessica said, her tone making it clear that it was actually a huge deal. "But I sort of put myself on the line here. You know, promised all sorts of great things about your work. That you'd take the job. That you'd do fabulous. That you were the best in the business. Stuff like that. So I'm counting on you. I'd hate for Alcosta to start thinking he can't trust my judgment."

Mia blinked, the weight of Jessica's words coating her doubts with a hefty layer of guilt.

"I'll get a hold of Alcosta and let him know how excited you are." Jessica grabbed her cell phone and started typing. "You get a proposal together. I'll set up the meeting. Just leave me a list of what you need done."

And with that, Mia was alone in the kitchen with her gorgeous view and the opportunity of a lifetime. Then she glanced down with a sigh at a nagging text from her mother.

By the time Mia had finished reading message eight of nine, she was sure of two things.

One, she was definitely going after the Alcosta job.

And two, no matter how old she was, her parents were going to drive her crazy.

His mother was driving him crazy.

A woman he'd dated a grand total of three time was stalking him.

His career was over.

A year ago, Spencer Lloyd had been on top of the world. Cryptographer, lieutenant and Navy SEAL, he'd known no other way to live but to the fullest.

One bomb explosion later, his vision was impaired just enough to put him out of the SEALs, his career was over and he was living life on the edge.

The edge of sanity, that was.

Getting out of hot spots used to be Spence Lloyd's forte.

The hotter, the better.

He'd once spent three weeks as a well-tortured guest of terrorists before engineering an escape for himself and six others, leading the way on a leg broken in four places.

He'd parachuted through heavy gunfire to take out enemy munitions before they destroyed a small city.

He'd helped rescue a kidnapped politician from a high-level prison, taking out multiple targets in the process.

Lieutenant Spencer Lloyd, former Navy SEAL and all-round fearless guy, had faced it all with confidence and equanimity.

But now, sitting in his superior officer's office on

the Coronado Naval Base for what was quite likely the last time, Spence wondered what he'd got himself into.

"Could you repeat that order, sir?"

A scowl between his bushy brows, Admiral Theodore Cade said, "Lieutenant, I need your help with my daughter."

Yeah. That's what Spence thought he'd said.

"Sir, you're aware that I'm in the middle of out-processing."

Leaving the military. Ending life as he knew—and loved—it. The Navy might accept an officer with compromised vision, but the SEALs could not. Better to leave with his dignity and his trident intact, he'd decided, than to be demoted off the team.

"The fact that you're transitioning into civilian life is the reason you've been chosen for this mission, Lloyd."

This must be a personal issue rather than a military issue, Spence realized.

"I'm breaking protocol by informing you of the benefits before I give you the details of this mission."

"Sir, I have no expectation of benefits or recompense for a favor."

"Which is why I'm making the offer. That, and because your talents, skills and expertise make you the right man for the job."

His abilities as a SEAL? As a cryptographer? Spence banished the questions from his head. He'd know soon enough, so forming any ideas beforehand would be a waste of time and energy.

"It's come to my attention that the position you're taking upon your release from the Navy is not as opportune as it seemed."

That was one way to put it. A huge disappointment

would be another. There weren't a bevy of challenging jobs here in the San Diego area that called for the skills of a former SEAL. And obviously Cade knew that already.

"In light of that, and in return for the personal favor I'll detail, I'm offering you an opportunity, a shot at a future where you utilize the talents and training the finest military experience in the world taught you. An opportunity to employ those skills in civilian life."

Was he going to sprinkle it with fairy dust and throw in a unicorn that did dishes, too?

"How?" Spence managed.

"A former SEAL of my acquaintance has started a premier security firm. This firm consists exclusively of former Special Ops personnel and handles the types of cases that require military expertise but the government finds itself unable to be involved with."

Spence had a sudden vision of that dishwashing unicorn doing his laundry, too.

"It sounds like an excellent opportunity," he said. "It also sounds, as you said yourself, exclusive. To offer that level of service, Special Ops won't be enough. It'll require a handpicked team."

A handpicked team he'd do anything but kill to be a part of. Spence had experienced the sensations often enough before ops and missions to recognize the tingle down his spine, the tightness in his gut. Excitement. Anticipation. And a bone-deep surety that this was something he'd kick ass at.

"I am serving as a liaison between the military, the government and the head of the newly established Aegis Security. As such, my recommendation will carry weight."

In other words, Cade was his golden ticket to the civilian career of his dreams.

"What do you need me to do?"

Spence would have made the offer even without the once-in-a-lifetime incentive, a fact that Cade knew perfectly well. His men were trained to do anything and everything asked of them. That was duty. But Spence was also acknowledging his acceptance of the confidential nature of the mission.

"It's come to my wife's, and therefore my, attention that our daughter is in a dangerous position. To be honest, I first considered Anne's concerns to be motherly overprotectiveness. But the key to a successful marriage is compromise. So despite my thoughts on the matter, I gave in to her request that I use my resources to access nonclassified information on an individual who's come into Mia's life. That research has led me to believe that my wife's instincts are accurate."

Cade lifted a manila file from his desk, hesitated, then held it out. Taking it, Spence continued to watch his commander.

Whatever was in the file was backup and details for later.

For now, he waited for his orders.

"I've already given orders to expedite your out-processing clearances. Details, such as lodging, transport, etc., are in this file." Cade handed over the file with the admonishment, "Keep in mind, this is a covert operation. You'll need to fit into the environment convincingly in order to secure your objective."

"And the objective is?"

"Gain my daughter's trust, keep her safe and end her association—on all levels—with Santiago Alcosta, while ensuring that her reputation is not damaged and her business not impacted. There is an event being held in San Francisco in three days. Your mission starts there."

"How deep is my cover?"

"Use your own name and whatever personal history you feel is necessary to make your role convincing. Your rank, your time in the military and your connection to me are all classified."

Maybe it was his near-civilian status, but Spence heard himself ask, "You're ordering me to lie to the target? To your daughter?"

Like any commanding officer giving a morally questionable order, Cade didn't even blink.

"Affirmative. This mission is and will remain classified. Standard protocols." Cade gestured to the door. "You have your orders. I expect them to be carried out, Lieutenant."

Chapter 2

All the best missions included careful planning, the right equipment, good weapons and the potential for danger.

This, sadly, was not one of those.

It'd taken him three days to prepare. Travel and arranging to stay at a buddy's apartment in San Francisco had been easy enough. Negotiating a concealed weapons permit as a civilian had necessitated pulling a lot of strings, and getting his hands on the main equipment the admiral ordered—a fitted tuxedo—had taken even longer.

As far as the potential for danger went, after reading through the file and then doing the basic research any covert op required, Spence had come to the conclusion that while Alcosta came from so much dirt and the man was filthy by association, Alcosta's own business practices were on the up-and-up. Since plenty of government agencies had reached the same conclusion, he was pretty sure that this mission was on par with a babysitting job.

A babysitting job that paid really well, Spence reminded himself. Besides, if he scored a position with Aegis, providing personal security would quite likely be part of the work description. Hopefully for high-level politicians, notable scientists and other high-risk VIPs, instead of his former commanding officer's do-gooder daughter.

But an assignment was an assignment, he reminded himself as he strode down the hallway toward the ballroom, his motorcycle boots echoing with each step.

The only problem was, in the week since receiving the admiral's orders, he hadn't quite nailed down the specifics of infiltrating the daughter's world. Maybe something with security. He'd figure it out once he'd assessed the situation. He hadn't earned the call sign Improv for nothing.

With no plan more solid than making contact, Spence stepped into the sun-drenched ballroom, watching people scramble around like confused ants, arms filled with linens, peacock feathers and, for some weird reason, paintbrushes.

"Mia, half the tablecloths are missing."

Spence looked around for his objective. Mia Cade.

According to the file, she was a willowy five-ten. Admiral Cade hadn't included a photo, so Spence found himself searching for a thinner version of the admiral.

But there didn't seem to be any white-haired, heavy-jowled women striding through the ballroom, with hands clasped behind their back while scowling at the workers scurrying around.

He did see a very tempting backside, though.

Her long, bare neck emphasized delicate shoulders and a slender back, wrapped in a vivid green tunic that draped over the sweet, tight curves of her butt encased in black leggings. He couldn't be sure of her actual height since her knee-high boots had heels, but he'd put it close to five-ten.

She was either the target or the woman he'd be making breakfast for.

He angled to the left, wanting a better look.

"Excuse me."

Spence shifted to one side to let a four-foot urn of flowers with legs pass.

Spence gave an appreciative hum when the sexy woman bent over to lift a cardboard box. Damned if that position didn't give him a few intriguing ideas. His smile spread as he wondered if she'd do it again, to music.

His mind added a bluesy beat while he watched the woman's backside as she handed the box off to a curly-haired blonde wearing a walkie-talkie and hoped like hell the sexy rear view didn't belong to Cade's daughter.

If luck was with him, the woman with the sexy backside had nothing to do with Mia Cade. Instead, he'd make contact with the target, she'd mention how cool it'd be to have a little security help and hire him, then introduce her sexy, dancing assistant, who'd want him working with her side by side.

Yeah. Spence could see that happening.

"Mia, the crystal is here but the cutlery is missing. Three waiters have called out sick and the, um, cellist? Is that what that says?" Tucking the box under one arm, the blonde held out a note. "Cellist? That's the big violin, right? The sad-sounding thing?"

Damn. The sexy view was Mia Cade. Lust punctured like a dart in a balloon.

The last time he'd had luck like this, he'd lost his night vision.

"Dude, you're right in the line of traffic."

While Spence sidestepped the man wheeling in a dozen cases of wine on a dolly, his fantasy hurried off, leaving the blonde with a box anchored under one arm and a clipboard in the other.

Disappointment piercing his gut like a piece of shrapnel, Spence lasered in on the blonde, figuring her as his best in with his target.

"Excuse me."

The blonde glanced up from the clipboard and pursed her lips as she got a good look at him. Brows arching, she gave a flirtatious flutter of her lashes.

"What can I do for you?" she purred. "I'm willing to do anything. Anything at all."

"I'd like to speak with the lady in charge."

The blonde stopped fluttering.

"You want Mia?" she asked, giving him a suspicious once-over. "Why?"

"I just need a second to talk with her. Why don't I help you with that?" He gestured to the box.

"You're here to help? Mia said Karen might send someone over. Great." Practically tossing the box his way, the blonde gestured with her clipboard. "The way Mia organizes things, these events are usually a walk in the park. But I'll be impressed if she manages to pull this one off."

Someone yelled. Spence glanced over as the guy ran his dolly through the puddle of broken glass, mangled flowers and splattered water. He arched a brow when the florist scooped up a handful of bruised posies and whacked the other man with them.

"Things do look a little disorganized."

"Mia's usually on top of everything. She has a reputation as the queen of organized. But this is a mondo major event and her latest assistant flaked." The blonde winced when the dolly guy pushed back. "This one only lasted three days—go figure. You'd think a person could handle a little constructive criticism while they're learning the ropes of a new job, right?"

"You'd think," Spence agreed, following her gesture to the small side room already piled high with boxes, and adding his to the stack the blonde gestured toward. "So, what's the problem?"

"The assistant couldn't handle a few accidents and mix-ups."

"What kind of accidents?"

"Nothing big. One time the ninny forgot to set the emergency brake on Mia's van and it rolled down a hill into a street sign. She sprained her shoulder when a stack of boxes fell on her in the storeroom. Once she slipped on ice in Mia's kitchen, landed on her butt while screaming her head off." The blonde rolled her eyes as if screaming was a stupid way to deal with a fall. "Throw in a minor bout of food poisoning, a broken stair rail and a minor electrical shock, and the gal claimed the job was jinxed."

"That's a lot of accidents," Spence agreed. "This was over what period of time?"

A month? Three?

"Six days."

"All of that happened in less than a week?" Spence stopped in his tracks. "Did this woman experience all of these *accidents* when she was with Mia?"

"Mia wasn't always there. But sure, Roxie was on the clock when they happened." The blonde gestured for Spence to move out of the storeroom. "Mia even offered hazard pay until this event was over. But no. Despite the fact that Mia has a huge event and a major client on the line, the woman was too much of a weenie to even try."

"Is that so?" Glancing around the makings of the huge event, Spence wondered if Alcosta was the major client.

"It is definitely so." With a roll of her eyes, she gestured for Spence to follow her as she skirted around the people mopping up water and mangled flowers. "You look like a talented guy, though. I'm sure that you can handle it."

He looked around the ballroom, noting the multitude of issues dripping off tables, spilling across the floor and arguing on the carpeted dais.

"I've handled worse." Figuring she could give him the ins and outs of the job, he offered up a friendly smile. "You seem to know a lot about the position and it's requirements. Do you work for Mia, too?"

"Nope. I'm Clair. I'm Mrs. Perkins' assistant. She's the head of the Forever Families Foundation. She hires Mia to coordinate events like this one. Turns out, Mia's great at finding ways to get rich people to dig deeper and donate more."

"Speaking of Ms. Cade, any idea where I might find her?"

The blonde gave him another strip-you-naked once-over before gesturing toward a narrow hallway.

"She's fighting with the chef over tonight's meal."

"Fighting? Sounds dangerous," he murmured. "I'll go do what I can to make sure she wins."

He headed for what he assumed was the kitchen, but

not before he heard the blonde murmur, "Mmm, I like the way you think."

Figuring he had a solid handle on both the job itself and the lay of the land, Spence formulated the rest of his cover as he strode into the kitchen. He'd thought the ballroom was chaos, but it had nothing on the bedlam that was the stainless steel monstrosity of a kitchen.

White-clad workers scurried through the cavernous space like confused ants, many of them cowering each time the bulbous man in the center of the room bellowed orders and insults.

Yet over the babbling, bellowing and other kitchen noises, one voice caught his attention. Intrigued by the husky tone, it took a few seconds for the words to sink in.

"I'm so glad you'll be joining us. Of course I'll save you a dance, Señor Alcosta." She paused just long enough for Spence to slip farther into the room. "Yes, absolutely. I'd be happy to meet with you Monday at noon. Your offices? Sounds great."

Looked like the intel was right.

Spence had never once questioned orders, but he'd figured the admiral was overestimating the seriousness if this particular mission.

But now, given the list of accidents Mia Cade had nearly missed, and that she was definitely in contact with Alcosta, Spence decided those orders might be a little more serious than he'd thought. Prepared to report for duty, Spence strode into the kitchen. His friendly smile froze when he saw the woman pacing, phone in hand, in front of the walk-in freezer.

Damn.

She was even better looking from the front.

Her features were both delicate and sharp, in a triangular face dominated by huge amber eyes, lushly lashed and tilted at the corners. Knife's-edge cheekbones seemed to point toward a wide mouth currently cajoling the chef with a creative litany of threats, praise and bribes.

Hair so black it reflected the overhead lights was cut almost as short as his but for a long sweep of bangs that swept across one arched eyebrow, curving nearly to her chin.

The front of the tunic crossed in front to gather at her hip, accenting her willowy figure. Throw in that husky voice that made even the mundane argument about lobster presentation sound sexy, and he was pretty sure she was the most tempting woman he'd ever encountered.

This was Cade's daughter?

Damn, Spence thought again, this time in pure appreciation. He'd give a lot to get a good look at Mrs. Cade.

Even as he thought that, the woman ended her call, slipped her phone into her pocket and gave the chef a friendly smile.

"Now, as we were saying…"

And they were off, arguing over something to do with lobster, arugula and risotto. He watched as, obviously losing the verbal disagreement, the chef opted for physical intimidation. They were about the same height, but the chef had a good two hundred pounds on her, so Spence quickly stepped into the room.

"Look, missy, this is my kitchen," the bull-shaped man growled. "I run it. I cook in it. I call the shots. You want me to cook this meal tonight, I serve it my way."

"Actually, Jacques, I appreciate creative license a great deal, but you signed a contract to prepare a very specific meal. A delicious meal I know everyone is looking forward to. That's what I expect you to serve tonight."

"Contracts be damned. I serve what I choose to cook, and people are grateful."

"Look, buddy," the woman he assumed was Mia snapped, jabbing her finger into the guy's chest. "The florist sent the wrong flowers. The supplier, instead of delivering midnight-blue tablecloths, sent navy. And the tapers are twelve-inch ecru instead of eleven-inch cream. I've had enough mix-ups for one event. So I suggest, very strongly, that you do what you agreed before I make you regret it."

Spence had seen that look on people's faces before. Usually right before they fired a gun. So he decided to intervene before the sexy brunette sent the chef to the hospital.

"Sorry," he said, offering up his most charming smile as he stepped between them. "I thought Ms. Cade was in charge."

"This is my kitchen, sir."

"My mistake." With just a twitch of his shoulders, Spence shifted into intimidation mode. His smile didn't change. His tone remained friendly. But from the pinprick of fear in the beefy man's eyes, he got the message just fine. "I'm just the kind of guy who believes in agreements."

"But—"

"And believe me, the last thing I ever want to do is let a beautiful woman down when she's counting on me to keep my word."

Those beady eyes shifted from Spence to Mia and back before the chef nodded so fast, his big white hat wobbled.

"The menu will be to your specifications, Ms. Cade. I'll get to work right away."

"I know Mia's got a lot to deal with, so while she's busy, I'll check back to see how it's going back here," Spence said, with just enough threat in his tone to make the chef's grimace quiver before he nodded his understanding.

"I'm glad we managed to get that settled," Mia said in a tone that sounded anything but. "Now, if you'll excuse us, we have a few things to deal with in the ballroom."

We, meaning she and he, Spence realized when Mia dug her fingers into his forearm and gave a subtle tug. Whether she'd had enough drama for the time being or to save his ego, she waited until they were out of the kitchen to turn on him like a rabid tiger.

Those fairy-queen eyes gleaming with outrage, she bared her teeth in a smile that radiated threat and warning.

"I have three questions for you," she said, her words as low and quiet as an unexploded IED. "First off, what exactly do you think you're doing interfering with me like that? Second, do I in any way appear incapable of handing my own business? And third, just for fun, who the hell are you?"

"First, I thought I was doing my job. Second, you actually appear capable of handling absolutely anything." He'd expect nothing less from one of Cade's daughters. "And third, I'm Spence Lloyd. Nice to meet you."

He held out his hand to shake.

She glanced at his hand, arched one brown brow and waited.

"You need a new assistant, right? I'm here to help you out."

For a solid three second, she simply stared.

"Did Karen send you? She usually calls me before she sends someone."

"I guess she didn't have a chance."

Obviously a strong believer in the talk-while-you-walk principle, Mia gestured for him to come along. Glad he'd passed the first hurdle, Spence followed in her wake, telling himself to focus on her words instead of staring at her.

"I'll need to see your résumé and a list of references, then. I don't have time right now but can you have them to me by the end of the day?"

"No problem." That'd give him time to gather enough intel to fake a few and figure out who Karen actually was. And speaking of intel… "Speaking of problems, I hear this job should come with hazard pay."

"Only if you're a wimp," Mia said dismissively, rolling her eyes. "Who tries to get out of forgetting to set the parking brake in San Francisco by claiming that someone is trying to kill them?"

Kill them? There were those red flags again, waving wildly for attention.

"Any chance any of those accidents almost happened to you, too?"

"What? Look, we have work to do." She shot him an impatient look. "I'm not sure if Karen went over the outline of tonight's event, but I assume you have the basics. So while I deal with the florist mix-up, you oversee the table setups." She gestured to the only set table in the ballroom, with its fancy-ass settings, complete with colored tablecloths, a round mirror, flowers, candles and class.

"You can handle that, right?"

No.

But he'd led twelve-man covert missions into enemy

territory with the goal of taking out insurgents without leaving a trace.

He could handle a few table settings.

"Tell me the order again." He gave a self-deprecating shrug. "I always like to double-check things."

"White floor-length tablecloths partially covered by what should have been shorter tablecloths in midnight blue but are navy instead, with the bead-rimmed mirrored tray in the center. Reverse order on the tables on the dais. Got that?"

Whiskey. November. Mike. Victor. Three Charlies and a handful of foxtrot. Spence nodded. "Got it."

"The florist knows to put the gardenia sculptures on the lower tables and orchids on the others, but I'd appreciate it if you'd double-check to make sure it's correct."

Sure. Just as soon as someone pointed out the difference between a gardenia and an orchid.

"You're sure?" Still assessing, those fairy eyes stared into his with enough intensity to make Spence wonder if the woman thought she could see into his brain. Still, when five seconds turned into ten, he felt a nervous tingle not even the hardest hard-ass commanding officer had ever managed with the darkest threats or demeaning insults.

"You want the tables covered with fabric, flowers and candles. You want me to order people around to make sure they do it right. Right," he added, "meaning your way."

Grinning, she shot one finger his way. "You catch on fast. We're going to get along great."

He liked the way she took charge without making a big deal out of being in charge. Unlike the insecure blonde, Mia knew her own power. Damned if that wasn't sexy.

"I'm sure we'll get along just fine," he agreed, his own smile slow and easy.

Something flashed in her eyes but was gone too fast for him to identify, replaced instead by professional friendliness.

"If you need anything, let me know. I'll be around."

"Actually, I need some time with you later."

Her eyes flashed again, but this time he could clearly read the caution. Smart woman. He appreciated a certain amount of caution, but not if it got in the way of his mission.

So he dimmed his smile down a few notches, going for safe.

"I just want to get a few things nailed down when you have time," he told her in his mellowest tone. "Job details, duties, responsibilities. That sort of thing."

"Oh. Sure, yeah. We'll get to that." She made a show of grimacing at her watch, then looking around the room. Spence followed her gaze, figuring her for one hell of an optimist if she actually believed she'd be holding a ball in here tonight. "Well. Lots to do. Busy-busy."

With her eyes still searching his, she bit her lip but didn't move. Good. It gave Spence longer to breathe in her scent, the rich notes reminding him of a garden in the moonlight.

"Just to clarify, this thing tonight is pretty formal, right?"

She blinked, her lashes so thick he was surprised she could hold those pretty amber eyes open.

"Seeing as I'm your right hand, I assume I should be here?"

"I actually prefer to have staff begin working with me at smaller events first. That gives me a chance to walk through my process with a little less pressure."

Spence looked around with an arched brow. She called

this pressure? Whether it was the look on his face, a sudden leap of faith or she really needed help, though, Mia finally gave a shrug.

"Actually, sure. I'm sure I can use your help. But it *is* black-tie." She gave him a look as hopeful as it was doubtful. "Can you get your hands on a tux by six?"

He could think of a dozen things he'd rather get his hands on—including the woman in front of him. Since none of them—including Mia—were on his mission list, he opted for a simple, "You can count on me."

Mia's smile flashed, both sweet and grateful, before she answered a summons from a frantic-looking woman waving from the other side of the room.

Spence indulged in a moment to appreciate the sway of her hips as she hurried across the marble floor before reviewing his current op-stat.

ASCOPE recon complete, he had a solid handle on the area, structure, capability, organization, people and event in question.

He'd made contact, established his cover and elicited trust. He'd verified the possibility of threat, garnered the necessary names and time frame to investigate, and had confirmed the connection with the enemy.

He considered this a good start for his first hour on the job, befitting years of SEAL training.

Now he looked around with a grimace; it was time to set some tables.

My.

My, oh my, oh my.

Mia pressed her lips together to make sure she wasn't drooling.

Karen had outdone herself, big-time.

Spence.

Mia knew she should have gotten his last name. But name or not, she was pretty sure she had his number.

Sexy, powerful and take-charge, the man had a gorgeous smile, piercing gray eyes and a butt so tight, she would bet she could bounce quarters off it. Add tousled hair with that hint of auburn and kissable lips that quirked in a sexy smile and Mia would rank him at the very top of the best-looking-men-she'd-ever-seen list.

If the guy was anywhere as good at handling events as he was at looking incredible, Mia was sure that her business was going to explode.

She watched him lean across the table to adjust the vase to the precise center, tilting her head to better appreciate the denim-clad view. The man's body was perfectly formed. Long, and lean with mucles sculpted in all the right places.

She knew she was objectifying a man she'd barely met. And she really should stop. Mia blew out a long, slow breath when he straightened, wondering if those shoulders were as sexy bare as they were covered in a black cotton tee.

Okay, she was sure everything about him looked good bare.

Not that she'd ever find out.

First off, the man worked for her now. So trying to see him naked was a really bad idea.

Second, with tonight's event for Forever Families as the latest example, her career was taking off, and big things were happening. Which meant she couldn't split her focus by dealing with other big things right now.

And third and most important, Mia had spent her formative years surrounded by strong men. Take-charge men. Men with major control issues. A half a lifetime watching them taught her to recognize trouble when she was staring at it.

"Mia?"

She'd always prided herself in being too smart to fall for a guy she knew was so wrong for her just because his body made her want to drool.

"Excuse me? Mia?"

Still, look at the way he moved. Pure poetry in masculine motion.

"Yo, earth to Mia."

"What?"

Thankfully Pierre chose that moment to roll a dolly of wine across the ballroom floor, obscuring her view of Spence and breaking the spell.

"I'm sorry, I was distracted. What did you say?" she said, giving Clair a distracted look.

"I had a few questions for you." The perky blonde aimed an arch look across the room. "If you're not busy, of course."

Huge gala, major client, important event.

Focus, focus, focus, Mia thought, ripping her thoughts away for the temptation of her new assistant. Instead, she gave Clair her most professional smile and gestured with her clipboard.

"Let's go over the checklist, shall we?"

"Is there anything to check off? I thought it was all falling apart." There was just enough maliciousness in Clair's voice to turn Mia's smile icy.

"Nothing's falling apart," Mia denied. "According to my notes, we're right on schedule."

"I thought there was an issue with the florist. And the menu. And late deliveries."

A big proponent of keeping all event planning in-house, Clair always reported every mistake, every ruffled expression and every single possible screwup to Lorraine—in duplicate. Mia knew plenty of event coordinators hated that sort of thing, but she told herself to be grateful. But Mia dealt with it by telling herself that Clair's tattling tendencies simply pushed her to use all of her organizational and efficiency skills, pushing her to work even harder to put on the best event possible.

"The florist is in the process of correcting their mistake and will have the correct arrangements delivered within the hour. The winery donated an extra eight cases in apology," Mia corrected, going down each item on the rest of her list, point by point. Her smile widened with every degree that Clair's dimmed. By the time she'd reached the end of her list, Clair was frowning and Mia's cheekbones hurt.

"And how's your list of tasks coming along?" Leaning from the waist, Mia made a show of checking Clair's clipboard. The other woman slapped it against her chest.

"Fine. We're doing great. I'm totally on schedule." In an obvious subject change, Clair made a show of looking across the room, blew out a breath and waved her hand to cool the air. "Now that we've settled that, spill. Where'd you get that yummy treat?"

"You mean Spence? He's my new assistant."

Despite her best effort not to, Mia followed Clair's gaze until she found him.

Spence.

Tall, dark and bossy.

Powerful enough to intimidate, but charming enough to get things done without needing to. She barely bit back a hum of appreciation when he lifted his arm to motion for the florist to stop and the muscles in his arm rippled. Who knew bossing a flower sculptor around could be so sexy?

Swiping her finger under her lower lip to make sure she wasn't drooling, she added finding an appropriate thank-you gift for Karen to her to-do list.

"Someone want to help me with these pedestals?"

Mia watched three men lift one of the pedestals, all straining to move it a foot to the right so they could set up the main art display. Spence grabbed the other himself, wrapping his arms around the carved post. His biceps bulged under the sleeves of his black tee as he lifted, effortlessly moving the marble cylinder three feet to the left.

Oh boy, did he have a way of moving.

Get to work, Mia reminded herself. She had floral arrangements to check, an ice sculpture to track down and eight artists to mollify. None of that would get done if she was ogling her new assistant.

"Is that really your new assistant?" Clair asked, as if reading her mind. "Talk about lucky."

"He does seem to be excellent at his job," Mia agreed.

"Who cares about his job skills?" Clair said dismissively. "The man is gorgeous."

"His job skills are what matter to me," Mia claimed, only half-truthfully. Because those shoulders did indeed make her wonder what other skills the man had.

"Are you sure? Because if you aren't interested, I'm going for it," Clair said, giving her a light shoulder bump. "I'll bet I'm just his type."

"He's not here to be hit on," Mia objected, not sure if she was protesting out of outrage over the poor man being objectified or if a part of her really did want to keep him for herself. Either way, as far as she was concerned, the objection stood. "He's here to help organize events, not to be treated like a hunk of meat. Speaking of events, we both have plenty of work to do."

Clair looked like she wanted to argue, but after a few seconds she rolled her eyes and shrugged.

"Fine," she said in a huff, tucking her clipboard under one arm and heading back to work. But not before she threw over her shoulder, "But you do have to admit, that is one sexy man."

"Ms. Cade?"

As Mia hurried across the room to meet the head of security, she made a point not to so much as look Spence's way. Still, she couldn't deny that Clair was right.

Spence was the hottest assistant she'd ever had.

Chapter 3

All that glittered wasn't gold.

Success sparkled prettily and brightly, too.

Mia inspected her latest masterpiece, a ballroom filled with generous donors and intriguing art, and gave a satisfied nod. Because yes, indeed, this was success.

Posh elegance glimmered and gleamed, from the damask-covered walls to the liquor-filled crystal. The string quartet—a minor point of contention between her and Lorraine—played a delicate tune in keeping with the ambiance. The waitstaff slid discreetly between guests, refreshing drinks, offering hors d'oeuvres.

The well-dressed attendees milled about, each person handpicked for their potential contributions. Donations, connections, introductions. Before the evening was through, Mia would wheedle a little of each from every guest.

Some would call it mercenary.

Mia called it good business.

Like her daddy always said, there was a perfect tool for every job. It was the leader's task to find that tool and use it—and use it right.

Speaking of good tools, Mia's stomach fluttered as she scanned the ballroom. Not that she was looking for Spence. She was just checking out the great crowd. Angling up on the toes of her strappy Louboutins, she shifted to the left to look around a six-foot redhead in Prada, then to the right to peer through a trio of tuxedoed guests talking investments.

"Trying to find the hottie?"

Mia froze.

Not interested in listening to any more from Clair, she decided to play dumb.

"Hottie? There are a some very handsome men here tonight. Which one do you think is the hottie?" Mia said, pasting on a friendly smile as she turned. "I mean, look at this crowd. I think it's a record turnout, don't you?"

Mia's words trailed off when she got a good look at Clair. Instead of her usual outlet special, fade-into-the-background dress, the blonde wore low-cut siren red.

"You look very different."

"You think?" Clair did a model turn, complete with one hand on her hip and the other behind her head. "Do you think Spence will like it?"

"You wore that for my assistant?"

"So, tell me everything you know about him. He's single, right? Does he have a real job? Not that running errands for you isn't a job. I'm sure there's plenty of things for him to do," Clair said, flicking her hand in the air with her usual dismissal of Mia's work. "I'll bet he's great on the dance floor. I can't wait to find out. I've rearranged the seating so he's next to me for dinner. It's not like you need him then, right?"

Before Mia could find a nice way to tell the woman to back the hell away from her seating charts and her assistant, Clair gave a low growl. Following the other woman's hot stare, it was all Mia could do not to give a growl of her own.

Oh.

Wow.

She'd had no idea that a man who looked so slurp-worthy in jeans could make her panties melt when he was wearing black tie.

In a tuxedo that fit as if custom-made, Spence surveyed the room with a calculation that would have made Mia frown if she wasn't so distracted by how gorgeous the man was.

From the hint of curl in his slicked-back hair to his sharp cheekbones and sculpted lips and the way his jacket perfectly hugged the impressive breadth of his shoulders, the man exuded a sexy power.

But something about the way he stood, as if ready to attack, made the back of her neck tingle.

And her belly quiver.

"You really only see that guy as a professional associate?" Clair murmured, incredulous disbelief clear in her words.

"He handled every job I gave him this afternoon, he averted three disasters, fixed two potential issues and intimidated Chef Porter. Since he walked through the door this evening, I've seen him charm three women into bidding in the art auction, introduce two patrons to attending artists and, at one point, he even made Mrs. Crane laugh."

"Aha," Clair exclaimed, jabbing one finger in the air. "There it is. Proof that you are interested in the man."

"No," Mia returned, waving that away with her French manicure. "That would be proof that he's the perfect assistant."

"Okay, fine. If you really have no interest in him, then you won't object if I go for it." Then, in case the "it" in question wasn't clear, Clair leaned closer to murmur, "I'll fill you in on the naked details tomorrow."

Mia wrinkled her nose. Of course she objected. The last thing she wanted to imagine was Clair climbing all over her assistant. Not when she wanted those delicious shoulders and the rest of him for herself.

"No need to share the details. But now, if you'll excuse me, I have to check the seating arrangements."

Before Clair could share one more detail, Mia hurriedly crossed the room, irritation clicking with each tap of her heels. Clair and Spence? There was an image she didn't want in her head. Now Spence naked?

That image flashed so large and vivid in her mind that Mia almost tripped over her own feet.

This was ridiculous.

Tonight marked an important turning point in her career. All her focus needed to stay not only on rocking this Forever Families event, but also on wooing Señor Alcosta. That left no room for lusting after a man she'd only met ten hours before.

Since her first priority was work, she'd do a check to make sure everything was on track before she cornered Alcosta for her next pitch.

With that in mind, she focused on doing her job, dashing between the kitchen, the musicians and the artists, ensuring that everything behind the scenes looked as good as the ballroom itself. Thanks to a gossipy sculptor, she was running five minutes behind by the time she was headed back to the ball.

She hated running behind.

If she wanted at least twenty minutes with Alcosta before dinner was announced, she had to hurry.

Hurry, hurry, hurry.

Double-timing it while mentally searching her timetable to make up the missing minutes, Mia almost didn't notice the man at the end of the hallway.

Spence.

Standing outside the side door to the ballroom, watching her with an intensity that made her shiver.

He was so tall, dark and sexy that her mind immediately pitched out the timetable and replaced it with a montage of erotic images.

Even as a tiny part of her wondered why the tuxedo didn't tame his delicious edginess, the rest of her brain just hummed with lustful appreciation at the way the expensive black fabric hugged his wide shoulders, at how the crisp white shirt accented his russet hair and gilded skin.

Since running away would be both cowardly and stupid, she shoved the images back, widened her smile and continued down the hall. Six feet from Spence, her stomach pitched one way, and her feet the other as her shoes hit something slippery. Mia instinctively bit back her scream of surprise as she caught air.

Torn between worry about damaging her favorite Louboutins and using that half second before she hit the floor to figure out how to finish the event to perfection while injured, Mia tried to grab the wall to slow her fall.

Her stomach swooped when, instead of a sconce, she gripped a handful of crisp fabric, her fingers digging into hard flesh. Warm hands wrapped around her, waist and hip, sweeping her off the floor to safety.

Spence.

He'd been all the way down the hall. How'd he move so fast? More important, how long could he hold her like this? Breathless, she stared into the intensity of those dark gray eyes.

Oh. My.

He looked even better up close.

Mia drew in a long, slow breath, trying to calm her racing pulse. But the air seemed to lodge in her chest, pounding in time with the heartbeat of awareness throbbing through her body.

"Are you okay?" Spence asked, his voice low, a soothing contrast to the intensity in his eyes as he inspected the empty hallway. "What happened?"

Happened?

One second she'd been hurling toward a guaranteed sore butt and bruised ego, and the next he'd been there, sweeping her into the safety of his arms.

His big, strong, muscular arms.

Mia had never been the type to lose her head over a guy's body. Then again, she'd never been rescued by one, either. Never been held as if she were a featherweight, cuddled so close she could see the deep gray ringing those smoky irises.

Close enough that she was tempted to rub her palm over the hint of whiskers carpeting those sharp cheekbones, just to see how they felt. To skim her thumb along

the fullness of his lower lip, teasing it open for her quest-
ing tongue.

"Mia?"

"Mmm?"

"Are you okay?" This time, enough concern coated
the question to make her blink. And realize how ridic-
ulously she was behaving, practically throwing herself
at a man just because he'd kept her butt from hitting
the floor.

"I'm fine. Well, embarrassed, but fine," she corrected
with a strained laugh. "I'm not usually so clumsy. I do
appreciate the rescue, though."

"What happened?" he asked again, his gaze skimming her from head to foot, leaving a tingling trail of
awareness in its wake. "You were really booking it down
that hallway. Did you lose your balance? Break a heel?"

Mia was too worried about ruining her favorite shoes
to take offense at the idea that she couldn't book with
the best of them.

"My Louboutins?" Horrified at the idea, Mia angled
to one side, checking her left shoe, then her right. It
wasn't until her second twist that she realized that her
breasts were rubbing against his chest. Her nipples, paying a lot more attention, hardened with tingling awareness.

Oh, God.

Embarrassed and more than a little turned on, Mia
told herself not to blush. But from the heat warming her
cheeks, she knew the warning was as useless as wishing
away her body's reaction.

Thankfully Spence didn't seem to notice. Even while
holding her tightly against his chest like she was pre-

cious cargo, the man didn't show any reaction other than concern.

"I slipped," she finally said, twitching just a little to let him know that it was okay to put her down. Not preferable, since it felt really good to be cozied up here in his arms. But she didn't want to be an imposition. "I always walk fast, so it's not that. There must've been something on the floor. One second I was walking. The next my feet were flying."

As soon as the words were out, she felt like an idiot. But he didn't look at her like she'd said something ridiculous. Instead, he cast a narrow-eyed scowl up and down the hallway before giving her a reassuring smile.

"You're okay now. Do you think you can stand?"

She wanted to say no. She wanted to claim anything that'd keep her in the hard, strong haven of his arms.

But the man worked for her.

Hoping he'd attribute her breathlessness to almost falling on her butt, Mia cleared her throat and tried a smile.

"I'm fine. Totally fine. You can put me down."

"Of course."

He let her down slowly, keeping one arm wrapped around her waist, her body pressed against his, until her feet hit the floor. Until she got her balance. Until she wanted to whimper with need.

For the briefest of moments, interest flared in those smoky eyes before his expression cleared. His hand still on her waist, he slowly stepped back to put some distance between them. Mia felt like she could truly breathe for the first time since her feet found air.

"Why were you in the hallway?" she asked, more in

hopes that words would put even more distance between them than out of any sort of curiosity.

"I was looking for you."

Concern replaced embarrassed lust. "Why? Is there a problem with the event?" A little more carefully this time, Mia headed for the ballroom. No amount of planning and preparation could prevent random problems from cropping up. "Is Lorraine looking for me?"

"No and no. The event appears to be operating on schedule, and to all appearances the guests are well entertained and content."

Needing to see for herself, Mia stopped just outside the ballroom to peer through the narrow side door.

"Everything looks just as it should," she murmured before frowning at Spence. "So why were you looking for me?"

His eyes locked on hers, he seemed to consider her question for a long moment, and then he smiled. A long, slow, melt-her-into-a-puddle smile.

"Do I need a reason?"

Anticipation doing a sexy little dance in her belly, Mia bit her lip and studied his face.

Was he hitting on her? She wasn't in a position to complain, given that she'd just massaged his chest with hers. But despite her obvious attraction to the man, she didn't want to give him the wrong idea.

Did she?

She wet her lips, studying his face.

The man was gorgeous and exuded an air of power that she admired in a professional capacity, but knew from experience to avoid at all costs in a personal capacity.

Before she could figure out how to tell him that without damaging their work relationship in the middle of a major event, his smile shifted from a sexy invitation to innocuous friendliness.

"Actually, Clair wanted my help with a few things," he said, a shrug clear in his voice. "I figured I should check in with you first, make sure we were clear before I agreed."

Clair? Oh, Mia knew exactly what Clair wanted his help with.

"Of course," she said, biting back the bitter taste of jealousy. "Lorraine is Clair's boss, and Clair is her right hand. Feel free to help her in any way she needs."

From his arched brow and the quirk of his lips, he obviously had a good idea of at least a few of Clair's needs. But all he said was, "I'm going to check the hallway where you slipped, make sure the floor is clean. Then I'll be inside."

She wanted to protest that she'd have noticed if there was something on the floor, but figured anything that kept him out of Clair's clutches for a few extra seconds was fine with her.

"Good idea," she murmured, stepping into the ballroom. She could feel his gaze on her, a tingling sort of awareness that made every step an erotic reminder of how his body had felt against hers.

Forget Spence, she chided herself.

The last thing she needed right now was to get her head—or her body—all messed up over a guy.

After all, she had her priorities. As her father always said, *A man at the top of the mountain didn't fall there.* If she wanted success, she had to work at it. And working at it meant doing whatever it took to accomplish the task at hand.

In this case, wooing her target.

Not wowing a hottie.

Her gaze tracking his progress across the room, Mia scowled. The last thing she saw before she was swallowed by the crowed was Spence being accosted by a fluff of blonde curls and flash of red satin.

So what if Clair hauled him off to a secluded corner and rode him like a stripper pole? The only interest Mia had in the man was his skills as an assistant.

Deliberately turning her back, Mia scanned the room for the one man she was invested in tonight.

Ah, there he was.

Santiago Alcosta.

Exactly as Jessica had described him when she'd coached Mia on her approach for the night.

Successful businessman. Wealthy philanthropist. Sophisticated playboy.

The man who, if this evening went right, would hire her to coordinate all funding for a brand-spanking-new children's hospital in Mexico City.

From the tips of his glossy black hair that was winged with silver and slicked back from a face almost too perfect to be provided by nature to the polished points of his snakeskin boots, he exuded confidence. Santiago was the epitome of charismatic power and wealth. All of that would play well in marketing the campaign and soliciting donations for the new children's hospital.

She had a million ideas and couldn't wait to get started. All she needed was the go-ahead—and of course, a contract—from Alcosta.

Ready to take the next step toward that, Mia ran her tongue over her teeth, checking for lipstick, smoothed her hand over her hip to ensure her dress was flowing just right, took a deep breath and then hurried across the room.

"Señor Alcosta," she greeted with a warm smile, holding out her hand. "How lovely to see you this evening. I'm so happy you accepted my invitation."

"My darling Mia," he greeted, the elegantly accented English rolling off his tongue like velvet. He lifted her hand to his lips, lingering over the kiss in a way that made Mia inwardly squirm a little.

"I hope you're enjoying the gala."

"I was indeed. But as lovely as this evening has been, it's infinitely better now."

"That's so kind of you," she said, a little surprised at the blatant interest in his eyes. Not because of any sort of false modesty—how could she pretend she didn't feel sexy and gorgeous after that encounter with Spence?— but because the man was old enough to be her father. "There are a number of people who'd love to meet you. Can I introduce you around?"

"I'd prefer to spend my time with the most beautiful woman in the room." He stepped closer, taking her hand and lifting it to his mouth. Mia pressed her lips together to keep from giggling when his mustache tickled her knuckles. She schooled her face to show nothing but respectful admiration when he met her eyes, though.

"You're definitely a charmer." She smiled, sliding her hand free to surreptitiously rub her knuckles against her hip in hopes of easing the itchiness.

"I worried you would not find enough time to spend with me this evening," Alcosta said, his expression theatrically morose. Without looking away from Mia, he lifted a finger to get the attention of a passing waiter, held up his empty glass, then dropped it on the man's tray.

Mia barely hid her grimace.

She was used to arrogance in men. Her father was one of the most alpha of alphas in existence. She'd seen him make raw ensigns cry. But—despite a few people wishing otherwise—he never treated anyone like they were invisible.

"I wanted to make sure I'd handled everything that had to be handled, so I could focus all of my attention on you," she told him. "I'd love to show you around the art displays. The silent auction is open for another hour and I'll bet I can find you the perfect match."

"Usually, I'm quite particular about my art. But I'm intrigued to see what you think will suit me."

"Challenge accepted."

Tucking her arm through his free one, Mia kept up a slew of friendly chatter as she led him from sculpture to sculpture. Before they'd reached the paintings, he'd slugged down three more drinks and was so effusive in his compliments that Mia was afraid he might be serious.

She sidestepped the suggestion that they take their conversation out on the balcony and gestured toward one of the three most expensive paintings.

"Isn't this gorgeous? It's my favorite here tonight," she said, studying the canvas. The colors were just as vivid and vibrant as the oils and acrylics, but there was something soothing about the watercolor that called to her. Looking at it felt like watching a brilliant garden through a misty rain. "It's soothing and exciting at the same time."

"Indeed," Alcosta said, his tone more dismissive than interested. Mia could feel his stare and knew he wasn't paying any attention to the painting.

She kept her eyes locked on the artwork while nerves

fluttered over her skin. She knew when a man was interested in her, and this wasn't the first time she'd had to discourage a potential client. But never one with a project—or an ego—the size of Alcosta's.

It'd take a delicate balance of flattery, diplomacy and evasion to avert the interest while enticing the business. Still working out the logistics, Mia gestured to the painting again.

"Would you like to meet the artist? She's as beautiful as she is gifted."

"I've already found the most beautiful woman in the room. Why waste time with anyone else?"

"You're too kind." Mia put another inch between them, looking around the room, looking for a polite escape. Her gaze landed on Spence again.

A tingle curled in her belly. He was talking to a group of people, including Clair, who was clinging to his arm like Velcro. But all the while, those piercing eyes were locked on her with an intensity that made her want to squirm. Nerves, she told herself. Just concern that Spence was doing a good job. Clair was obviously keeping him busy.

"Kindness is not necessary when the truth will suffice," Alcosta said, pulling her attention back to him as he lifted her hand again. Mia braced herself, but he didn't kiss it this time. Instead, he just held it and stared at her until she wanted to brush at her face. "I'll be happy to bid on this painting if it makes you happy. And in return, you'll help me find the perfect place to display it. We can discuss it over dinner, perhaps? My suite, tomorrow night?"

"I appreciate the invitation, but I have a prior commitment." With her jammies, her laptop and a pint of

Chocolate Chunk Delight. "I do hope you'll bid, though. This painting suits you so well and would be a wonderful addition to any art collection."

"Ah, collections. As a connoisseur of art, seeing these paintings is only one of the reasons I was eager to attend this evening. I understand that you have access to the famed Penz collection. I lost a lovely Monet to the senator in an auction and have envied him that painting ever since."

"Monet was an amazing artist," Mia said with the same care she would use dancing in a minefield.

"Your expertise in tonight's gala gives me the idea to include something similarly in my own series of fundraisers. Perhaps a more intimate affair, one with a more exclusive guest list. You are related to the senator, yes?"

Ah, Mia almost sighed. Damn.

She really didn't want to go there, but didn't see a lot of options.

"Senator Penz is my uncle," she confirmed.

"A great man, your *tío* Penz, and one I'd be honored to meet. I believe his presence would bring a great deal of attention to our cause, as well as highlight his support of the arts. This is what they call a win-win, yes?"

"I'm so sorry, Señor Alcosta, but I don't feel comfortable using my family's connections for profit."

For a brief second, something flashed behind the charm in his dark eyes. Something so cold and cutting, it sent a tiny shiver of fear through Mia's system. Before she could figure out why, it was gone, leaving only a lingering chill.

"I confess I am disappointed." Then, exchanging his empty glass for a full one, he gave an easy shrug. "But I am sure you have many other ideas that might be equally intriguing."

"I really do have a long list of fabulous fund-raising ideas to share with you at lunch on Monday. I'm excited to integrate your art benefit into the list. I can think of numerous ways to make it an event you'll be excited about," Mia said, hoping that'd appease him.

She didn't know if his "ah" was an acknowledgment or agreement, but at least he dropped the subject. Instead, Alcosta waved one elegant hand toward the dance floor.

"The music is almost as lovely as the artwork. If you won't have dinner with me, at least grant me the pleasure of a dance?"

"I'd be delighted." Mia laid her hand in his.

When her body recoiled at the touch of his hand on her waist, she reminded herself that this was business. Important business, which she was an expert at handling. To prove it, she spent the entire dance weaving a subtle, skilled pitch of how her services would benefit his hospital charity event, while being careful to keep her every word and action completely professional.

"You'll sit next to me at dinner, of course?"

"Actually, I have duties to attend to," she decided on the spot. "But I'm sure that I'll see you after the meal."

He gave her another one of those piercing looks that made the hair on the back of her neck stand at attention.

"If I didn't know better, I might think you were not interested in spending time with me." Alcosta's laugh was chilling. "Except, of course, for business."

Mia was skilled enough to keep the *well, duh* from her face, but couldn't help but wonder why he'd think otherwise. It wasn't like she'd hit on the guy or they had a long-term relationship. Still, she'd worked with the wealthy long enough to know to step carefully around this type of narcissistic arrogance. Especially if she wanted his business.

She caught sight of Lorraine in her hot-pink and huge diamonds as the older woman gave a thumbs-up from across the room. She followed that with patting her hip, then miming eating, then another thumbs-up.

Lorraine. With her extensive connections, her propensity to gossip and, most of all, her elite Winter Ball.

Lorraine. Who wanted Santiago Alcosta for any variety of reasons, not the least of which were his charm, mustache and notoriety.

Mia sighed.

Yeah. She definitely needed Alcosta and his business.

Before she could figure out how to maneuver this new tightrope, she felt a presence at her side. Her breath caught in her chest, tiny goose bumps dancing over her suddenly overheated flesh.

She didn't need to look to know it was Spence standing next to her. She didn't need to see Alcosta's glare, either, to know the man didn't like the interruption.

Before she could say anything, Spence leaned in close, his breath warming her cheek like a gentle caress.

"I'm sorry to interrupt, Mia, but when you have a moment…" he murmured, his hand a whisper of warmth on the small of her back.

Without waiting for a response, or even for an introduction, he left.

"I'm sorry," she told Alcosta, following his gaze as he watched Spence walk away. "Apparently I need to check on some event details."

"That man? He works for you?"

"He's my boyfriend," Mia heard herself lie. She leaned close enough to make it seem like she was sharing a secret, but not so close that it seemed like she was flirting. "He's got a few issues with jealousy. We're working on them, but sometimes he backslides."

"He does appear to be quite a brute," Alcosta said, inspecting Spence with a look of derision. "And not at all your type."

"The heart wants what the heart wants." Or more realistically, in her case, the body lusts.

"Mmm, and sometimes the heart shows a person's taste in ways nothing else could," he murmured before giving her a look more leering than charming. As if weighing his chances of pitching an affair seconds after meeting her supposed boyfriend.

Mia realized that she didn't like Alcosta. If he'd been any other client, she'd have made one last donation pitch, said her polite goodbye and that'd be the end of it.

But he was simply too important to her career.

Spurred by desperation, she went with the lesser of two evils.

"You know, I just remembered that my uncle is due for a visit to the West Coast. I would be happy to ask him to arrange it to coincide with your fund-raiser."

"Indeed?" Alcosta's smile cleared the irritation from his face. "That would please me greatly."

"We'll talk about it more on Monday," Mia promised. "But if you'll excuse me for now, I have duties to attend to."

It took another few minutes to extricate herself from Alcosta's company, putting Mia just enough behind schedule that she decided to wait to report to Lorraine until after she'd checked in with the kitchen.

And then she'd find Spence and explain that she'd added *fake boyfriend* to his job description. A job she'd bet he was excellent at, she thought with a sigh. Her job, she reminded herself, would be keeping firmly in mind the "fake" part. Because she had a feeling that pretending with Spence would be temptation personified.

Chapter 4

"There you are, hot stuff," Clair said, her words on the slurred side of bubbly, thanks to a few too many glasses of free-flowing champagne. "I've been looking all over for you."

The blonde expressed her appreciation at finding him by making a grab at Spence's ass, this time hard enough for those talons she called fingernails to dig into his skin.

This job should come with hazard pay.

"I'll bet your boss is saying the same thing about you," he murmured, shifting to the left so he didn't lose his view of Mia through the crowd. "Didn't you say that—it's Lorraine, isn't it?—that she had a long list of work for you to do tonight?"

As he'd expected, that's all it took to set her off in a bitch-fest about how overworked she was, how unfair her boss was and, after she'd snagged another flute of champagne from a roving waiter, how much she liked the way his muscles flexed when he moved.

Clair reminded him a lot of Lori. He'd only dated a handful of times months ago—well before his accident—and had made it clear that he had no interest in a long-term relationship. When he'd been on duty, living on base and traveling for various military ops, that message had been easy to reinforce. Then she'd got word of is injury and, what? Figured that despite his strong assurances that he had no interest long-term relationships, he'd suddenly be desperate to settle down?

He glanced at Clair and sighed. Some women just didn't like to take no for an answer.

But now that she'd removed her talons from his flesh, Spence pressed the mental mute button and watched Mia. He supposed, in a room filled with brilliant colors, she figured the black dress made her fade into the background. It didn't. Instead, the way the fabric draped and folded over her curves gave the impression that she'd just slid out of bed, naked and well loved, before wrapping herself in a velvet sheet.

His throat went so dry at the thought, he was tempted to grab one of those glasses of champagne for himself. But he never drank on duty.

Of course, he'd never worn a tux while on duty before, either.

His assignments had never included rich snobs, highbrow art and hiding his identity from his assignment, a too-sexy-for-her-own-good VIP.

A VIP that felt like heaven in his arms. A warm, lush heaven. His mouth went dry at the memory of those intriguing eyes looking deep into his, those full lush lips being within kissing distance.

She was an endangered VIP, he reminded himself, scowling as he forced himself to focus on the reality at hand instead of on an irresponsible, and more to the point, unattainable fantasy.

Reality wasn't what she'd felt like when he'd caught her. The reality was that Mia could have been seriously hurt in that fall. A fall that might—or might not—have been an accident. After he'd let Mia go, he'd done a careful check of the hallway and found a series of almost infinitesimal drops of oil.

Left behind by careless kitchen worker? The hall did lead from the kitchen, so that was a reasonable assumption. But Spence couldn't dismiss the concern churning in his gut.

That churning deepened as he watched Alcosta approach Mia, his smarmy smile doing nothing to hide the predatory look in his eyes.

The tension filling Spence's gut now had nothing to do with lust and everything to do with concern. His first instinct was to stride across the room and plant himself directly between Alcosta and Mia. Better yet, to wrap her in his arms, mark her as his in a way that'd force the other man to back off.

Or else.

But he doubted that Mia would appreciate his interference. There was a good possibility that interfering would piss her off. Maybe enough that she'd fire him.

His jaw clenched when Alcosta shifted closer to Mia, trailing the back of his hand along her bare arm.

To hell with pissing her off.

He wanted that man away from her.

Before he took a single step, though, he watched Mia introduce Alcosta to a nearby group before unobtrusively gliding away. Spence's sharp appreciation of the graceful brushoff was blunted by the fact that Alcosta's eyes never left her.

Maybe he'd haul the guy outside and give him a little warning about what was and wasn't appropriate.

Except that wasn't the job at hand.

Damn. He was seriously losing perspective on this.

Spence scrubbed a hand over his hair, but the move did nothing to relieve the frustration churning in his gut.

What the hell was his next step?

Once, he'd had a solid handle on protocols. He understood a clear chain of command. A team of experts by his side, covering his back, offering up their shared expertise while they fought in the deepest pits of hell for their country.

Maybe staying in the Navy and riding a desk wouldn't have been such a bad idea after all.

Something to consider, he decided, while absently sidestepping Clair's wandering hand again.

For now, he had his orders.

As if he needed a reminder, his cell phone chimed.

He glanced at the readout.

"I have to take this," he murmured.

Ignoring Clair's disappointed pout, he stepped to the door. Not into the hallway, though. He wasn't letting Mia out of his sight.

"Sir."

"Report," Cade barked through the phone line.

"I'm on duty, at the gala, focused on the target."

"Threat level?"

He'd usually lay it out, fact by fact. But Spence hesitated, brutally aware that this wasn't a typical assignment. The admiral might be his commanding officer and an employer of sorts, but this was about the guy's daughter. So Spence needed to temper his words accordingly.

After hearing about that slew of accidents around her, he'd still leaned toward this being a fluff job: a way to appease the admiral's wife and, more important, a way to score himself a prime new career.

But he didn't believe Mia's little slip and slide down the hall had been an accident. Not with the oil conveniently dribbled over the floor.

"Sir, I've made contact with your daughter and am currently serving as her assistant. This not only allows me to work closely with her, but also offers me insights into her business with the opportunity to insert myself into her dealings."

They both knew that wasn't the actual question. But until Spence had completed a thorough recon of the situation, he was hesitant to assign a threat level and worry the man.

"Do you require any backup?"

"No, sir. I will require proper references and a résumé that support this position, though. Through someone named Karen?"

"Consider it done. And Alcosta?"

"Present. Reports show that he usually travels with an entourage, but he's solo here. Could be because of the ambiance of an event like this. Could be reluctance to donate the required five grand per person."

Could be that Alcosta was reluctant to hit on pretty women half his age when he was surrounded by his employees. But given that the guy's eyes had been crawling over Mia in a way that made Spence want to drop-kick him, that last one was doubtful.

"And Mia?"

His gaze still locked on the woman in question, Spence watched with appreciation as she convinced one guy to buy a painting of a red dot, instructed a waiter to make one last round and signaled someone in the dining area to begin the music. All at the same time.

The light of the chandeliers glinted off her skin, making it look like alabaster dusted with diamonds. Obviously in her element, she sparked with an energy Spence recognized. He'd felt it plenty of times. That assurance that you were doing exactly what you were meant to do, exactly how you were meant to do it.

Damned if he didn't miss feeling like that.

"She runs one hell of a show." Then, remembering who he was talking to, he amended that to, "She has a firm handle on the workings of high society. The people, the entertainment, the games, if you will. She does her work behind the scenes, yet still remains front and center."

He reviewed the mental debate he'd had since discovering the drops of oil in the hall. His assignment was specific—to protect Mia from Alcosta. He had no proof that someone had deliberately spilled oil on the floor, and no reason to believe that the incident was connected to Alcosta.

Holding back the intel until he'd done further reconnaissance was standard protocol. It had nothing to do with reluctance to describe the incident aloud—especially to Mia's father—until he was sure his intense physical reaction was under complete control.

"She's a pretty thing, isn't she?" Protocol obviously had nothing on a father's pride.

"Pretty enough to garner quite a few admiring looks." He'd keep his to himself. "Including from Alcosta."

"You're confirming the man is interested in more than my daughter's professional skills?"

Spence tore his gaze away from the gentle curve of Mia's back to scan the crowd. He didn't have to look far to find the man in question, drink in hand. His dark, hooded eyes watched Mia with a predatory hunger that made Spence's fist clench.

"Affirmative."

The harrumph came through the phone line loud enough that Spence was surprised it didn't ruffle his hair.

"All the more reason for you to stay on point. I want that man kept away from my daughter."

Spence could sympathize. He wanted the man away from Mia, too. But that wasn't an actual mission.

"Have you determined the actual threat?" he asked, slightly desperate for something to focus on besides watching the most gorgeous woman he'd ever seen.

"Using various resources at my disposal, I've instigated a level-two background check and, again, found no known intel linking this man to any crimes,"

It took all of Spence's training not to protest. Years of service had developed his habit of trusting intel, of following orders and to bow to the chain of command. But instincts honed on the battlefield had taught him to trust his intuition over all else. And everything he had—training, instincts and intuition—said that with proof or not, the man was bad news.

Not just bad news for Mia.

Criminally bad news.

"Sir—"

Cade cut him off. "However, my original order stands. You are to use whatever means necessary to prevent any personal contact between that man and my daughter. Any means, Lloyd. Do you understand me?"

Torn between relief and tension, Spence could only grimace. As happy as he'd be to carry out those orders, he had to accept—bitterly—that in these circumstances, he was a civilian. Cade had warned him when he'd taken this assignment that those constraints meant he wouldn't be able tap into the usual tools he'd accessed with the SEALs. No automatic weapons, no sanctioned takedowns, no covert attacks. He was on his own with nothing more than a pistol and his wits.

No question that Cade's goal here was his daughter's protection. But it was still a test. The man was watching Spence's methods, waiting to see if he could assimilate his Navy training into the civilian-security realm before he recommended him to Aegis.

Good, Spence decided. He worked better under pressure. He'd just look at this as a new version of Hell Week and kick ass. Just like he had in BUD/s, testing to become a SEAL.

As the tempo of the music slowed, shifting dancers off the floor, Spence watched Alcosta stare at Mia with a feral hunger, and nodded. Yeah. He'd do whatever it took to keep them from getting personal.

But…

"I'll keep her safe and ensure that any contact she has with Alcosta is business only." Hearing Cade gear up his protest, Spence pointed out, "You said it yourself, sir. According to the known intel, the man is clean. If she's planning to work with him, Mia will know that. Which means that any overt interference in her business will be problematic. I've established myself as her aid. So it shouldn't be a problem to finesse my way into any business interactions she has with him."

"Business?"

"Business and personal," Spence corrected.

"Very well. I'll provide the necessary support to your cover and will pull some strings, call in some favors and see what I can do to pull in deeper intel. But you're on the front lines, Lloyd. You are to assess the situation, mitigate the threat and, most of all, to keep my daughter safe. That means you stick to her side like glue."

"Yes, sir." Spence hesitated, not quite comfortable with deceiving Cade's daughter to such an extent. As if reading his concern, the admiral harrumphed.

"You have your orders, Lloyd. Carry on."

The line went dead. Not bothering to sigh, Spence shoved his phone in his pocket again and strode into the crowd.

He'd only made it three steps before Clair grabbed on to him like a barnacle.

"There you are," she declared, wrapping her arms around his so she could press her breasts against his biceps. "I've been looking everywhere."

"Sorry. I'm busy right now."

"Too busy to dance?"

Absolutely.

"I need to check with Mia. I'm sure there's something she needs me to do," he added before Clair could object. "Hey, she is the boss. Gotta do the job, right?"

"I wouldn't think a big, strong man like you would like taking orders from a woman."

"I live to follow orders," he deadpanned, giving her an absent smile. "If you'll excuse me."

* * *

Spence gave himself a moment to breath deeply her scent, roses at midnight, before clearing his throat. She spun around fast enough that her skirt slapped at his legs, sending that little wrapped-in-a-sheet fantasy he'd had into full gear again as he imagined the garment hitting the floor.

"Oh. Spence. Hi." Those full lips spread into a smile edged with nerves. The same nerves danced in her eyes. Why?

"Everything okay?"

"Sure. Fine. Just, you know, winding into phase three," she said with a wave of her hand. Phase three, he remembered, was the fancy dinner part of the evening's event. "I was just thinking I should talk with you, though."

"Here I am. Let's talk."

She opened her mouth, but after a few seconds, closed it and shook her head. "Bad timing. Let's ensure phase three goes smoothly, and then I'll fill you in."

"Is there a problem?"

"No, no. I've already explained to Lorraine that I'll miss the meal because I'll be handling some behind-the-scenes tasks. She can handle it just fine. She's a skilled hostess, and has a strict code about soliciting funds during meals. And she has Clair as backup. So she won't need me in there."

"And me?"

Mia slanted him an amused look and arched one brow.

"I'm guessing Clair would say she needs you in a number of places. If you want to join her for dinner, there is an open seat available."

"I'd rather grab something to eat with you in the kitchen." Or anywhere else, for that matter.

"Oh, I never eat at these things. I'm always too amped up to try to put anything in my stomach."

"And if you were sitting with that crowd at the dining table?"

"I'd pretend to eat while chatting up everyone within speaking distance," Mia said, laughing as she gave a self-deprecating shrug. "But this evening, I think my time will be better served elsewhere."

She studied the room, and he noticed a tiny frown between her brows when her eyes landed on Alcosta. Probably because the guy was wearing jeans and a sweater instead of black tie. He was obviously not one of Mia's subcontractors. Had he crashed the event?

Alcosta's expression was somewhere between indifferent and annoyed.

Mia, on the other hand, looked outraged.

Gauging her mood, he blocked her path before she could storm over to kick the intruder out.

"That guy, Alcosta, right? What's his story?"

He figured the wide-eyed look Mia gave him was meant to be questioning, like she didn't know what he was getting at. He was sure of it when she only smiled and said, "He's a client. A very prestigious client who rightfully expects not to be accosted at an exclusive event."

Actually, Spence thought, the guy looked like he deserved to be accosted at all kinds of events. But he kept that to himself.

"Who's the guy with him? He looks intense." Intense, pissed, pushy. Pretty much all three rolled into one, Spence decided, watching the other man wave his hands to emphasize some point. From his one-shouldered shrug, Alcosta didn't seem to care. Which only pissed the guy off more.

"I don't know who that man is," Mia replied, biting the words off between clenched teeth. "But I do know he doesn't belong here."

She'd managed two steps toward the confrontation before Spence grabbed her. Since her arm felt like silk beneath his hand, he let it go as soon as she met his eyes. "I need to tell him to leave. He isn't on the guest list, he didn't pay and he's clearly annoying one of our guests."

Right. Like Spence was going to let her go head-to-head with a guy who was obviously pissed, probably confrontational and possibly dangerous.

"I'll handle this," Spence assured her, adrenaline spiking. He was looking forward to it. A little confrontation, the potential for a fight, a chance to poke into Alcosta's life? Yeah. He was looking forward to all of that.

"But—"

"Leave it to me."

Leave it to me?

Those words echoed in her head while Mia did what Mia did best. Organize, maneuver and entertain, all with a charming smile.

The smile was hard to hold in place, though, with all the thoughts of Spence that were racing around in her head. She watched, wide-eyed, as he strode toward those arguing men, determination and strength clear in his every step. Enough determination and strength that he barely made it halfway across the room before the gate-crasher caught sight of him. One look at Spence, and the guy scowled, jabbed his finger toward Alcosta's chest one last time, then hightailed it out the door.

She held her breath when Spence followed. Held it until she was dizzy. It wasn't until she caught sight of Lorraine sending a critical stare her way that Mia forced herself to exhale and, more important, get back to work.

It was silly to worry, she told herself as she signaled to the waitstaff to open the dining room doors. Then after Lorraine announced the meal, she helped usher guests out of the ballroom.

This was a charity ball. Not a seedy bar.

But that man wasn't on the guest list. So what was he doing here? Definitely not checking out the art.

Lorraine didn't believe in ruining the ambiance of events with any sort of security system and used her own people to welcome guests at the entrance and ensure they kept crashers—or as Lorraine put it, cheapskates—out. Still, Mia made a mental note to research security options for upcoming events.

Her lips quirked as the thought of how intimidating Spence had been striding across the room flashed through her mind.

She could probably hold off researching security while she had a man like that around. He was an entire security force in and of himself.

Smiling and chatting, she subtly ushered the guests toward dinner, all the while wondering where he was. How long did it take to shove someone out the doors and warn them to stay out?

Focus on your job, she ordered herself. Spence was a big boy. No, correction. He was a big, strong, gorgeous man. One who practically oozed control and power. She didn't care what he did as long as he didn't disrupt the event, didn't upset any guests and, most especially, didn't offend any of her potential clients.

Speaking of potential clients, Mia figured it wouldn't hurt to check in with Señor Alcosta, smooth any ruffled feathers, make sure all of his thoughts about this evening—and more important, about her skills as an event coordinator—were upbeat and positive.

She worked her way through the crowd, sharing a friendly word here and a compliment there as she made her way toward her goal. But as she reached the wide glass doors leading to the dining room, she saw Alcosta offer Lorraine that charming smile of his as he pulled out the chair on the other side of him for Clair.

A little of the tension drained from her shoulders. Okay, this was good.

A win-win.

Lorraine and Clair would entertain Alcosta, hopefully keeping him happy enough that he would forget the jerk in the ballroom. And giving Lorraine this time with Alcosta would be one more jewel in Mia's coordination-queen crown, proving yet again that anything the client wanted, Mia made happen.

Mia took another few minutes to ensure that Lorraine and all of her guests were satisfactorily settled, their chatter a loud hum over the duet of cutlery hitting china and the string trio.

Then she got back to work.

The same nerves that snapped in her stomach echoed in her voice as she instructed the staff to tidy the ballroom, replenish the bar and reset the seating.

Then Spence stepped through the double doors at the far end of the ballroom.

"What happened?" she asked, hurrying so fast across the marble floor that she almost slipped again. "Are you okay? Who was that man? And what took so long?"

"Nothing happened. I'm fine. I wasn't able to apprehend the intruder or discover his identity, as he went through a series of side doors to a running vehicle in what appears to be a prearranged exit strategy." Both frustration and disgust shimmered in Spence's eyes for a moment before he blinked them away and continued in that same official tone. "Not knowing the intruder's purpose, I deemed it prudent to do a search of the building and the perimeter. Other than a pair of drunks getting it on in the ladies' room on the far side of the building, all's five by five."

Five by five?

She knew that expression. It was military speak that meant that everything was fine. Mia's eyes narrowed with suspicion as she asked, "Do you have experience with the military?"

Spence blinked. He ran one long-fingered hand through his hair, then gave her a curious smile.

"Why would you think that?"

"The way you answer questions. Those short, specific responses answered in perfect order." Not to mention the way he'd taken charge and his search of the perimeter.

He frowned, silent for a second, as if replaying his words in his head. Then he shrugged.

"I'm not in the military," he said, sounding honest enough that Mia didn't feel comfortable pressing the issue. "I'm experienced working security. Am actually waiting to hear on a new security position, as a matter of fact."

Oh.

Ignoring the disappointment sinking in her belly, Mia nodded. "So that's why you're volunteering? Something temporary until you hear about the new job?"

"In part," he agreed, sliding his fingers along her arm.
Tingling little jolts of awareness shot lust through her
system, making Mia want to lean in for more before she
realized they were in the bartender's path as he tried to
wheel a dolly of cartons through.

"Let's get out of the way," Spence said, gesturing toward the patio doors.

She stepped out onto the patio just ahead of him and
breathed in the chilly night air so the scent of jasmine
wrapped around her. Portable heaters stood every few
feet, offering an oasis of warmth amid the cool evening.
Chairs, deeply cushioned and welcoming, were grouped
in welcome.

But Mia ignored them. She wasn't looking for comfort
right now. Instead, she walked toward the low wrought-
iron fence that hugged the patio on two sides. The or-
nate curlicues and twists of metal reached her waist and
blended with the soft blackness of her dress as she turned
to face Spence.

Behind him, she had a clear view of the ballroom and,
more important, of the closed dining doors beyond. She
could gauge the progress, be on hand and get information at the same time.

With the light behind him, Spence's face was shadowed. The darkness seemed to leech away that slick,
sleek gentlemanly veneer, leaving only raw male power.
Mia gave herself a second to adjust to the change, struggled to ignore how much she wanted to reach out. To
run her fingers through his hair. To rub her palms over
his shoulders, down his chest. To press herself against
that strong, hard body, just to see how it felt.

"In part?" she forced herself to say, picking up their
conversation again, both to quiet the sudden, desire-

spiked nerves dancing in her belly and because she really wanted the rest of the information. "What are the other parts of why you've come to work for me?"

He took a second before answering. Mia couldn't see his eyes, but she felt his stare. She had to force herself not to fidget under the assessing weight of it.

"Most of my work, security and otherwise, has been pretty down and dirty. I need to up my game, learn the ins and outs of working with people in a variety of social elements. Like this one. You've got the creative and eccentric artists, you've got servers and staff, and high-society muckety-mucks. Like that guy, Alcosta. I'll bet that's a guy who understands the need for security. If he was doing a party like this, he'd want to know it was covered tight."

"If that's one of his priorities, the fact that someone waltzed right in here and accosted him didn't make a very good impression," Mia pointed out, tapping her fingers on the railing as the worry took hold.

"Actually, I see it working in your favor. I scoped the setup prior to the event. Providing security, what there was of it, is firmly in Forever Families' list of responsibilities. So that guy getting in is on them," he pointed out, stabbing his thumb over his shoulder toward the ballroom. "On your side, though? The minute you saw that intruder, you took steps."

"*You* took steps," she muttered. "And you didn't catch him."

"I ejected him all the same," Spence said stiffly, insult practically dripping from his words. "Which Alcosta saw. Bottom line, that's the kind of thing that makes you look good."

"Okay. Okay," she decided, her fingers now smoothing down the fabric of her dress instead of tapping out worry. "You're right. This is a good thing. I can work this to my favor. I can weave it into my pitch on Monday, too."

"Pitch?"

"Mmm," she murmured, mentally revising her presentation outline. "Alcosta has hired me to create a series of events to raise funds for a children's hospital. I'll give my final pitch in a couple of days."

"And you're going to incorporate security into the mix?"

"I think it'd be a strong selling point and add an air of exclusivity and panache to the entire presentation. I'd need you to take point on all of the security, obviously. And to commit to working with me until the end of the events. What do you think? Can you stick around and work with me for the next month or so?"

Even as Mia told herself that this was a business discussion, the silly, giddy, crushing-on-him-big-time, way-too-hot-for-a-guy-she-barely-knew part of herself held her breath.

She wanted him to want her. So much, she wished he'd say he was interested in more than business with her. An unrealistic hope, the logical part of her mind pointed out.

Mia's breath lodged in her chest at the idea of her and Spence getting physical. No connection other than their bodies. No commitments other than pleasure. Those big, strong hands caressing her. Those intense, dark eyes watching her.

Oh, my.

She could get on board with him being physically interested in her.

Except he worked for her, she reminded herself, hoping the warning would take hold before she did something stupid. Like touch him.

Her fingers itched to skim that hint of stubble on his cheeks. Thankfully he answered before she could reach out and make a fool of herself.

"I think this is a great job that'll give me plenty of opportunities to up my game. I'll learn the ins and outs of working with high society, I'll get a solid behind-the-scenes understanding of how charitable programs function and I'll get to meet a lot of people." He offered her a smile that was so full of charm, she didn't need light to see it. "And who knows, if the security gig doesn't pan out, maybe we can work it out so I stay with you permanently."

Permanently? Delight fluttered in Mia's belly, then quickly dove into rock-hard dread at the memory of her earlier lie. As much as she'd rather keep it to herself, to just pretend it hadn't happened, she knew she couldn't. Not if Spence was going to continue working with her. Especially not if he was going to participate in the Alcosta fund-raisers.

"I have a confession to make," she said, the words as quiet as the night wind dancing through the trees. She wet her lips, her fingers twisting in the fabric of her dress as she tried to force herself to make the confession. But the words wouldn't come.

"What's your confession?" Spence prodded, stepping closer and shifting to the side just enough that the lights from the ballroom glanced off his face. Mia almost wished he hadn't moved. It was harder to make an idiot of herself if she could see his expression.

"Maybe it'll be easier if I give you the context first.

See, earlier this evening, a potential client—a really important one whose business I really, really need—expressed an interest in me. Actually, he expressed a little more interest than I was comfortable with."

"Did someone get pushy with you?" Spence asked. The words were quiet and calm, but there was something beneath them that sent a chill down Mia's spine.

She angled just a little closer to the heater.

"Oh, no. Nothing like that. And I'm usually better at shutting that kind of thing down. But this time I got flustered, I think, because the client is so important. Really, really important."

"Mia. You're rambling."

"Probably because this is a little embarrassing," she murmured, biting her lip as she tried to figure out how to admit the rest. Finally she just blurted it out. "When you came over to talk with me, he misinterpreted our relationship. Or rather, I encouraged him to misinterpret it. And now that it's been misinterpreted, I'd like to keep it that way."

Grimacing, Mia tried to mentally rephrase that in a way that made sense. She wasn't sure she could follow that line of babbling herself, so she had no expectation that he would. Before she could try, Spence nodded.

"So to sum up, the guy hit on you and wasn't taking no for an answer. Because you want his business, you didn't want to offend him, so you claimed I was your boyfriend?"

Relieved that he seemed more amused than irritated, Mia drew in an easy breath of cool night air and smiled. "Exactly. I swear, I've never done anything like that before. But I've worked really hard on the Alcosta campaign and didn't want to offend him before I'd even pitched my ideas."

"Alcosta?"

A little unnerved at the icy look in his eyes, Mia slowly nodded.

"You told Alcosta that we're in a relationship? That I'm your guy?"

"Yes." No longer relaxed, Mia tried a placating smile.

"Excellent." Before Mia could do more than frown at the change in tone, he angled his head and smiled. "Tell you what, if you're going to incorporate security into this pitch, we need to solidify our story and strategy ahead of time."

"Ahead of what time?"

"Ahead of that meeting time," he said, steely determination lurking just beneath the friendly tone. "I'm going with you. This way, I'm there to answer any questions and you won't be alone with Alcosta. At all."

Chapter 5

"What do you mean, you're dating your new assistant? How the hell did this happen so fast?"

"It's not fast, really," Mia lied. "It's pretty casual, so I hadn't told you about him before. Kind of like how you keep everything about your boyfriend, including his name, a secret."

After a lot of tossing and turning the night before, Mia had decided to keep up the fiction of her and Spence having a relationship in front of Jessica. It wasn't right to ask the woman to fib to her boss, and Mia wasn't willing to walk back the lie, so this just seemed easier.

Or at least it'd seemed that way in the wee hours. Now the bright morning light streaming through the kitchen windows seemed to emphasize every flaw in that thinking.

Or more to the point, it emphasized the irritation on

her roommate's already flawlessly made-up face. With her hair falling in loose curls over the shoulders of what Jessica considered casual Sunday wear—a silk maxi dress and designer heels—the blonde looked like she wanted to throw something.

"And where the hell did this guy come from? How'd he end up being your assistant?" Jessica asked, shooting out the next question with a bang before Mia had even responded to the first. "I thought you were letting me find a new assistant for you. I'm supposed to be helping you out, Mia. Don't you trust me?"

Teeth clenching, Mia bit back her automatic curse. Years of built-up frustration due to her family's guilt, guile and straight-up manipulation made her want to scream. But she knew Jessica wasn't deliberately trying to guilt-trip her, so Mia kept her tone light and her expression friendly as she explained.

"I appreciate all of your help, Jessica. I know how busy you are with your own work." Not to mention her even busier love life, since it'd kept her away from the apartment for two days. "Lucky for both of us, I mentioned my predicament to Spence and he offered to help out. He's perfet for the job."

"Perfect, is he? I guess that means you don't need my help any longer." Jessica's pretty face rearranged itself into a pout as she dropped into a chair with enough force to jar the table, sending Mia's tablet skittering across the slick surface.

Mia clamped down on the urge to grab her tablet and move it to a safer place. She'd had enough experience with drama to know that the second she chose the expensive tool she needed to basically run her business over her pouting roommate, things would get ugly.

"Of course I need your help," she said instead. "I don't know what I'd have done this last week without it. Especially with crafting the proposal for your boss. If I get that contract, added to all the events I have coming up, I'm going to need all the help I can get."

"That's true. You're going to be so busy training this boyfriend of yours, you'll probably have twice as much work for me," Jessica said, her teasing facial expression at odds with the irritation in her eyes. "I'd set aside this afternoon to work on your client and vendor database. I still need all of your contact information to get started, though."

No, Mia mentally groaned. Not the database.

Yes, she needed to put all of that information into a database. It was the biggest to-do task on her list, and had been for over a year. And it wasn't like it was top secret or anything. But it was *hers*.

She'd collected many clients' details over the years, with everything from their favorite restaurant to their favorite flowers to their pets' names. Her vendor information was complete, with notes on which subcontractors were friendliest, which were leeches and which ones needed big tips to do their jobs. Potential contacts, networking information, family connections. All of those notes, those index cards and those scraps of paper stuffed into a file needed to be input into an easily searchable database.

But she wanted to do it herself.

"Actually, I have a couple tasks that are much more important than the database, if you've got some time?" she told Jessica. To give herself time to think of them, she bent down to peer through the oven window. The cranberry-pecan muffins looked as done as they smelled.

Perfect.

"I've incorporated everything you told me about Señor Alcosta's preferences to incorporate as many cultural elements from his homeland as possible into my proposal. I have a list of venue options for Señor Alcosta but need their availability confirmed. I need quotes from three liquor vendors, to solicit set lists and demos from all of the local mariachi bands and a cost analysis for each event I've outlined, focused on the donation levels necessary to hit our goal," she listed as she pulled the tray from the oven using a vivid teal-and-green-striped oven mitt, pouring the ruby-studded golden mounds into a waiting basket.

All tasks she could easily do herself, but if Jessica took them on, Mia would have more time to perfect her presentation.

"If I'm doing all that, what's your guy doing?"

Mia almost said *security*, but caught herself at the last second. For some weird reason, Jessica was already feeling threatened by Mia having a new assistant. No point in making things worse.

"I figured I'd work with him one-on-one. You know, show him the ropes, use these first couple of weeks as training for bigger events," Mia hedged.

"Did you check his references? I'll do it myself," Jessica decided, pulling her cell phone out of her dress pocket. "Give me his name, his address, phone number—any pertinent information I can use to run him. Better yet, you have his application, right? I'll do a background check on him and on his references this morning."

"That's all taken care of." It wasn't, but for all she

knew, a wife or girlfriend should show up in that background check and ruin her fictional relationship.

"I hope you did a thorough job. It's your reputation—and mine, now—if he's incompetent," Jessica muttered, kicking the table again. "Of course, all that one-on-one training probably has its benefits. I hope you're not paying him for that."

"And I hope you're not insinuating that I don't know what I'm doing," Mia snapped, finally at the end of her rope. The only thing that irritated her more than someone trying to tell her how to handle her business was someone trying to tell her how to run her life.

"No, no." Looking horrified, Jessica waved both hands in the air as if clearing the slate. "I'd never do that. I admire what you've built. You're totally great at your job or I wouldn't have recommended you to my boss. I guess I'm just a little protective. You know, because I don't want to see some guy take advantage of you. And I'd especially hate to see anyone screw up your business or lose you a huge account like Alcosta International."

Surprised—and a little touched, once she got past the irritation, at how serious the other woman was—Mia offered a conciliatory smile.

"I'm not about to let anyone take advantage of me," she vowed. "Spence is a great guy. He's clever and strong. He has a take-charge personality and a great sense of humor."

Not to mention a tight butt and shoulders to die for.

"I can't wait to meet this paragon."

"I think you'll like him," Mia lied. Then, because she didn't see any way around it, she admitted, "He's coming by this afternoon. You can meet him then."

"You invited him here? To our apartment?" Her eyes

wide with outrage, Jessica reminded her, "Don't you remember our agreement? No lovers, no overnight guests, no uncomfortably sexy scenarios."

That hadn't so much been an agreement as the rule Mia had laid down after listening to Jessica go into detail about how one of her hotel room sexcapades had resulted in a shattered lamp, torn curtains and a broken bed frame.

Mia, on the other hand, had never even had sex hot enough to tear up the sheets, let alone do property damage.

Besides, it was her apartment, and up until a month ago, had been her office, as well. So she had every right to invite over anyone she wanted, especially anyone she might be dating—for real or otherwise. Those and a dozen other responses ran through Mia's mind. But pissing off Alcosta's assistant before she'd even had her morning coffee wasn't a good way to get it.

So she swallowed her comments and offered a placating smile before getting up to pour coffee into an oversize cobalt mug. Doctoring it with sugar, cream and a dash of cinnamon, she handed it to the woman who held her career in her manicured hands.

"This is just a business meeting, so the furniture is safe. Spence is handling the details on a few of my smaller events this week so I can focus on the presentation for Señor Alcosta," she explained. "I don't have a lot of extra time, so it seemed smartest to have him come here, where all the files and information are, instead of meeting him somewhere else."

With narrowed eyes, Jessica considered that as she took her first drink of coffee. By the second sip, she'd stopped tapping her foot against the table leg, and by the third her face was irritation-free and her body had relaxed.

"Well, I guess this is good, then. Anything that gives you more time and energy to focus on Santiago is great."

For a brief second, Mia considered asking Jessica if her boss was always a lech, but dismissed the idea. Dealing with perverts probably ranked right up there with property-damaging sex in Jessica's list of things strong women did.

"I didn't get a chance to talk with you Friday," Jessica continued. "But Santiago mentioned again how beneficial he thought it'd be if your uncle was attending his events. He's sure he can lure in a lot of dignitaries if they think a senator will be attending."

Mia's spine automatically stiffened.

She wasn't using her uncle as a bargaining chip, dammit. She wanted to get this job—every job—on the basis of her skills and reputation as a stellar event planner. Not because her uncle was a senator. Or her father an admiral, or her brother-in-law a fighter pilot.

But…

She covered her hesitation by getting up to top off her own coffee. Taking a little extra time stirring in a dollop of coconut milk, she considered the pros instead of the cons.

She knew perfectly well that networking was one of the strongest lynchpins in the art of soliciting large sums of money from people. Maybe it'd help if she looked at this as just another form of that. And agreeing to invite her uncle didn't guarantee his attendance. But it could cement this contract, would get her points for her willingness to meet the client's wishes and might pacify Jessica out of her snit.

"I'll give my uncle a call this evening. I'll mention the scope of the event and see if he might be available during that time frame. No guarantees," she cautioned when Jessica clapped her hands. "Even if he is available, he might not attend. He's very particular about that kind of thing."

"Why not?"

"It's a quirk of his. He doesn't like to imply support of any cause unless he's 100 percent behind it." Mia smiled in memory. "Once, he refused to attend my sister's ballet performance because they were doing *La Bayadère* and he was taking a stand against Russia."

"This is totally different," Jessica assured her. "I mean, who doesn't support hospitals for children?"

Actually, it was exactly the same, but Mia didn't bother pointing that out before Jessica glanced at her watch and gave a delicate yelp.

"I've got to go," she said, leaving her empty coffee mug on the table as she hurried out of the kitchen. "I'm meeting my hunk in an hour and I don't want to be late."

"I thought you were hanging out here today."

"I was planning to spend the day helping you. But now that you have someone to replace me, I'm going to give my hottie a good-morning treat before his flight."

"Where is he flying off to this time?" Mia asked, not surprised when Jessica shook her head.

"No, no, no. I can't tell that." Jessica stopped to lean her elbows on the short bar that ran between the kitchen and living room and offered a naughty wink. "But if you want, I'll tell you what we'll be doing. In great, vivid detail."

"No, no, no," Mia shot back. The last thing she wanted before a one-on-one session with the hottest man she'd ever met was to talk about someone else's wild, passionate sex life.

"Your loss," Jessica said with a laugh, heading toward her bedroom. "I could have inspired hours of work-time kink for you and your new hottie."

"During work time, he's my assistant." Nonwork time, too. More's the pity.

"Your call. Still, you might want to primp a little. Maybe punch up the makeup, wear something girly," Jessica threw over her shoulder. "You might not want bust-up-the-furniture passion, but if you're dating this guy, you do want him more interested in you than in the work."

No. She definitely wanted him interested in the work.

Mia caught a glance at herself in the etched mirror over the fireplace and frowned.

She'd given her hair its usual swipe of serum and finger-comb after her shower, so the short strands stood this way and that in gamine-like tousled disarray. Since she planned to work from home all day, she'd gone for casual, the front hem of her forest-green tee tucked into the waistband of her favorite boyfriend jeans, a chunky quartz-crystal necklace on a leather band and her favorite hoop earrings, the ones her father claimed were big enough for a bird to perch on. A smudge of liner and a swipe of mascara were all she'd bothered with for makeup.

But she looked fine.

Wrinkling her nose, she sighed and headed for the bathroom.

She wasn't changing her clothes, but it couldn't hurt to put on a little more makeup. Play up her eyes, add some gloss to her lips. Maybe even a light mist of perfume.

After all, a little interest in her wouldn't be a bad thing, would it?

By the time she'd fluffed the couch pillows for the third time and moved her files from the coffee table back to their usual spot on the bookcase in the kitchen, she had to admit that the idea of Spence being interested in her probably was a bad thing, since just thinking about it was turning her into a basket case.

Thankfully Jessica had swept out of the apartment, so she wasn't here to see Mia's dithering. Knowing you were acting like a giddy fool was one thing; being teased about it was another.

But it was kind of nice, Mia admitted to herself. For the first time in as long as she could remember, she was interested in something besides work, something beyond proving her professional success.

The doorbell rang.

All the air in the apartment disappeared. Her stomach doing a wicked 360, Mia grabbed on to the back of the couch to steady herself.

He's just a guy, she repeatedly reminded herself. A savvy assistant, here to assist with her events. A strong security specialist, who's expertise would ensure her success. A key component in proving her business acumen.

That's it. That's all. That's everything.

The viselike tension in Mia's chest eased, the spots clearing from her eyes as she took a deep breath. In control again, she gave her tee a little tug, lifted her chin and pulled open the door.

And all of those levelheaded thoughts were instantly overwhelmed by sensations, her mind going blank but for a low-level sexual buzz.

Like her, Spence wore jeans and a tee. But oh, wow, what his did for his body. The pale blue shirt stretched tautly over broad shoulders, the sleeves wrapped tightly around biceps so impressive, Mia was tempted to squeeze them to see if they were as hard as they looked. Denim stretched from slim hips to scarred work boots. She tore her gaze off the acre of his long, long legs to focus on his wrist and sighed. How could a utilitarian watch on a battered leather band be so sexy?

"Hello."

At his greeting, Mia tore her gaze off the sprinkling of hair on his arm to meet Spence's friendly gaze.

"Um, yes. Hi. Thanks for coming over," she greeted, grateful that her voice sounded normal. "I appreciate you giving up a Sunday to help me out."

"I'm always ready to report for duty," he said, his smile doing dangerous things to Mia's libido. "Show me what you want and how you want it done, and I'll make it happen."

Oh, if only.

She waved him into the apartment, touching the tip of her tongue to her upper lip to keep from sighing. The man worked for her, she reminded herself. This was all business. Despite the story she'd spun for Alcosta—and, by association, Jessica—Mia knew there were too many pitfalls in workplace relationships to willingly step into one.

"I looked over those event notes you emailed me," he said as he followed her down the short hallway to the living room. "My schedule is clear to handle everything on your list, and I have a few ideas for security on the bigger events."

"Great. I can't wait to hear your thoughts."

Nope. She couldn't fire him.

And since she couldn't climb on and gyrate with him, either, she'd have to settle for doing a kick-ass job with him.

So, this was where Admiral Cade's daughter lived. Not bad.

Spence looked around the living room, automatically noting the exits as he appreciated the energy of the space. Part of it could be Mia. She definitely added a tempting spark to every room he'd seen her in so far.

Today, she glowed as much as she sparkled.

The dewy gleam of her pale, silken skin emphasized those huge eyes with their thick, smudgy lashes. The hint of gloss touching her full lips tempted, making him wonder if they tasted as good as they looked.

Earrings big enough to fit a baby's fist swung from her ears, brushing the sharp angle of her jawline, drawing his eyes to the elegant length of her neck.

Trying to quench the heat flaring in his loins, he drew in a cooling breath and reminded himself that he was on assignment. But he couldn't help but wonder how the woman could make jeans and a T-shirt look so damned good.

He forced his attention back to the apartment. Clean white trim accented the cool blue walls and bleached wood floors, making the small room look larger than it was. The open floor plan added to the feeling of spaciousness, with a short tile bar separating the living room from the kitchen on one side and three closed doors that probably led to the bedrooms on the other.

Since wondering what Mia's bedroom looked like was a sure path to trouble, Spence deliberately turned his gaze away from those doors to check out the rest of the room. Purple, blue, teal—the colors made a bigger impact than the furniture itself. A fire flickered, low and comforting, below a white marble mantle. The room's pillows, rugs and knickknacks echoed the fire's friendly warmth.

It gave him an odd sense of contentment. Almost like a homecoming. Probably because it was nothing like the barracks he'd spent his adult life in, he told himself, trying to shake off the strange longing. He was just drawn to the place because it was a total contrast to Lori's overly trendy, minimalist apartment. He'd only been there once, but he still got a chill just thinking about all the chrome and Lucite.

"This is a great place," he said, meeting Mia's gaze again. "It looks like you."

"Does it?" Her smile flashed, those fairy eyes satisfied as she looked around the room. "Thank you. I like it here." Mia gestured for him to take a seat before asking, "Can I get you something to drink before we get started?"

"Coffee, black, if you have it."

"I do," she assured him, hurrying into the kitchen. After Mia punched a couple of buttons, the rich, heady scent of coffee filled the air, telling him she was a woman who believed in being prepared. "I made some cranberry muffins to go with it. Fresh this morning. Sound good?"

"You didn't have to go to the trouble." He sat on the couch, the deep cushions welcoming him to sink in and get comfortable. That seemed to be a theme with Mia. Comfort with class.

"No trouble," she assured him, pouring his coffee into

a glossy emerald mug before meeting his gaze across the small kitchen island. "You're giving up your Sunday morning to meet with me, the least I can do is offer you something to eat."

"You gotta do what you gotta do when you're building a career," he pointed out with a smile.

"Isn't that the truth," she agreed, setting his mug of coffee and a basket overflowing with golden muffins on the table. "I'll get the paperwork so we can rock working our careers."

Paperwork. Spence took a drink of coffee to hide his lack of enthusiasm. He'd rather order bartenders and florists around. Actually, he'd rather dodge bullets and blow up buildings. But apparently this was where his career was.

He was intrigued by that little tripping incident in the hallway at the gala. Adding that to the list of "accidents" involving Mia and her business over the previous six weeks, he thought it was worth looking into.

Cade, unfortunately, thought otherwise.

Dismissing the accidents as a byproduct of his daughter's propensity to rush through life and her habit of hiring unqualified people, the admiral ordered Spence to keep all his focus on Alcosta.

Not for the first time since his meeting with the admiral, Spence wondered if he'd made the right decision. Yeah, the promise of security work, the lure of duty alongside fellow military types—men who understood the nuances of protocol and skilled focus of teamwork, while facing untold dangers and protecting innocents—loomed brightly.

But so far, he was lying to a gorgeous, appealing woman, organizing party favors and chasing party crashers through fancy ballrooms. Not exactly an auspicious start to his new career.

Although, as he watched Mia bend at the waist to dig through a short filing cabinet wedged between the refrigerator and the kitchen table, he had to admit that the view here was a lot more appealing than any he'd seen in his years of travels.

Get a grip, he told himself, watching as Mia pulled out a big stack of what he assumed were event files. That the folders came in an array of colors, from red to purple to green, didn't surprise him.

She was clearly a woman of deep sensuality, he could tell, from the rich textures and vivid colors filling her apartment to the delicate scents wafting from the lilies in the corner and the wind chimes getting a workout in the San Francisco air just outside the window.

What did surprise him was the disarray the folders seemed to be in, stuffed in the cabinet in no apparent order, all with papers sticking out here and there.

Mia turned back, her arms filled with files. Seeing his surprise, she gave a half smile and a shrug.

"My roommate, Jessica Alexander, has been helping me with the office work lately," she said, wrinkling her nose as she set the files on the coffee table, sorting through the stack of papers, setting some aside and tidying the others. "She's great with concepts, but a little messy when it comes to little details like organization."

Alexander. It only took a second for Spence to flip through his mental files. Alcosta's assistant. Party girl with debt up to her baby blues, a reputation as a maneater and a history of catfights.

She was doing work for Mia?

That was a surprise. None of the reports hinted at the woman's generosity.

Looked like the admiral definitely knew his daughter. Still, Spence decided to take a closer look at Ms. Alexander.

"If you've already got help, do you really need me?" he asked, totally serious despite his light tone.

"I really do. Jessica really doesn't have time to do much. She has a demanding day job and this super-intense relationship. And, well, as much as I appreciated her donating her time, the type of work I do isn't actually in her wheelhouse."

"Donating time?"

"Didn't Karen tell you?" Her expression horrified, she dumped the pile of folders on the small oak kitchen table and hurried over to face him. "Oh, man. We should have talked about this before, but I don't usually bring someone in midevent, so I was distracted."

"No worries," he assured her. "What do we need to discuss?"

"Most of my assistants are volunteers," she admitted, biting her lip. "Actually, all of them are. Maybe it's because most of the work I do is to raise money for charities, but I try to keep my overhead as low as possible."

Excellent. The tension he hadn't even realized was balled in his gut eased. He felt bad enough working for the woman under false pretenses; he'd be damned if he'd take her money, too. Now he didn't have to come up with an excuse.

"My long-term goal is a security gig," he reminded her. "Helping you out will add some range to my skill set and it'll look great on my résumé, but it's definitely short-term."

"Oh." For a second, her bottom lip trembled and she looked sad enough to cry. Then, so fast that he wondered if he'd imagined the distress, she smiled. "Well, don't forget that I'm bidding on a huge fund-raiser tomorrow. If I get it, the series of events will kick off in three weeks. So as long as I can count on you to commit to the next month, we'll be fine."

Spence didn't know why he hesitated. He'd agreed to protect Mia until the end of Alcosta's fund-raiser or until they found something to nail the guy with—whichever came first.

But when it came to Mia, he was loathe to make any promises he might, for any reason, have to break.

"I'm all yours," he finally said.

"Are you, now?" Her smile started slowly, slipping from sweet to wicked with a flutter of her lashes.

Damn.

He could fall for those eyes.

So, yeah. Maybe that was the reason he'd rather avoid making her any promises. Because the woman tempted him to consider stupid ideas.

"Well, then," she murmured, her voice a throaty temptation. "I'll have to make sure that I make good use of you."

Before he could respond—or even temper his response down from the X-rated version in his head—she hurried back to the kitchen to grab the stack of files off the table.

"We've got three small fund-raisers, two solicitations meetings and my Alcosta presentation," Mia said, suddenly all business as she finished sorting her files and settled on the couch next to him. "You ready to learn the ropes?"

"Like I said, I'm all yours," he said again, just for the hell of it.

"Then let's get started."

Two hours later, Spence was sure of three things.

One, whatever doubts her family might have, Mia knew her stuff. Location options, wine choices, weather conditions, even the rates of exchange—she reeled off lists. Names, dates, themes and brands—she had them solid. For every event booked, she'd memorized the details. Every question he asked, she easily answered.

Two, this woman worked her ass off. Between the planning, the organizing, the coordinating and the execution, even the small events took a minimum of forty work hours. And she had three small events and one large one each week—not even counting the Alcosta fund-raiser, if she got the job.

And three, if he made it the entire month without giving in to his attraction for her, it'd be a testament to his miraculous willpower.

"I feel so comfortable handing over these events to you now," Mia declared, leaning back on the couch with a smile. "I think you're going to do great."

"Thanks. I'm good at coordinating details and strategizing results." Usually they were battle strategies, but he was nothing if not adaptable. And speaking of...

"Now that we've covered everything you need me to handle over the next of couple weeks, how about that Alcosta fund-raiser?"

In the process of tidying the stack of files she'd copied for his use, Mia gave him a questioning look.

"What do you mean?"

"What's the deal with this other event you're trying to get?"

"Actually, it's a series of events. A cocktail party, silent auction, golf tournament, fashion show and wine tasting, ending with a Monte Carlo Night–style gala. The tone for all events is luxurious indulgence," she said, getting up and hurrying into the kitchen for her computer tablet and a basket holding yet another stack of files. "Most fund-raisers of this caliber take months to plan, but Señor Alcosta is in a time crunch."

"Why the time crunch?"

"His previous funding fell through, and if he doesn't come up with the money for the children's hospital in the next six weeks, he'll lose the land and his investors." With her arms full, she settled onto the couch, next to him, with a bounce. Her knee brushed his thigh as she tucked one foot under the opposite leg and gave him a rueful smile. "If he likes my ideas, he's all but promised me the contract. Most big, established event planners were already booked. Even if they weren't, they'd probably say it was preposterous to try to pull off an event of that magnitude in that short of a time."

"You obviously aren't worried." Spence glanced at the folders, impressed to see that they were not only color coordinated, but cross-referenced, as well. But he'd put in enough time with event details today to earn her trust. Time to dig for information. "You'd think a guy like Alcosta would have enough connections to get around that sort of issue."

"I thought the same thing," Mia said, her attention focused on pulling up the Alcosta fund-raiser timeline on her tablet. "Jessica told me that he has plenty of connections, but he hates to call in favors. It's lucky for me that she convinced him to give me a chance since this type of an event will really catapult my business. It's going to be fun, too. A man like Alcosta, with his air of mystery and all that charm, is sure to be a real draw."

Charm? Mystery? Spence had to unclench his jaw before he could respond.

"He is the guy who hit on you, right?"

"I wouldn't say that he hit on me," she corrected, wrinkling her nose as she gave him an embarrassed look. "More like he implied that he wanted to hit on me."

"Implied it strongly enough that you needed a fake lover?"

"Fake boyfriend," she corrected, with her flush fading as she arched her brows in challenge.

"I haven't been called a boy in decades," he told her, appreciating that she met his gaze head-on, even as a hint of color washed her cheeks again. He couldn't resist the urge to see if he could get that hint to bloom into a full-on blush. "I think I prefer the term *lover*."

Instead of blushing and backing down, Mia rolled her eyes. "Just like a man to only be interested in one thing."

"Believe me, my interests are many and varied." Almost as many and varied as the sexual positions he was currently imagining her in. With a body as lithe and long as hers, the possibilities were pretty damned intriguing.

"There's only one of your interests that I need right now." Her words were sharp and decisive, but Spence could see the desire in her eyes. It made it damned hard to ignore his own.

"Tell me what you want," he encouraged, shifting on the couch so his arm lay across the back cushions. The move brought him just a little closer. Close enough to see the pulse dancing, fast and furiously, in Mia's throat.

"I really want to do an amazing job with the Alcosta account," she said faintly.

Just what he'd wanted to hear. Spence's smile was slow and just a little wicked.

"We'll have to be pretty convincing, then," he said, glad she was sticking with that idea. By pretending they were a couple, he had the perfect excuse to stay close to her side.

"Convincing?"

He took the tablet from her hands and set it on the coffee table, then shifted even closer. Close enough now to feel the heat pulsating off her body. To smell the soft scent of powdered vanilla emanating from her hair.

He knew the move was questionable from the standpoint of an officer serving under her father, but as the man pretending to be her assistant, Spence felt like he was on pretty solid ground.

"You told the guy we're in a relationship. We'd better be able to put on a good show to make sure he doesn't think you lied to him."

"It's not like anyone is going to be watching for us for public displays of affection," she pointed out with a breathless laugh.

"You never know."

Both to cement his position, and because the temptation was just too great, Spence reached out to skim his palm along her jaw before sliding his hand into her hair.

It was like running his fingers through silk.

Before he could do it again, she jumped to her feet. Her expression wary, she watched him slowly stand until he towered over her.

"Well, I think we covered everything we need to go over today," she said, her words coming in a rush.

"Wait." He wrapped his hand around her arm before she could move, slipping his fingers down until they curled into hers.

He could feel her trembling. He stared into her eyes, noting the gold sparks in the whiskey-dark depths, seeing the passion igniting those sparks into flames.

He could heard the alarms blaring a warning in his mind. He knew this was a dangerous move, one that could jeopardize his mission and, with it, his future.

But for the first time in his life, he was unable to resist risking both.

His eyes locked on hers, he lowered his head enough so their breath mingled. He gave it a second, watching her irises flare, feeling her breath come faster. Then he rubbed his lips over hers.

A single soft whisper of a kiss.

Swaying just a little, she pressed her hand against his chest to steady herself. Figuring she was anchored good enough now, he took her mouth again.

This time, he wasn't as gentle.

His lips took hers, teeth scraping as his tongue delved deeper into the welcoming, delicious warmth of her mouth. He felt her gasp, tasted it. Welcomed it. *More* was all he could think as his hands gripped her biceps to hold her still.

Sliding from tentative to bold in one sweep of the tongue, she met his kiss with the full force of her own passion. The effect on him was instantaneous. So hard that he felt like he'd snap, Spence forced himself to let her go.

Her eyes were huge, staring at him in glazed wonder. He waited for her to yell, to berate him. To say something. Anything.

"I should leave," he finally said, both to break the silence and because, dammit, he had to get out of here.

Even as he stepped away from the welcoming warmth of her body, a part of him waited—desperately hoped—for her to call him back.

"You should leave," she whispered in agreement instead. As if to ensure he did, she took a step of her own, putting more space between them.

A chill poured over him, seeping into his bones like regret. Whether it was regret for the kiss, or that it had ended, was up for debate.

Yeah. He'd better go. Before he did something even stupider than kissing her. Like telling her the truth.

Pausing only long enough to grab the stack of files she'd made for him, he headed for the exit.

"Spence…?"

He knew what she wanted to ask, and figured the least he could do was save her the words.

"It was just part of the act. Practice, in case we have to prove anything," he assured her, pausing at the edge of the entryway. "Don't worry about it."

"Right. The act." She managed a hint of a smile before grabbing her tablet and hugging it to her chest like a shield. "For the account. For the job."

"Right." He took one last look before heading for the door. "The job is what matters."

Chapter 6

"So, I dug deep on Alcosta. Dude's a dirtbag, for sure. His records are clean, but there's plenty that isn't in the records. A lot of travel, which could be reasonable given he's a real-estate mogul, so he has business all over the place. But these trips? These trips carry the stench of bad business."

That was something Steve Miggins, better known as Smidge to his friends, knew plenty about. Spence had served with Smidge his first year in the Navy, before the other man had been booted out for hacking into the Navy's personnel database for a home address and marital status of a pretty little blonde he'd wanted to hook up with. Now Smidge wrote code and designed algorithms for a huge online store, and kept his hacking to the occasional favor.

Which was why Spence had tapped him. He figured

while Cade was searching on the high road, he'd dig into the low road. Smidge had no compunction about circumventing legal channels to dig for information. That, and because Spence needed someone to alter his own records. After that first night, he'd realized that Mia might, and Alcosta would, check into his personal and professional history. Cade ordered knowledge of his military service to be off-limits, so Spence had tapped Smidge to create a false career trail, heavy on the security work. Now, thanks to Smidge's talents, Spence's fake work history would not only stand up to a basic internet search, but to all but a high-level background check.

It paid to have friends in low places.

"So, you didn't find anything solid? Nothing I can take to Cade to prove that the guy is dirty?"

And more to the point, use to cut short this mission so he could move on to his new career. Somewhere far, far away from the temptation that was Mia Cade.

"Nope. I got lots of hints, but nothing solid."

"What are the hints pointing to? Something about his traveling?"

"He goes to a lot of hot spots, you know? Places where drugs and crime rule the day. These trips are supposed to be tied to real estate deals, but he's not buying anything. Just traveling."

"Does anything pop up after a trip? Money moving through his bank account? New crimes associated with anywhere he visits? Anything like that?"

"What do I look like, a rank beginner? If something that simple had popped, I'd have said so. Still, there's no way the guy smells this bad for no reason. It'll just take me a while longer to figure it out."

Resigned, Spence leaned against the lamppost in front

of Alcosta's office building as he spoke to Smidge on the phone and considered the mission. Cade wanted his daughter safe from Alcosta. Which had nothing to do with whether the man was dirty or not.

So as far as Spence and Mia went? Temptation or not, they were together until she finished working for the guy. Together, pretending to be a couple whenever they were around the guy. Couples were friendly. Hugging, kissing, sexing.

Mia's face flashed in his mind, the appeal of those huge eyes, the taste of that wide, mobile mouth. The feel of that lithe body pressed against his.

Four more weeks working with her, ignoring the desire that wound so tightly in his gut that he couldn't think of anything else? Pretending he didn't imagine her naked half of the time, and coated in whipped cream the other half.

"Go wide. Look deeper into Alcosta's family. Anyone he's connected with. Grudges, conflicts, feuds toward him, and toward anyone he's close to," he decided. "Any information is useful information."

"Aye-aye, sir," Smidge retorted before laughing. "So, you're buddying up with Cade's daughter?"

"I'm protecting Cade's daughter," Spence snapped. "On his orders."

"Right. Orders."

"This is my shot, Smidge. A chance to work with Aegis."

"Dude, Aegis is huge. After you mentioned them, I did a little research. Founded last year by a former SEAL, the company offers security on par with the military. Comprised completely of former Special Ops personnel, it's run by Lucas Adrian," Smidege recited, obviously reading the information from his computer. "That's big shit, man. You know who Lucas Adrian is, right?"

"Navy SEAL, lieutenant in Naval Intelligence who flushed out an on-base blackmail ring running ops on everyone from captains to ensigns on three separate naval bases. He led his team in five separate strikes on enemy bases in Afghanistan and took out numbers two and six on the President's hit list," Spence recited.

"Good man, you did your homework."

No homework necessary. Lucas Adrian's fabled reputation had made the rounds long before Admiral Cade had waved the guy's company like a carrot on a stick.

"Still, seems like a crazy assignment," Smidge assessed. "You're what? Covering a potential target by playing secretary? That's gotta make the ole ego smart."

Maybe a little. But one of the first things he'd learned as a SEAL was that ego had no place on a mission. The only thing that mattered was the target.

"I want a spot on the Aegis team. This assignment is my job interview. Get me information," he repeated. "Any information I can use to nail this down."

"You got it," Smidge promised.

Spence hung up and shifted, his body on full alert.

Target sighted.

And damn, that target looked good.

Her form was long and lithe in a traffic-stopping red dress that hugged her waist before flaring into a fifties-style skirt that showed excellent legs. Shiny black heels with skinny straps matched the bag hooked over her shoulder. Nearly as dark, her hair spiked this way and that around her gorgeous face. Despite sunglasses that covered half that face, he could tell she was looking around.

For him?

Damn, he hoped so.

"Gotta go."

He shoved his phone into his pocket and strode across the street to meet Mia.

She looked even better up close and personal.

"Good morning," she greeted, those amber fairy eyes glinting through the lenses as she gave him a long, intense stare.

He could feel the questions hovering in the air between them as she studied him. A dozen responses came and went unspoken, because none mattered.

Telling her the truth would blow the mission, destroy his chances of a career with Aegis and seriously piss off the admiral.

Telling her he'd keep his hands to himself was iffy. He didn't plan to touch her again, knew it'd be the stupidest thing he could do. But everyone knew what road good intentions paved.

A long night of consideration told him that apologizing was probably the smartest choice. But he couldn't. Not because he wasn't willing to add yet another lie to the list he was feeding her. But because he was pretty sure any words that implied he regretted kissing her would freeze on his lips.

So he took the only option possible. He waited to see what she'd do.

"So, this is it," she finally said, giving him a tentative smile. "Ready to take me to the meeting?"

He could think of a dozen places he'd rather take her, but given their current circumstances, they were all off-limits.

"Ready as I'll ever be. Need any help with that?"

he asked, indicating the large portfolio-style case she carried.

"Nope." She shot him a bright smile. "I've got this. I'm ready to rock this presentation. I had a lot of energy to burn last night, so I went through it all again, polished it up and added some great elements."

He'd used his excess energy in the gym, beating his body into submission.

"Anything I need to know?"

"Nope." She shook her head as they stepped into the cool, airy office building. "I went over it twice with Jessica and it's perfect. We'll hold five events over the course of four days, culminating in a Monte Carlo–themed dinner gala and auction that'd make last weekend look like a country dance. We only have a little more than three weeks to prepare, but I'm sure we can do it. It's going to be great."

Mia gave their names to the receptionist. While they were escorted up to the twelfth floor by a snooty woman whose hair was wrapped so tight it stretched her face, Spence digested that.

Three weeks. Five events. Four days.

Pure hell.

Spence's only consolation was that after today, Mia should have little reason to be in Alcosta's company. She wouldn't need babysitting; he'd be busy pretending he knew what he was doing on her other events, and they would have little contact.

There it was, the cloudy silver lining.

Holding tightly to that, Spence followed Mia into a set of plush, overdecorated offices.

"Please wait here for Mr. Alcosta," their escort said

before sliding through a set of heavily carved walnut doors.

After taking one look around the room, with its curvy velvet couch, gilt picture frames and thick rugs, Mia didn't seem as sure of herself as she had downstairs.

Spence leaned against the wall next to the exit, watching her take a deep breath. She pulled out her presentation outline to review it, opened the portfolio, shuffled the papers, clipped them together, added her business card, took it off, then put it back.

"You nervous?"

Mia looked up with wide eyes.

"I usually thrive on presentations. On painting my vision for clients to see and convincing people that they did the right thing by taking a chance on me. I love the rush of it." She blew out a slow breath and, since apparently talking helped more than shuffling papers, shoved her report back in the bag. "But there's a lot riding on nailing this series of events. And Alcosta has a reputation."

Yeah, he did.

But Spence didn't think they were talking about the same thing.

"What kind of reputation?"

"According to Jessica, who should know, since she works for him, Señor Alcosta is extremely picky," Mia explained. "So as comfortable as I am with pitching events, as sure as I am that I have some great ideas that'll really work, I am a little concerned about getting it just right."

"From what I've seen, you're damned good at the event side of what you do. I'm sure you're just as good at the pitching side."

"Thank you." Surprised pleasure sparked in her eyes

as Mia reached out to take his hand and give it a squeeze. There was so much gratitude in the gesture that it practically dripped from her fingers. "I'm so glad you're here, though. I know your ideas for security will really make an impact."

Spence knew that, once accepted, missions left little room for a crisis of conscience. So he only allowed this one a few seconds before squashing it like a bug.

"I'm glad you think I'll make a difference. I promise to do my best."

"Actually, Jessica didn't think it was a good idea to bring you. She said it might change the dynamic, perhaps even shift Alcosta's focus."

Since he'd seen just what parts of her body Alcosta was focused on at the party the other night, Spence didn't see that as a bad thing.

"When I was adamant that you'd attend, she suggested that you wait out here while I meet with him," she admitted slowly, rolling the corner of her lower lip between her straight white teeth.

No.

First, she needed to stop biting her lip. It was just too tempting for him.

And second, she wasn't going in there alone. Spence's orders were to guard her from Alcosta at all times, and he couldn't do that unless he was in the same room.

"So, what? You're letting your roommate call the shots when it comes to this particular client?"

"No," she denied in a snappy tone. "I'm considering my roommate's suggestion based on her knowledge of this particular client. Professionals don't bring their boyfriends to presentations."

"That sounds like a quote."

Her lips twitching with humor, the irritation faded from Mia's eyes.

"Okay, it is a direct quote. Still, Jessica is Alcosta's assistant. She knows the man's mind and understands how he works. I shouldn't ignore that."

"You said you wanted to integrate security elements into your pitch," he reminded her. "A guy like Alcosta is going to want to know he's safe, right? Which means you need me to give him the details."

As excuses went, Spence figured that was pretty lame. But it got him what he wanted, since after another indecisive second nibbling temptingly on her bottom lip, Mia nodded.

"Okay. That's a good point. Let's keep the focus there. I'll introduce you as my security expert and use the incident at the Forever Families charity ball as a presentation point." She went on to outline the other points she wanted him to make, along with suggesting that he stay far in the background so that Alcosta would see him as wallpaper. The decisive way she gave those orders emphasized that she was in charge and would be calling all the shots.

He wasn't sure why the admiral was so dismissive of his daughter's skills as a businesswoman. As far as Spence could tell, she had one hell of a handle on getting things done.

"Be invisible, speak when spoken to, pay attention and look competent but not intimidating," Spence summed up when she was finished. "No problem."

"You actually mean that." She leaned back in the chair and studied his face, surprise creasing her brow. "No male ego, no power tripping, no condescending knowledge that your superior skills should be front and center since security is obviously more important than petty party planning?"

"Petty party planning?" Spence laughed. "You know better than that, right?"

"Of course I do. But in my experience, big bad alpha guys who focus on the safety and well-being of others tend to be somewhat dismissive of what I do," she told him, her shrug doing nothing to dismiss the hurt she felt over that attitude.

"Maybe all your experience is with the wrong kind of guys."

Those big brown eyes melted like chocolate in the hot sun, her expression both curious and considering. A soft smile played over her lips, making him wonder what he'd need to do with that mouth to make consideration overcome her curiosity.

Off-limits, he reminded himself, forcing his thoughts in a different direction.

"Either way," he said abruptly, "I'm here. I'm going in with you. We'll make it work."

Irritation chilled the warm admiration in her gaze.

Good.

He didn't want her thinking he was anything special. Fighting the battle of his own interest in her was challenge enough. Fighting it on two fronts would be nearly impossible.

"You're right. This will work," she decided, and then tapped her fingers on the leather portfolio, her short, clear nails making a determined *rat-a-tat-tat*. "But if at any time I get the feeling that Señor Alcosta would be more comfortable with you not there, I'll give you a signal to step out. We'll use a code word."

"A code word?"

"Yes, a code word. If at any point, I think it'd be better if you leave so I can finish the presentation, I'll mention the weather. You know, like 'It's been a warm day,' or 'Isn't it sunny out?' Whatever seems natural to the conversation."

"Whatever seems natural?"

"Exactly." Mia's smile made it clear she knew he hated the idea and didn't care. "You can handle that, right?"

Orders.

Spence was used to taking them.

Taking them from two conflicting sources was a new experience, though. It was going to take a little adjustment.

Before he could voice the agreement he knew Mia expected, another tight-faced assistant stepped into the room.

"Señor Alcosta is ready to see you now."

Alcosta's office was even heavier on the ornateness than his reception area. Bloodred rugs thick enough to sink their feet. Thick-topped tables covered in urns of flowers edged the walls, and a dark gilt-edged desk, heavy on the curlicues and big enough for an orgy, dominated the room. Alcosta rose from a black leather chair, sweeping around the desk with a smile that gleamed as brightly as the mirrors covering one wall.

He barely spared Spence a glance, instead focusing on Mia like a laser.

"Ms. Cade," Alcosta greeted. He took her hand in both of his, held it for an irritatingly long second before lifting it to his mouth.

For the first time in his life, Spence wished he carried a handkerchief. He needed something to wipe the smarm off Mia's knuckles.

"Señor Alcosta, I'd like to introduce my assistant and head of security, Spencer Lloyd," Mia said after she'd extracted her hand and returned the man's greeting.

"Mr. Lloyd," Alcosta said with a chilly inclination of his head, before focusing on Mia again. "I'm certain that with your skill and knowledge, you are more than capable of impressing me with your plans, Ms. Cade. There was no need to bring the hired help."

Hired help?

Ouch, Spence thought with a grin.

"Given the amount of money we're targeting, I've planned the events around a very exclusive guest list, including my uncle." Mia's smile was pure charm, her voice holding the same level of persuasion that Spence imagined sirens had used to lure sailors to their deaths.

Alcosta's face certainly lit up, a cunning sort of greed replacing the lust in his eyes.

"Your uncle would attend?"

"I can't guarantee his attendance," Mia said, patting her hand in the air as if to tamp down Alcosta's excitement. "But given that I'll be inviting him, I wanted to ensure that every event takes the possibility of his presence into account. Hence, a focus on security."

Well, that won Alcosta over. As the man waved a hand toward a trio of leather chairs grouped around a low glass table, Spence made a mental note to check into whomever Mia's uncle was later.

"Please. Be seated. Both of you."

Like Alcosta, Spence waited for Mia to settle in one of the plush club chairs before deliberately moving one of the others closer to her and taking his own seat.

After a brief moment, Alcosta took the third seat, angling it so Mia could get the full impact of his questionable charm. He offered her a friendly smile before turning his gaze on Spence. His eyes were like a snake's. Cold, black and assessing, as if he were deciding just where to strike.

Spence smiled.

Message received.

He'd seen that look on men's faces before. Men who considered him the enemy.

Good.

Winning the battle was all the sweeter when the opponent put up a good fight.

Mia wasn't sure what was going on, but she felt a lot like a juicy bone sitting between two big, hungry dogs. And while Spence had barely said a word, it sure seemed like he was winning. Tension wound tightly in her belly, because Alcosta didn't strike her as a gracious loser.

And he'd already lost to Spence once, even though he didn't know it. Biting her lip, she slid a sideways glance at her companion. As glad as she was to have him as a buffer between her and Alcosta, she hoped having him here wasn't a mistake.

Oh, not in the way Jessica had said. She had enough faith in her negotiating skills to handle any shifting dynamics. At least, she did, as long as she was focused and at the top of her game. Which was why she was worried this was a mistake. How could she focus on anything when Spence was sitting there, looking so gorgeous?

Obviously a man who took business casual seriously, he'd paired a dark blue dress shirt and tie in the same hue with a pair of crisp jeans and boots. His hair glinted mahogany with just a hint of curl, and unlike yesterday his face was shaved clean of that sexy scruff.

He lounged more than sat in the chair, his body at ease and his expression mellow. But Mia still felt like he was ready to pounce. As if the smallest thing would set him off.

Like yesterday. She'd spent the entire night replaying that kiss, and she still couldn't figure out what'd triggered that. And she was desperate to know. After all, without knowing why he'd done it, how could she get him to do it again?

Which wasn't what she should be thinking about now, she reminded herself, forcing herself to ignore the tingling brought on by the memory of Spence's mouth on hers.

She was here to wow Alcosta so he'd sign off on her plans, give her a big, fat check and let her get to work. She wasn't here to obsess about her assistant/security specialist/fake boyfriend.

Thankfully, dangling her uncle's name as a potential guest seemed to have caught Alcosta's attention enough that he hadn't noticed her slip into fantasyland while he'd taken his seat.

"Please show me your brilliant plan, Ms. Cade. I'm looking forward to cementing our relationship in both pleasure and profit."

Mia felt rather than saw Spence's disdain, but her own smile didn't falter. Cheesy comments, leering looks and horrible decorating taste aside, the man was her client. Her very wealthy, if slightly eccentric, going-to-launch-her-to-success-with-his-huge-event client.

With that in mind, she opened her portfolio and offered Señor Alcosta the embossed folder that contained her proposal, both in bullet points and in detail with enough information to make her plan very clear. The proposal was deliberately vague on specifics like vendor names or contact information.

Mia had heard plenty of stories of wealthy clients stealing a planner's event ideas, their vendor contacts and even their staff. Señor Alcosta seemed like a nice enough guy, but her daddy hadn't raised a fool.

As he leafed through the folder, she began her pitch. Despite the older man's neutral expression throughout, it only took the ten-minute overview for her to see she'd hit a bull's-eye. Not just because he began nodding so much that he looked like a bobblehead, but because he'd made enough notes throughout the folder to assure her that he was enthusiastic.

It was all Mia could do not to bounce in her seat as she finished the broad overview of her plan.

"I think these five luxury-retreat-themed events over a three-day weekend will not only impress the donors into digging deep into their pockets, but by offering both a weekend price point and individual event tickets, we'll draw a much larger guest list than if the weekend were billed as a single event."

"Mmm, yes, as you say, that's a clever plan," Alcosta agreed. "But what of the time constraints? Will this not cause an issue with attracting enough patrons? As I'm sure you recall, there is a deadline looming, in barely over a month my company will lose the property, as well as the entirety of our hard-earned bureaucratic support, unless the five-million-dollar threshold is met in time."

Spence shifted hard enough that his chair scuffed on the carpet. Ignoring him, Mia handed Alcosta the PR proposal she'd created.

"Which is why I'd not only schedule ample press coverage, but would call in multiple favors in order to publicize the event. A longer lead time would be better, of course. But I'm quite confident that I'd be able to generate enough excitement and interest in the event to attract enough donors," Mia assured him. "And as you can see from my outline, I'd actually use that time frame to gently pressure generosity in our patrons—especially those who aren't able to attend in person."

"And the actual work of the event? In my experience, I'd estimate a bare minimum of three months, promotion notwithstanding, to successfully implement an event of this magnitude."

Spence's snort was quiet enough that Mia hoped she was the only one who'd noticed it. Before he could ask the question she saw teetering there on the tip of his tongue, she reached for her portfolio, making a point of smacking Spence in the knee with it when she reached inside to pull out her itemized proposal.

"Well, yes, three months definitely would have been ideal," Mia agreed, handing Señor Alcosta the thick proposal with a rueful shrug. "But I'm a big believer in making the most out of what you have. As you can see by this outline, I've called in a few favors to book the ideal venue. The Napa location is easy traveling distance for most of our Northern California donors, but I have a tentative hold on a block of rooms at a nearby hotel, pending your approval. I've also checked the availability of all of the subvendors I'd like to use and asked my top choices to earmark the dates for us. All of this is tentative, pending your approval, of course."

And she'd had to call up every marker she'd had in her arsenal, in addition to promising everything in return, right down to her very soul, to pull it off. But she figured her soul was a fair price to pay for an opportunity like this.

"Since this will be a high-profile event—especially the Monte Carlo gala—that targets a wealthy and powerful guest list, one of the key components is security. My security specialist has outlined that plan."

With that, she gestured to Spence to take over. Abandoning his casual pose, he stood with almost military precision to describe his strategy for securing each event. Like she had with much of her plan, he gave broad strokes rather than details, since they hadn't committed to a specific location. He wound up his short narrative by reminding Alcosta of the incident at the Forever Families gala.

"Your guests should not only be safe, but comfortable in the knowledge that they won't be accosted. I doubt you were thinking about donating money to the cause last week when that guy crashed the party and got in your face, right?"

Obviously less than thrilled at the reminder, Señor Alcosta grimaced.

"Is all of this really necessary?" he asked distastefully. "It sounds only one step up from hulking guards and metal detectors."

"As Spence said, your guests' comfort and safety will be paramount, and can be done without adding to the cost."

Mia thought Alcosta was going to argue. She didn't understand why he wasn't jumping at the idea of solid security, and held her breath until he gave an expressive shrug and waved his hand.

"The security sounds adequate. Let's move on to

the guest list, shall we?" Alcosta suggested, dismissing Spence's contribution with a flip of the page as he turned to that section of Mia's proposal. As she had with her vendor list, Mia had kept it informatively general by offering detailed résumés of known philanthropists and organizations she planned to target, in addition to numerous smaller groups and lesser-known donors. Included in that section were projected attendance and funds she anticipated, both from each event and for the fund-raiser as a whole.

"A larger donor pool might be preferable," he murmured, running his finger down the page as he read.

"Unlike the event plans, the guest list is more fluid," Mia explained, none of the tension she suddenly felt obvious in her voice. "I'd be happy to work with your assistant to ensure that your own contacts are invited, as well."

"My contacts?" Alcosta looked like he didn't much like that idea.

"Human nature is such that people often donate more money and more often to someone they know. Your business and personal contacts, especially those from your own country, are more likely to have a personal investment in the building of your hospital."

"Yes, yes," he said, waving her words away as if they didn't matter. "But my desire to raise funds here, using your services, was in order to access people I couldn't reach on my own. I've already discussed this venture with the businessmen of my acquaintance. Is it not contrary to our purpose to invite and, quite honestly, fund their attendance?"

Used to that question, Mia explained the advantages versus the potential costs until Alcosta was finally satis-

fied. She was tempted to check her brow to see if she'd
worked up a sweat trying to get his agreement.

Desperate to move on to the after-event portion of
her presentation before he changed his mind again, Mia
quickly took a sip of water to wet her dry throat.

"What about inviting your family?" Spence asked
before she could change the subject. "Big fund-raiser
like this, you must have a lot of relatives that will want
to be here."

No, no, no. Mia held her breath. She should have
warned Spence that family was an off-limits topic for
Señor Alcosta.

"Ahh, family. Both a blessing and a curse, isn't it?"
His jaw tight, Alcosta shook his head. "But sadly, no.
Traveling to the United States is not an option for most
of my family."

Mia leaned forward to pour more water from the iced
pitcher so he couldn't read her expression.

"Some families are more curse than blessing, that's
for sure," Spence agreed. His tone was so conversational, Mia paused, midpour, to check his expression.
She couldn't read anything there, either, though.

"Your family sure has a reputation," he continued,
leaning forward to brace his elbows on his knees, hands
dangling between his legs as he gave Alcosta an easy
smile. "Drug cartels, smuggling and, what was it your
cousin went down for? Leading one of the largest human
trafficking rings in Colombia?"

Something bright and mean flashed in Alcosta's
eyes before they flattened. He considered Spence with
a snakelike disdain that made Mia feel as if he were deciding exactly where to strike to cause the most pain.

"My cousin's sins are not my own. I, unlike many

in my family, strive to help people. To offer support and good influence. That very operation for which my cousin was arrested, for instance, resulted in the death of many people, some of them family members. Leaving behind the devastation of grieving widows and orphaned children."

Mia could all but see Spence's taunting rejoinder. One that'd match the disdain so clear on his face. While she agreed that the Alcosta families crimes were horrible, Santiago wasn't his family.

"Spence," she murmured, mentally digging her fingernails into his arm to emphasize her warning.

"No, no," Alcosta said with a generous wave of his hand. "It's good to bring this into the open."

"As disturbing as incidents like the one Señor Lloyd mentions might be, they did help me become the man I am today. After that incident, I reached out to help those left behind. I offered financial support, I helped many relocate to safer places. I even all but adopted one orphaned boy, giving him a home and education." He paused to offer Mia a pious smile. "While I condemned the crime, I know full well how hard it is for family members who, through no act of their own, are judged by their relations."

Mia gave a hum of sympathy, empathy all but pouring through her.

"Yeah, a family like that, you gotta admit staying out of the dirt is a challenge," Spence said, clearly not at all empathetic. "If nothing else, it must give you all a lot to talk about at those big Thanksgiving dinners."

"Perhaps we'll have something new to talk about next year. A cautionary tale describing what happens to people who speak of things they know nothing about."

Enough. Seeing her brilliant career trajectory going down in flames, Mia hurried to interrupt what was quickly devolving into nasty byplay.

"Spence, thank you for the security outline. I'm sure it'll go a long way to ensure that everyone's focus at these events is on the ambiance, the sunshine and the great weather."

"Unless it rains."

"It won't. Not if it knows what's good for it," she said, grinding out the words through her smile.

For a second, she thought he'd ignore her. Finally, with just a hint of an eye roll, he subtly reached into his pocket. A heartbeat later, his cell phone rang. He made as if reading the display before giving Alcosta an apologetic grimace.

"Sorry, but I have to take this call." He gestured to Mia with his phone and told Alcosta, "If you have any security questions for me, just send them through Mia."

Then he brushed his hand over Mia's shoulder. Even though she knew it was just for show, he rubbed his thumb along her jaw. The light slide of his finger over her skin sent a shimmer of desire tingling through Mia's system. Her stomach jittered. Her breath tangled in her throat. Her lips trembled into a smile and her eyes locked on his for a long, heart-stopping moment before Spence tore his gaze away.

She was so caught up in the sensations that it took her a few deep breaths to refocus after he strode out the door. Two more and she was able to relaunch into finishing her pitch. It took her twenty minutes, but finally she'd said all she had to say and was able to take a deep enough breath to loosen the knots tangled in her stomach.

"I much admire your ideas and think that we'll do

good work together," Santiago finally said after she'd finished outlining all of the events and answering all of his questions. "There are only two adjustments I'd like to make."

Although her fingers were itching to pull the contract from her bag, Mia pulled out a fresh pad of paper instead. Pen poised, she smiled and asked, "Just let me know what they are and I'll make them happen."

"First, although I will be working at your side through every element of this fund-raiser, I'd also like you to work closely with my assistant. As you know, Jessica is well-versed in my preferences and my business."

"Absolutely," Mia agreed.

"Excellent. Second, as much as I appreciate your attention to detail and consideration for all elements of this fund-raiser, I believe my own security is sufficient for these events."

Mia's stomach tightened right back up again. She'd been afraid of that. Still, the sympathy she felt over everything he'd faced—and overcome—was still front and center in her mind. And she thought her family was a challenge?

But while sympathy might make her feel closer to him, it didn't blind her to the pitfalls of doing this job without Spence as a buffer.

"I have every faith in your security, Santiago. But if I can be frank? A number of the guests, my uncle included, will be more comfortable attending if my company is providing the security."

As she'd hoped, all it took was mentioning her uncle to change his mind.

"Very well," he said slowly. She could tell from the look in his eyes that it really wasn't very well and knew they'd be revisiting this again. "Finally, third, I have a question."

Her already uneasy stomach began churning in response to the look in his eyes, yet Mia still smiled and asked, "Yes?"

"I would like very much for you to join me at dinner tonight to celebrate the success of our joint venture. We could discuss future work together, other ways we could collaborate. No need to bring your security friend." He said it like he was joking, his tone light and teasing. But the look in his eyes warned Mia that he was anything but resigned to her being in a relationship.

The uneasiness in her stomach knotted tightly, the tension spreading to her shoulders so she felt as stiff as a board. But Mia managed a friendly smile.

"I appreciate the invitation. I really do—" she started to say. Before she could finish her refusal, he shook his head.

"No, no. No need to explain," he said, waving his hands extravagantly. "We will be spending a great deal of time together over the next few weeks. I will sweep you so far off your feet that you will forget even the name of your friend. You'll see that I can do so much more for you than that man could."

Good thing she didn't want a man doing things for her, Mia thought as she got to her feet. Still, she'd had enough experience with bloated male egos to know she had to tread lightly.

"But if you were busy showing me the world, how would I produce the most successful series of fund-raising events ever held, and all in your name?" she asked with a laugh, repacking her portfolio as fast as she could. "I'm sure it's better this way. After all, it's going to take all of my time, and every bit of help I can get, to do justice to your vision of these events, and to your name."

"You'll do an amazing job, I'm sure," he said as he got to his feet. "I am just as sure that you'll soon be tired of your friend and ready to enjoy my company."

Fat chance, Mia thought with a friendly smile. If she was sure of one thing, it was that she'd never be tired of Spence in any way, shape or form.

Chapter 7

With the same care she'd take sneaking away from a ferocious, napping tiger, Mia escaped Señor Alcosta's office. She'd never felt as triumphant, stressed and disgusted at the same time.

She had her signed contract and a big fat deposit. She had the biggest events of her career to pull off in the shortest time she'd ever been allotted. And instead of her preferred method of working on her own to do so, she'd have to work side by side with a guy old enough to be her father, who was trying to oust her fake boyfriend from her bed so he could show her the world.

Ah, well, Mia sighed. Nothing came without a price, and since it was pointless to whine about getting what she wanted, she set it aside.

Instead, she started compiling her to-do list for the rest of the day as she hurried toward the elevator. She'd made it tentatively, in anticipation of getting the contract, but she had to integrate the changes Señor Alcosta wanted, then nail down the details.

Mentally adjusting the list, reordering her planned phone calls and debating whether to call her uncle tonight, or wait till morning, Mia punched the elevator's down button.

"How'd it go?"

"Oh." She gasped so hard, she almost sucked off her lipstick. "I didn't realize you were still here."

"What kind of boyfriend would I be if I left you at the mercy of a guy like that?"

Hands in his pockets, Spence straightened from his position against the wall opposite the elevator and held out his hand for her portfolio.

"The same kind of boyfriend who'd make me carry my own bag?" Mia guessed, half laughing. After a second—because despite antagonizing Alcosta, he'd actually been helpful in there—she handed him the large leather portfolio.

When the elevator doors opened with a *ding*, Spence waved her in and waited, silently leaning against the wall again, until the doors closed.

Mia pressed the lobby button before glancing at Spence.

She started to launch into a description of how her meeting had ended, but her words caught in her throat.

He was staring at her, those dark eyes so piercing that she wanted to squirm. Instead, she arched one brow in question.

He just smiled.

But it was that intense, sexy smile of his that made her want to sweep her tongue over his bottom lip to see if he still tasted as good as he looked. She'd bet money that he did.

She shifted from one foot to the other, clasped her hands together, then let them fall to her side again. She knew it was stupid, but she wished she was the one carrying her portfolio so she could use it as a shield.

Remembering his little act of sexy make-believe in Señor Alcosta's office, her chin tingled as if he'd just reached out to touch her again.

Or maybe that was just wishful thinking.

"Well?" he finally asked, his voice wrapping around that single word in husky invitation.

Mia wet her lips.

"Well, what?"

His smiled widened.

"Well, how was the rest of the meeting?"

Oh. Well, damn.

Mia wondered if he could hear the sad *wah-wah* of her ego deflating.

"It was good enough to garner a signed contract, a nice advance check and enough work over the next three weeks to make sanity iffy and sleep a fond memory."

"Congratulations." His smile shifted from predatory to pleased. "That's great."

"Thanks." Thinking of how much she had to do, and how much was riding on doing it well, Mia blew out a long breath. "I'm glad you'll be handling the bulk of the current workload. It's really going to help give me time to focus on getting everything done for this huge extravaganza."

"For the next three weeks, anything you need, I'm your man," he said as the elevator doors opened to the lobby.

She liked the sound of that.

There were so many things she needed. A candlelit, full-body massage. Practice finger painting whipped-cream designs on a sexy, hard body. A mind-blowing orgasm or ten.

"We should celebrate," she heard herself suggest as they walked through the lobby toward the exit. Afraid he'd think she meant they should celebrate the way she really wanted to celebrate, she quickly added, "We can get a drink, maybe something to eat, discuss the upcoming week's schedule, that sort of thing."

"Sure. Food sounds good," he agreed. "Where would you like to go?"

Before she could decide, he wrapped his arm around her shoulder, yanking her against his side.

Mia yelped.

So much tension shot through his body that she could feel it seeping into her own muscles.

"What're you doing?"

"Just a second," he murmured, pulling her to the side of the lobby, behind a six-foot palm. He shifted their bodies so they were face-to-face.

Her breath caught in her chest.

Was he going to kiss her again?

Her mind racing, she bit her lip. What if he did? Should she let him? Sure, she'd been obsessing with their first kiss since he'd closed her front door. But obsessions and fantasies aside, the bottom line was that the man worked for her.

Hitting on him was all kinds of wrong. But him hitting on her?

She breathed in his scent, soap and an ocean breeze, and decided that him hitting on her was probably fine.

Just fine.

"Spence—"

"Quiet," he ordered, staring over her shoulder with eyes narrowed in concentration.

"What?"

"Over there." Still holding her with one arm, her portfolio with the other, he gestured with his chin. "It's the guy who'd got in Alcosta's face at the ball last week."

"Here?" Mia started to turn around, wanting to get a look for herself. She froze, the man forgotten when Spence wrapped her tighter against him. "What are you doing?"

"Using you as camouflage," he said, looking away from his prey just long enough to give her a smile. "The guy ran from me once already. I don't want him getting away again."

"Again? What do you mean, again?" He wasn't going to chase the man through this building, was he?

"He crashed your party last week to confront Alcosta, and now he's at the man's office. If the guy means trouble, what do you think the chances are that he wouldn't show up again at one of your Alcosta fund-raisers?"

Mia frowned.

Well, that burst her sexy little fantasy.

"Are you sure it's the same guy?"

Taking her cue from Spence, instead of twisting around to check the other man out this time, Mia dropped her purse so, when she bent down to pick it up, she could look over without being obvious.

She shivered.

It was the same man, all right.

And he wore the same dark scowl.

"He looks mean," she murmured.

The man was about her height, but almost as broad as Spence. Even in a pricey suit, his muscles rippled in a way that screamed brawler. Cell phone against his ear, he paced in front of the elevator, enough anger in his steps that she was surprised he didn't kick the metal doors to hurry it up.

"I'm going to follow him, see where he goes."

"No," Mia protested. "He could be dangerous."

"So can I."

Oh, God.

Why did that turn her on?

"Maybe you should call security instead of following him," she suggested. She knew the words were futile before they even left her lips, but she'd had to try.

"No point." He wrapped her fingers around her portfolio. "Wait for me in front of the building."

"Hold on." She made a grab for him, but his sport coat slipped through her fingers. "Spence, please."

That stopped him.

He stopped and gave her an impatient look.

"This is what I do." He headed for the elevator without a backward glance, leaving Mia standing there, with worry crawling up and down her spine as she watched him check the elevator the guy had taken before hurrying to the stairwell.

Oh, damn.

Mia ran after him toward the elevator, her heels sliding precariously on the marble floor with each step. As soon as she reached the closed doors, she realized she had no idea what she was doing. Resisting the urge to follow the angry guy's example and kick the doors, she stared at the light indicating up, blew out a breath and turned on one heel.

Damn Spence.

What had he been thinking, running after that man without a clue about what he might be getting into? Granted, the danger in a midtown San Francisco office building was minimal, but still…

She left the building in a huff. Once she hit the fresh, cool outdoor air, she paused. Was she really going to wait? Why? She had work to do. A lot of important work. Spence knew how to reach her when he was done chasing his imaginary bad guy.

But instead of leaving, she paced in front of the building until her heels pinched her toes. Still, Spence didn't come out. Her fingers gripped the handle of her portfolio so tightly, they hurt almost as much as her feet.

Where the hell was he?

Was he okay? What if the man was armed? Spence might have security experience and be plenty smart, but even more than Alcosta's confession, she'd done enough research of her own into his background to know that even if he was clean, his family ran with plenty of scary people. Drug lords, smugglers and the like. What if the guy Spence had followed was one of them?

A trickle of terror lodged in her gut. Her stomach clenched tightly around that fear to keep it from spreading to the rest of her body.

This was why she'd always refused to date a military man, she remembered. She'd had no choice in growing up with a father who dedicated his life to danger, but there was no way she was giving her heart to a man like that by choice. She'd learned young that loving someone in the military meant living with worry.

And what did worry get you?

Stress, stomachaches and worry lines. And more important, wasted time.

To hell with that. She'd learned young that she didn't want any of those. She'd learned, too, that the best way to avoid them was to focus on something else.

Mia looked around and saw a big cement fountain in front of the building that had a benchlike rim for sitting. She made herself comfortable, resting her portfolio against her legs and a notepad on her lap, and then pulled out her cell phone and got to work. The app she used for planning synced between her tablet and phone, so while it might be a little harder to work this way, she'd manage just fine.

And so she did.

By the time she'd finished her first phone call, she'd confirmed the main location for the bulk of Alcosta's events, and she had herself under control. Spence was doing his job. She was doing hers. No big deal.

After her second call, she'd booked her preferred caterer, confirmed their appointment to solidify the menu the next week and had negotiated a 10 percent discount by promising to use the company for her next three events. And her mood had gone from tense to elated. She'd rather have a go-getter working for her than some slacker who hid behind her, asking what to do. So he'd chased after a creeper. He was right, that guy could ruin their event.

By her third call, she'd not only found her equilibrium again, but she was back on cloud nine. A good thing, since the call was turning out to be a bust.

"Are you sure you can't handle those dates, Frank? When we discussed this last week, you seemed confident that you'd have no problem providing flowers for these events."

As she listened to his litany of excuses, she drew a line through the florist's name and, after debating the other three listed, she sketched an arrow to her second choice. Impatient to get on with nailing down her biggest vendors, she ended the call. Before she could dial her second choice, a tingle raced over her flesh.

She looked up.

"Oh." She blinked against the sun. Even with his features obscured by the light, she could read Spence's expression. Pure frustration, with a hint of satisfaction. "I guess you didn't catch the guy?"

"I lost him after he went into one of the offices on Alcosta's floor where he met a woman. I didn't get a good look at her, but I'd recognize her voice if I hear it again."

"My roommate, Jessica, works there. I could describe the guy, see if she knows who he is."

"No."

When she arched her brow at his abrupt response, he amended, "He might hear about it. Whoever he is, I don't want him tipped off."

"You make it all sound like a Bond movie." Mia laughed, sliding her notepad into her bag and getting to her feet. "He is probably seeing one of Señor Alcosta's employees and thought the person would be at the ball the other night."

"Could be," Spence agreed. "But even if that's true, the guy still needs a talking to. I'm not having him bust into one of your events again to make a scene."

Mia's eyes widened. She knew it was his job. She knew perfectly well that he was a responsible guy who was naturally protective. But his vehemence made her feel all soft and warm inside. Being so antimilitary when it came to the men she dated, she'd never been big on that alpha attitude, but it sure looked good on Spence.

Good and sexy. She gave him a quick once-over, her eyes lingering for a long moment on his shoulders, broad enough to block the sunlight. Oh yeah, he was so, so sexy.

"So?" At her blank look, he added, "Ready to do it?"

Horrified that her thoughts might be clear on her face, Mia slapped her sunglasses on.

"Do what?"

"Celebrate? Let's go get that drink."

Right. They'd talk business, go over her plans and, sure, toast the new contract.

One drink wouldn't hurt.

"And food. We definitely need food," Mia said, gathering her portfolio and composure. And vowed that by the time they reached the restaurant, she'd have a handle on her libido, too.

Because hot or not, hitting on people who worked for her was off-limits.

Spence sat across from Mia in a quaint Italian bistro, the scent of sauces and spices redolent enough to mask her tempting perfume. Too early for the dinner crowd, and too late for lunch, there weren't a lot of people in the restaurant, so it was quiet.

The better to enjoy Mia's company.

He leaned back, one arm wrapped around the back of his chair as he listened to her summarize her meeting. He liked the way her eyes lit with delight when she detailed her progress so far, and tried to ignore the temptation of her mouth and the way it moved as she spoke.

On top of gorgeous, she was smart and savvy, with a wicked sense of humor. She was a lot more fun than any woman he'd ever dated. Which was probably why he'd never dated a woman for more than a couple of months.

Not that this was a date.

This was business. On two levels, all business. He just had to remember that.

"So, I'm solid on the jobs you need me to cover this week. How about the Alcosta event? What do you need me to do for that?" he asked when she finished her summary and stopped to take a sip of her ice water.

He wasn't surprised when she pulled out a detailed task list. But he was when she didn't hand it over as he reached out. Instead, she pulled out her pen.

"I have to make some changes," she said absently, her attention on the notes she was scrawling across the pages. Spence leaned across the table to see how much more she wanted to do, then frowned.

"You just booked the biggest event of your career and you're cutting back on the amount of work you want me to help with? Are you sure you're doing this right?"

"One of the requests Señor Alcosta made was that in addition to having his assistant, Jessica, involved, he wants to personally assist me with a lot of the event details." She glanced up and gave him a reassuring smile. "Don't worry. I'm not taking any key jobs from your list. I'm only having Señor Alcosta help with a few tasks that I'm already taking point on."

Mia and Alcosta, together? Just the two of them? Without him standing between them, doing his duty to protect Mia from any danger—real or imagined? Sure, any danger was more imagined than real at this point, but orders were orders.

"No."

"Sorry, what?"

"No," he said again. "You're not deliberately arranging your schedule so that you're alone with that guy."

She set the pen down with the same care he'd use diffusing a bomb and gave him a steady look.

"Again, what?"

"Alcosta hit on you at a party and it made you so uncomfortable that you claimed to be in a relationship with me," he reminded her. "I wasn't at that meeting because you need a security presentation. I was there as a shield. My money says he hit on you when I left, too."

He paused to give her a chance to deny it. She fluttered her lashes, then took another drink of her water. He smirked before continuing.

"You've got the contract. You've got the deposit. You've got your golden opportunity to send your company into the stratosphere."

"In other words, you don't think I should make any concessions."

Spence narrowed his eyes, trying to read her tone and body language. He didn't want to piss her off, but he wasn't going to lie.

"No. In other words, I don't think you should be alone with Santiago Alcosta. He has a crap reputation. Maybe he got a raw deal, being judged for his family's crimes. Maybe it's just a matter of time before he's caught. Maybe that guy at the party, the one in the office today, was just delivering a message or asking for a raise." Spence shrugged. "I don't give a damn which it is. The bottom line is associating with Alcosta carries a risk. It's my job to mitigate that risk and ensure that you're not harmed while dealing with him."

That was as close to a speech as Spence ever got, and he wasn't sure what to do now. Bow? Wait for applause? Duck?

"So, you're protecting me?"

"Yeah." Spence nodded. "I'm working for you, assisting with your business and helping raise money for some good causes. But bottom line, I'm going to protect you."

Tension gripped his shoulders. He wasn't a man who shied away from confrontations. Actually, he reveled in them. But Mia was different. And not just because pissing her off could get him fired—on two levels.

He waited, wondering if she was going to explode. A lot of women would get pissy being talked to that frankly.

But Mia only tilted her head to one side and, lips pursed, gave him a considering stare. For the first time since he'd met her, he could see the resemblance to her father. Finally she arched her brow and nodded.

"Okay."

"That's it? Just okay?"

"Sure. I mean, not that I'd let you tell me how to run my life or my business. But you're right about Señor Alcosta," she admitted with a grimace. "I'm not afraid of the man and don't think he's a criminal. But I'll work a lot more efficiently and do a much better job knowing I don't have to fend off passes that will eventually make for a very uncomfortable working relationship."

Spence's lips twitched. Her tone made it clear that Alcosta would probably be the uncomfortable one.

"And that's the bottom line?"

"Rocking my job?" Mia laughed. "Of course. It sounds like that's your bottom line, too."

The tension eased from his shoulders and Spence relaxed again.

"I have to admit it is."

"I like that," she said with a smile that sent that tension surging once again, this time quite a bit south of his shoulders.

Spence stared into her eyes, drowning in the image of what it'd feel like to hear her say those words in the dark. Just the two of them, tangled in cool sheets while the hot night air wrapped around their naked bodies.

The sound of his cell phone ripped him out of fantasyland and back to reality.

Saved by the bell.

Not caring that it was rude, he grabbed it from his pocket like it was a life preserver. As soon as he glanced at the readout, he grimaced. He should have stayed in fantasyland.

"Do you need to get that? I don't mind," Mia said, waving her pen at her notes to indicate she had plenty to do.

"I guess I should," he said, choosing the lesser of two evils. Then, steeling himself, he moved a polite distance away and answered.

"Hello, Mother."

"Spencer, darling. I've been trying to reach you for days."

"I've been working."

"Working? At that gym? Spencer, you're so good at so many things, why would you settle for teaching rich men how to lift weights?"

Even if he hadn't been sitting there with Mia, he wouldn't have corrected her. Instead, he just said, "A job's a job."

"You could do better. You really need to consider your future, dear. Just the other day, I had a long chat with a darling woman. Your girlfriend, Lori. She and I talked for a good quarter hour, Spencer."

"She was never my girlfriend," he corrected, glancing over to meet Mia's unapologetically amused stare. "And should I ask how you got her number?"

Mistake, he realized as soon as the words were out of his mouth. By investing even that much into her rant, he fed her rant. Knowing there was only one way to stop the train before it jumped the tracks, he said, "I'm at lunch with a woman right now, so I need to go."

"A date? Spencer, you're talking on the phone while on a date? What is wrong with you? Where did I go wrong. You hang up right this minute. No, wait. You call me back this evening, young man. You call to tell me all about this woman or I'll show up on your doorstep. You know I will."

"Goodbye."

He put the phone on silence before shoving it deep in his pocket. Her smile even wider now, Mia propped her elbow on the table, rested her chin on her fist and arched her brow.

"Rough phone call?"

"My mother," Spence confirmed with a grimace. "She's recently gotten into the habit of calling at least once a week to share her thoughts on my life."

"Oooh, interfering parental phone calls." Mia breathed with a wide-eyed nod. "Those are always fun. Even better are the unannounced interfering visits. Although those, at least, are often accompanied by muffins."

"Muffins?" Spence laughed.

"My mother was big on bringing a basket of muffins as the excuse for her in-person interference."

"I guess I'm lucky that my mom still lives in Pennsylvania."

"That's where you're from?" At his nod, Mia asked, "How long have you lived in California?"

"I left Philly for college at UC San Diego. It was close to my priorities. Surfing and, um, school," Spence corrected, fumbling that last word into a lie. He'd gone to UCSD so he could be near the Coronado Naval Base while getting the degree so he could join the Navy as an officer. Spence frowned at the realization that the Navy, and more to the point, the SEALs, had been his be-all and end-all as far back as he could remember. It's all he'd had. All he'd wanted. A part of him was afraid that it was all he was.

Mia blinked in surprise, either at his odd phrasing or his sudden silence. Spence couldn't blame her. He was surprised, too. Both at his realization, and at how easily he'd dropped his natural caution.

"And your mom's weekly phone calls are a new thing?" she asked after a few more seconds of silence. "Is that because you're making changes in your career?"

"How do you know that?" Not that Spence was surprised at her insight—Mia was an amazingly insightful woman—but he was impressed that she'd nailed down his mother with so little information.

"Believe me, I'm an expert on the topic of parental interference in all its many forms."

If only she knew just how many forms there were, he thought, trying to ignore the guilt trickling like ice down his spine. That guilt, and an uncomfortable need to open up to Mia as much as he could, prompted him to share a little more.

"For years she seemed perfectly content with the *live and let live* policy she'd adopted when I went to college. But, yeah, as soon as she heard I was going to change careers and focus on security, she's been on a rampage. She's desperate to have a say in what that career is. If she can't control my career, she's determined to marry me off. Or, failing that, to convince me to move back home."

"Didn't you tell her that you're rocking the event-planning business on your way to launching the next phase in your new security career?"

"Hell, no. I told her I was on a date," he confessed with a laugh. "But I kept your name out of it, so don't worry."

"So, I'm your date?" she asked with a flirtatious flutter of her lashes.

"Just like I'm your…" He'd choke before he said *boyfriend*, but throwing out the word *lover* would be like tossing a live grenade on the table between them.

"My boyfriend?" she said with a flutter of her lashes.

"God."

Mia's laugh echoed off the restaurant walls, pulling a reluctant smile out of him.

"Don't worry about it. Believe me, I understand interfering mothers," Mia said, still laughing as she swiped a hint of butter over her sourdough bread. "Mine considers it her sacred duty to poke into my life as often as possible. She criticizes everything from my hairstyle to my choice of roommate."

"Mine used to be pretty good about staying out of my life. She still is now, except when it comes to things like my career, my failure to provide her with grandchildren or what I had for breakfast," he said, ripping a slice of bread off the loaf. "I take it your family is big on interfering, too?"

"They are. My mother more than my father. He's okay as long as he considers me a contributing member of society. Besides, he's not the interfering type," Mia explained before biting into the bread.

Damn, Spence thought derisively. If she only knew.

"My mother seems to feel like a failure if I'm not living life the way she's decided I should," Mia continued with a shrug.

"She doesn't know you very well, then," he said. From what he'd seen over the last few days, Mia had built herself one hell of a life, with no failure anywhere to be seen. "You're doing what you want, you're good at it and you're obviously having a good time. That sounds about as far from failure as it gets."

"Thank you. I don't understand why your mom is against your career, either. I know you're working in event planning to build your résumé, but why security?" Mia asked as their meals were served. "Was there a specific reason you chose that career path?"

All he'd ever wanted was to be a SEAL. Suddenly feeling adrift, Spence stared at the hefty portion of chicken parmigiana in its bed of thick pasta. Things change, he reminded himself. Deal with it.

Still, it took him a second to pull himself out of the loss and meet Mia's gaze again.

"That's a family thing, too," he told her.

"Your family is in the business?"

"No, my family drives me crazy. I figure one of the reasons that my mom is—or was—so good at letting me live my life was because her parents and siblings are total busybodies. I chose—" since he couldn't say the Navy, he went with "—San Diego to get as far away from my family as I could."

And with the SEALs, he'd found his true family. One he'd lived with, learned with, traveled with and fought with, side-by-side. Even more than his birth family, his SEAL brothers had helped him figure out how to be his own man. How to push beyond the limits his family imposed and reach for new heights.

He'd be damned if he'd give that up and live an average life—no matter how much his mother nagged.

"Oh, yeah. I can so relate to that. Getting way from my family became priority number one when I was ten years old. Don't get me wrong," she quickly added, twirling pasta around her fork. "I do love them. I just love them better if they are far enough away to keep their interference to a minimum."

"Distance means there's less chance of showing up for dinner and finding your mother's current daughter-in-law pick seated next to you. Or cousins who constantly want to borrow your truck or your tools or your cash."

"Exactly," Mia agreed. "Now I might get a nagging phone call about general life choices but it's better than coming home to find my mother has replaced my living room furniture with 'something of quality and taste.' Life is better without family interference, isn't it?"

"Much better," he agreed, looking around the room in case she could see the guilt in his eyes.

How the hell did this woman draw so many feelings from him? Before Mia, he hadn't realized he even had that many emotions.

"I never asked—why'd you leave your last job?"

A shaft of misery shot through him, piercing and sharp.

"I was injured on the job. While I was recovering, my position closed," he finally said, trying to stay as close to the truth as possible. He had no problem doing whatever was necessary to get the job done, but he didn't like lying to Mia.

"I'm sorry," she said quietly, those dark eyes sympathetic as she reached across the table to lay her hand over his. Since her touch ignited feelings a lot hotter than comfort, he slid his hand free after one tempting second.

"I was, too. Sorrier that it left me open to that family pressure we talked about." At her questioning look, he explained, "My employment changes opened up a lot of suggestions from my family. Safe suggestions, ones that require that I move back to Portland. Suddenly I'm uniquely qualified to manage the neighborhood grocery store, to run my cousin's construction business or to help my brother-in-law start up a computer-repair business."

"None of which you have any interest in."

"Exactly." He took another drink of his beer. "I like security work. It's what I'm trained to do. It's what I like to do."

"Then you should do it."

"Instead of event planning?" he asked with a teasing smile.

"After next month, yes," she said with a smile. "I learned at a very young age that the only thing that's certain in life is that it's uncertain. So if there's something you want, something that's important to you, you need to grab it while it's there. Otherwise, by the time you think you're ready for it, it might be gone."

What if what you want is off-limits?

"Very wise." He studied her over his beer. "Wise and maybe a little cynical. What happened at that young age that got you thinking like that?"

Mia held up one finger while she swallowed a mouthful of pasta, then washed it down with a sip of wine before patting her mouth with her napkin.

"My dad is in the Navy, so I grew up bouncing from military base to military base. State to state, country to country. My life pretty much changed every two years until I went to college."

"Sounds rough."

"In a lot of ways, it was fabulous," she hastened to assure him. "We traveled, saw so much of the world and other cultures, and learned independence in a way I don't think I appreciated as a child."

She glanced down at her plate for a moment, nibbling on her bottom lip instead of her pasta, then shrugged.

"And yeah, there were rough parts. A little too much togetherness, for one. But mostly there was a lot of stress involved in my father's work. He was gone more than he was home. Everything he did, right down to the time of reveille, was hush-hush. And most of it was dangerous. I never knew if he'd come home from whatever secret location he was at, doing whatever secret thing he was doing."

"I'd imagine that oftentimes secrecy is as much to protect the families as it is to ensure the success of a mission." Actually, he didn't have to imagine. He knew it for a fact, since that secrecy and the many varied reasons for it had been an integral part of his training.

"Oh, sure. I have no doubt the world is a lot safer because of men like my father. I don't question his choices. Actually, they helped me make a few of my own."

"Like what?"

"Like the choice to never get involved with a military man. Both my sisters carried on the tradition and married officers. Me? I won't even date one. I had enough of that growing up."

A shaft of pain speared through him, but Spence ignored it.

"What about former military?"

"Nope. No way." Mia laughed. "According to my father, once military, always military. I can't imagine the mindset and training ever fade completely."

No.

He didn't imagine they would, either.

As Spence finished his lunch, he listened to Mia's stories about the various places she'd lived and told himself that this was for the best.

He might have fooled himself into thinking he had a shot with a woman he was lying to by convincing her down the road that it'd been for her own good. But once she knew the truth, his career alone would ensure that she'd want nothing to do with him.

Good.

His life was a mess. He needed all of his focus and energy to build a new career. The last thing he needed to add to the mix was a relationship. Or even an attempt at one.

It'd be a hell of a lot easier to accept, though, if he didn't have that same sinking feeling in his gut that he'd had when he'd been informed that he was off the SEAL team.

Chapter 8

Spence had been on a lot of missions over the course of his career, but this one just might be shaping up to be the roughest. He'd felt closer to danger in the last two weeks since he'd enjoyed pasta with Mia than he'd ever felt in combat.

Standing in a state-of-the-art kitchen in a palatial house overlooking the San Francisco Bay, he watched Mia pacify a hysterical florist, direct the bartender's setup and oversee the gardeners as they arranged topiaries among the tables strategically arranged over the stone patio. All the while, musicians calmly rehearsed for the next morning's sunrise breakfast event.

Like everything she did, Mia juggled them all with skill and grace. He had no problems admitting that. He just wished she'd do it all without looking so damned good.

And what was he—a Navy SEAL decorated with honors—doing to further his own career?

Instead of a being shot at by angry terrorists from a bunker in the desert's blasting heat, he was placating a grumpy caterer in a Northern California mansion while the wind played through the palm trees.

Given a choice, Spence would rather be shot at.

As if hearing his plea, his cell phone rang. He glanced at the readout and, much to the caterer's obvious relief, excused himself.

"Yo, Smidge. What've you got?"

"Yo, Improv. I dug deep and scooped up some deets."

Spence felt his first tingle in two weeks that wasn't sexually inspired.

"What kind of deets?"

"Deets like search trail. I can't pinpoint who's using the server, but someone in the Alcosta empire has been doing a lot of digging over the last two years on a certain Senator Luis Penz. Keeping tabs on the guy's location, tracking his voting records, his charitable preferences. Digging into his background, his family, who he hangs out with. That sort of thing."

Interesting.

Spence had done a little digging of his own on the senator. Never married, Mia's mother's brother was a former captain in the Army, and as strong a proponent for human rights as he was antidrug. From everything Spence had gleaned on Penz, the senator was so clean, he glowed. And he'd sponsored a number of bills targeting areas that would put a pretty tight squeeze on operations like Alcosta's.

Would Alcosta try to bribe Mia's uncle into changing his stand on those bills?

Tied in with the other info Spence had found—that Alcosta's reason for rushing this fund-raiser was as thin as smoke, that Mia was the only event planner he'd considered for it, and the real-estate mogul was facing some major financial challenges—bribery made a lot of sense.

"Send me the intel."

"Encrypted?"

"Of course."

Juggling the new information, he slipped the phone into his pocket. He could run it by Cade, see if his commander had inside information. More to the point, he could lay out the fact that a bribery scheme meant Alcosta was only using Mia as a conduit to meet with her uncle. A dirty plan, but not particularly dangerous.

Which would mean that this torturous babysitting duty was unnecessary.

Spence watched Mia wend her way around the patio, her spiked heels echoing each step as she checked the view from each table. Probably ensuring that every diner had a chance to watch the sunrise they were paying so much to enjoy, Spence realized.

That was Mia.

The consummate hostess: she worked her ass off, not just for her client, but for the guests and, most of all, for the charity she was raising funds for. And she did it all with that sweet smile, making everyone from the guests to the servers to the guy delivering the cocktail olives feel good.

She wasn't a pushover, though. He'd watched her call out a vendor on subpar equipment, fire a bartender who'd smarted off to a server and charm a client out of arguing about their bill.

The woman was hell on wheels. Or, in this case, on sexy pink sandals. In yet more coordination, she wore a strappy white sundress with a full skirt embellished with pink flowers that matched her heels. He'd put money on the fact that her lingerie matched, too.

Tiny little straps of white lace edged in hot-pink satin, wrapped around skin like silk, just waiting for him to slide the garment off those long limbs with his teeth. He'd nibble his way up her legs and nibble his way down her arms.

Spence blew out a deep breath.

Nope.

Not going there.

He shoved his hands into the pockets of his jeans and stared out at the ocean, waiting for the white-capped waves to soothe that vision from his mind so he could refocus on the issue at hand.

The possibility—probability, if Smidge's intel was correct—that Alcosta's goal was to get a face-to-face with Penz in order to bribe the man. It was a solid lead and a viable conclusion.

But if he suggested that to the admiral, the man might very well void this assignment, deciding that as it hadn't been finished, Spence wasn't deserving of the promised reward.

Scowling at the impressive arcing majesty of the Golden Gate, Spence realized that given the admiral's reputation, that that sort of outcome was a strong possibility.

In addition, the minute the admiral decided that Spence had served his purpose, he'd pull him from this assignment. That Spence was, for all intents and purposes, a civilian wouldn't matter. If he didn't follow orders, Cade would simply out him to Mia.

Spence could just imagine her reaction. After the shocked fury, she'd be hurt. And the last thing he wanted was to hurt her. Not because he thought they had a future, he reminded himself. Despite his attraction to her—and her intense reaction to that one kiss they'd shared—they weren't even a couple.

But she was a special woman. An amazing one. And if he couldn't have a future with her, he at least wanted her memory of him to be a good one.

Better to catch Alcosta in the act and move on the crime rather than on supposition. He'd cement his position with Cade and be able to leave Mia's life quietly, without her realizing a thing.

Content, if not satisfied, Spence returned to the kitchen to make sure the caterer was ready for the next morning, and then headed down the long, narrow hallway toward the atrium.

He'd just stepped into the luxurious glass-enclosed room, with its jungle of greenery and wicker, when he spotted Mia.

At the sight of him, her smile glowed brightly enough to dim the rays of the setting sun.

"There you are."

As always, the sound of her husky voice touched off a cord of desire low in his belly. Steeling himself against it, he waited and watching her hurry toward him. She was moving so fast, her skirt swished against long golden legs with each sway of her hips.

"I'm finished for the evening," she said by way of greeting when she reached him. "How about you?"

"Just went over the final numbers and instructions with the caterer," he confirmed. "He agreed to add three vegetarian options and a fruit sculpture, just like you wanted."

"You really are good at this. Are you sure you've never had any party-planning experience?"

"The only party I've ever handled was a bachelor sendoff. The extent of my planning was to make sure there was plenty of beers, enough foot-long subs for two dozen men and that the stripper was willing to…"

"Willing to what?" Her brows arched, Mia leaned closer and gave a low "Hmm?"

Deciding it was time to change the subject, Spence tapped the clipboard in her arms.

"Obviously you're better at party planning than I am. So? Are we on schedule?"

"Chicken?" Mia laughed.

"Absolutely. So, the schedule?"

"We're fine," Mia confirmed, still laughing a little as she gave her list a quick glance. "Early morning events can be tricky since so much has to be done the night before, yet still be fresh. But I think we're set on this one."

"This is the arts council, right?"

"Right. They're hosting this breakfast to honor their donors."

"Honor them while trying to elicit more donations?"

Noting the distaste in his voice, Mia shook her head, with one hand pressed against his arm.

"Allow them the pleasure of supporting something they believe in while showing gratitude for all they've done," she corrected in a prissy tone that made him grin.

"Nice."

"I thought so," she said with a flutter of her lashes.

Silence fell as, together, they turned to watch the sun drop down behind the water. Bleeding shades of purple, magenta and orange washed the sky, seeming to pour a feeling of peace and ease over them as they waited for night to fall. It wasn't until she sighed that he realized she was so close that it'd only take lifting his arm to give her a hug. To feel her entire side pressed tightly against his. To breathe in her scent while her body meshed with his.

Spence took two decisive steps to the right.

Distance. He needed distance.

"It's a great view," he said, tossing out the first words that came to mind.

Her eyes a mystery as she turned her gaze on him, Mia simply nodded.

"I'll bet sunrise is just as nice. Your donors are going to enjoy it a lot."

Her gaze locked on him as if she were peering deep into his soul, in search of answers to a question he hadn't heard.

Spence almost squirmed before he steeled his spine. He was a SEAL, dammit. It was ridiculous to get nervous over a sexy woman giving him intense looks.

"The sunset is a pretty good draw. I'm surprised this place isn't booked tonight," he continued, gesturing to the grounds. He felt like an idiot, but at least talking business seemed to pull her attention from his soul.

"Since it's a morning event, I was able to negotiate the rental on this location for a twenty-four-hour time frame at the same price they'd charge for an evening event," she told him. "This gives us time to begin setup this evening, hold tomorrow's event and have plenty of time for cleanup afterward."

"Smart. You really are good at this," he complimented her.

"I heard how well you handled the caterer's complaints. I'd have to say that you're getting quite good yourself." She smiled up at him, the soft evening light glinting off her skin like gold dust. "What do you think? Ready to take this on as a permanent career?"

"I've learned a lot, but I don't think I have the personality for it," he said honestly. "As you probably heard in the caterer's report, I'm better at confrontation than negotiation. And I suppose that I prefer keeping people safe to making them happy."

"Between the two of us, we're doing both," she said, turning to rest her elbows on the balcony railing so her profile was shadowed, the setting sun reflected in the blue-black depth of her hair. "And I suppose it's an interesting way to spend a Thursday evening. But tell me. Given your druthers, how would you spend tonight if you weren't working?"

Stripping her naked and making her cry out with pleasure topped his list of ideas. But Spence went with the safer answer of, "If I wasn't working, I suppose I'd hit a bar. Maybe a club. Something with music."

"I'm guessing you're looking for music a little livelier than the string quartet we had practicing here earlier?" Her tone was conversational, but there was something underneath that rekindled nerves he'd already squashed twice.

"A string quartet is fine at these fancy events, but it's not much to dance to."

"You like to dance?"

"I'm good on my feet. And I'm good with my body."

"Is that so?" Mia asked, the wicked quirk of her lips matching the spark in her eyes.

Spence mentally winced.

Damn. He'd managed to sideline his desire for the last three weeks. By watching his words and carefully coordinating their time so they were rarely alone, he'd kept his hands—and his fantasies—to himself. So what the hell was going on tonight?

He couldn't pinpoint what was different, but he definitely felt like he'd lost all control of where this situation was going.

"What kind of music do you prefer showing off your moves to?" she asked.

Spence stared into those whiskey-colored fairy eyes and wondered when the hell she'd moved so close. He had to force himself to focus on the actual conversation.

"Rock. Nothing beats rock, on or off the dance floor."

"I noticed how much you liked it at the fifties' sock-hop fund-raiser we held last week for the library."

"You caught that?"

He didn't know why he was surprised. She'd stopped by every event he'd handled, spending anywhere from a half hour to the entire fund-raiser helping out. But he hadn't seen her at that one.

"I spent most of my time with Lawrence, the head of the library association. But I caught a few minutes of the event." She waggled her brows. "You and Mrs. Ogilvie really cut up that dance floor."

"Give me a seventy-year-old librarian and a good band, and I can hand jive with the best of 'em," he quipped.

"And how do you do with the younger crowd? How about we go dancing together?" she suggested.

"I don't think that's a good idea."

"You don't?" She was close enough now that he could see the moisture glistening on her lips. "Why not?"

"If I get you on the dance floor, I'm going to try to kiss you again. And that could get out of hand, fast."

Well, that was the flat-out truth.

Spence watched Mia's expression, trying to gauge whether he'd irritated her or not. He knew he was making some assumptions with that statement, but it was where his mind was. And he was seriously tired of lying to her.

"Then let's go."

"I beg your pardon?"

"Let's dance." She skimmed her palms up his chest, her fingers drawing little circles when she reached his shoulders. "We'll move to the music, enjoy ourselves and see where the steps take us."

"I beg your pardon?" There was so much needy desire buzzing through his head, Spence was sure he'd heard her wrong.

"I want to dance with you."

"You what?" Despite his body's instant, rock-hard reaction, Spence was still sure he hadn't heard her right.

"I want you." Mia's smile was candy-sweet, but the light in her eyes was pure challenge. "Do you want me?"

Spence would rather take a bullet than hurt her, but he knew a trap when he teetered on the edge of one. Truth or lie, either way he'd be in trouble.

The upside? She didn't wait for his response.

"What do you say? Want to see if we're any good together?"

The downside? Her words were tempting enough to destroy his resistance.

He stared at that gorgeous face, with her full lips tilted in a mischievous smile and those fairy eyes glowing with challenge. Refusal was on the tip of his tongue, but then he looked closer. There was just a hint of nerves lurking there, just beneath the desire.

That vulnerability hit him even harder than the desire, melting the rest of his resistance like fire-melted wax.

Where was a sniper when you needed one?

See if we're any good together?

Mia would have cringed if she wasn't frozen with the shock of hearing those words come out of her own mouth. So many times had this little scenario played out in her fantasies, and not one had included a stupid phrase like *let's see if we're any good together*.

Here she was, standing on a romantic balcony at sunset with the guy who'd starred in all of her sexiest dreams, and she dropped a lame line like that?

Her only defense was that she'd never seduced a man before.

At least not in real life.

Sure, over the last three weeks, she'd done it about a million times in her imagination. Compared to the million-and-a-half in which she'd imagined Spence seducing her.

But Spence worked for her, so she'd kept those seductions exclusively in her mind. But whether a new security gig kicked in or not, Mia knew he had no intention of continuing to work for her after next weekend's events were over.

She'd watched him from the garden as he dealt with the caterer, as he took his phone call, and all she'd been able to think was that this was it. As busy as the next week was going to be, this was her last chance to be with him. So she'd decided that if he wasn't going to make the first move, she would.

Her stomach churned.

What had she been thinking?

"Look, Mia…"

She held her breath while he considered his response.

"I'm flattered. And it's not that I'm not interested. But I think that's something we really need to think about," he hedged. "For now, why don't I walk you to your car? You must be ready to go home."

Despite the thrill zinging through her at his admission that he actually was interested, Mia rolled her eyes. That was a stall if she'd ever seen one.

"I'm staying here tonight."

"What?" That stopped him dead in his tracks.

"The mansion boasts twelve bedrooms. I have so much to do tomorrow to ensure the fund-raiser kicks off successfully that I thought it more logical that I simply stay on location so I get started bright and early."

"You're sleeping here tonight?"

"I have a bed here tonight," she corrected, touching the tip of her tongue to her upper lip as that sank in. When she saw his eyes blur, she smiled and gestured toward the stairs. "Want to join me?"

"I really don't think that's a very good idea."

It wasn't ego that kept Mia from being insulted by his refusal. It was that she could see how much the words cost him. Tight jeans did nothing to disguise his growing enthusiasm for the idea of being with her.

"Are you saying you don't want to make love to me?"

"I'm saying that there are a lot of factors that we should consider before taking that kind of step."

"Don't you sound all uptight and official." Now Mia didn't have to fake being amused. Not with all this laughter bubbling up inside her. "And as sexy as that is, I'd rather act than talk."

She could practically see the refusal on the tip of his

tongue and almost groaned with frustration. There were so many other things she'd rather see his tongue doing. But apparently offering herself up like a free sample wasn't enough to tempt him.

Fine.

Whatever.

Unable to stop the pout from sliding across her face, she crossed her arms over her chest and gave a dismissive shrug.

"My mistake. Call it a result of testing the champagne spritzers," she excused. "Let's just forget I said anything."

When she saw the apology on his face, she threw one hand up before he even opened his mouth.

"Look, I don't want you to feel bad or uncomfortable. So, like I said, let's just forget the whole thing." She tried a smile, hoping it came across as friendly instead of pained. "Now, if you'll excuse me, I'm going to get some work done."

Before he could say anything, Mia hurried across the patio to escape through the French doors. She'd lock up later. Right now, all she wanted was to get as far away from Spence as she could.

She was all the way to the marble entryway when he caught her. He grabbed her arm with one large hand, swinging her around to face him. Mia's skinny heels slipped on the slick floor, forcing her to grab on to Spence's shoulder to keep her balance.

Before she could ask what the hell he thought he was doing, his mouth crashed down on hers.

He tasted like sunshine. Hot, edgy, bone-melting sunshine. She met the demand of his kiss with her own edgy needs, scraping her teeth along his bottom lip as her fingers dug into the rigid muscles of his shoulders.

God, what a body.

Desperate to touch as much of that body as she could in case he changed his mind, she skimmed her palms down his arms, her hands curling over his biceps, delighting in how hard they were, even relaxed.

That boded well if things went the way she wanted.

In hopes of encouraging that to happen, she shifted just a little closer, the full fabric of her skirt rustling against his jeans as she angled her thigh between his. The move brought her chest close enough to his that all she had to do was take a deep breath to bring the tips of her breasts into contact with his chest. It felt so good that, with her next deep breath, she gave a little wiggle, teasing her nipples into needy awareness.

Spence seemed to like the move, too, because he gripped her arms tighter, lifting her just a little so she balanced on her toes. Then he deepened the kiss.

Oh, oh, baby.

She gave a breathless moan when his tongue swept between her lips. Their tongues mated, dancing, dueling, delighting with wild abandon.

The kiss seemed to last forever and it ended too soon as he slowly pulled his mouth away.

Her eyes still closed to better revel in the sensations swirling through her body, she felt his shortened breath against her face. She had no idea what she'd see when she looked at him, so Mia wanted to draw this moment out as long as she could.

Then he covered her breasts with his hands, squeezing lightly as he rubbed his palms over the nipples pebbled against her bodice.

"Oh," she keened, her eyes flying open to meet his intense stare.

"Show me."

Her breath coming in hard gasps, Mia shook her head to let him know she didn't understand his request.

"Show me your room."

"My pleasure," she murmured.

She was so light-headed from his kiss that it took her a few seconds to make sure she wouldn't fall right off her heels. Then Mia gestured toward the staircase with a deep breath and led the way.

Hoo, boy.

Her heart pounded so loudly that she was surprised the sound didn't echo off the vaulted ceiling as they climbed the curved staircase. Spence followed in silence, just a step behind her as she led him down the hallway to the bedroom she was using.

"Decadent," he murmured, looking around.

She'd barely noticed the sensual décor, having chosen the room more for the attached office, figuring the desk would come in handy as she worked into the night, than for the ambiance.

Her teal overnight bag stood out like a sore thumb against the lush fabrics, slick wood and erotic art. Suddenly shy and wondering why she'd thought she was the seductive type, Mia bit her lip to keep from making an excuse for her choice.

"It reminds me of you," he said, shifting to the side so his body angled behind hers, his breath teasing the sensitive flesh on the back of her neck. "Strong lines, sensual textures, vivid color all combined in a sexy invitation."

"Do you think so?" It wasn't so much his words that

made her feel so bold, but the emotion behind them. She could practically feel the desire pouring off him.

Mia moved into the center of the room and turned so she faced him. Obviously letting her call the shots, he leaned one shoulder against the doorframe and watched her with an edgy sort of patience that made her feel like her time in control was limited.

Like she did any time she wanted to make a big impact in a limited amount of time, Mia went for broke. She kept her smile soft, sweet even, and her eyes locked on his as she skimmed the fingers of one hand down the side of her bodice, tracing the curve of her breast on her way down to her waist. She traced the same path up, and on her way down again, she released the zipper. From there, all it took was a flick of each finger to loosen the straps from her shoulders and let gravity do its work.

He gave a low grunt of approval when the fabric puddled at her feet, leaving Mia standing there in her pale pink lace panties, matching bra and sassy fuchsia stiletto slides.

She gave him enough time to get a good, long look. Waited to see the blur of need in his eyes. Then she smiled.

"Now what do you think?" she asked, arching one brow. "Does the room still remind you of anything?"

"What room?" he asked, his words distracted as he strode toward her. In a blink, he was there, close enough to feel the desire radiating off him, warming her. His scent teased. His eyes seduced.

Mia shivered.

"I've wanted you since you kissed me," she confessed with a breathless moan. "Once I realized you weren't going to do it again, I figured I'd better take matters into my own hands. So to speak."

"Good call."

With that, he reached out. Mia held her breath, surprised when he only skimmed the line of her jaw with his knuckles. He stared into her eyes as he leaned closer. Slowly, softly, he brushed his lips over hers.

This time his knuckles traced the side of her throat as he deepened the kiss, his tongue sliding gently along her lower lip.

Mmm, so good.

He skimmed his hands down her sides, teasing at her waist and making her ache for more. Hoping to hurry him along, she opened her mouth, sucking his tongue inside. His groan rumbled through her body like an aphrodisiac.

Mia thrust her hips from side to side so the delicate lace of her panties rubbed against his soft denim jeans. Proof of his interest pressed, impressively hard and long, against his zipper.

"You do want me," she said, releasing his mouth with a husky laugh. "I wasn't sure."

"Believe me, you can be sure." He swept kisses along her jawline, whisper-soft and enticing.

"Why didn't you show me before?" she asked, not really caring once his mouth reached the erotic softness behind her ear.

"I knew it'd be wrong if I did," he murmured, his words a husky rumble against her throat.

"Wrong how? It feels so good."

"You're going to regret it. Not now," he decided as his teeth grasped the delicate lace of her bra strap and pulled it off her shoulder.

"Probably not tomorrow," he added, tugging the other strap down, his teeth scraping along her flesh and sending little rivulets of pleasure spiraling through her system. "But soon. Very soon, you're going to wish we hadn't done this."

He sounded so serious. Even as his fingers teased, slipping in and out of her bra cups to skim her aching nipples, Mia heard the gravity in Spence's tone. Why was he so intense?

Breath coming fast, Mia forced her eyes open and her mind to focus on something other than the pleasure surging through her body.

"Are you married?"

"No." His fingers stilled on the edge of her bra.

Impatient that he was delaying her pleasure with this little game, Mia blew out a heavy breath.

"Engaged? Living with someone? Seriously involved?"

"No." He shifted his head, his lips brushing whisper-soft kisses along the side of her throat.

"Are you a creeper who peeks through the windows of elderly women in nursing homes?"

"No."

Mia shivered at the feel of his laugh as it blew a soft gust of warm air against her skin. Before she could think of any other scenarios that would make her regret finally reaching the heights of orgasmic pleasure he'd been leading her toward, Spence added, "And before you ask, I've never broken the law, either."

"Well, that covers everything," she decided. Since all that was left was guilt, like he thought he was taking advantage of her or something silly like that, Mia decided it was up to her to move things along. "Time to quit worrying and start doing."

"You're the boss," he quipped with a smile.

"Indeed, I am." And she liked it.

To ensure the talking portion of their evening was over, she shifted away from Spence just enough to reach between her breasts and unclip her bra. Her eyes locked on his, she gave a tiny shrug to loosen the lace so it fell between their bodies.

His eyes stayed on hers for a heartbeat. Then, as if unable to resist, his gaze dropped.

Pleasure poured through her as his pupils dilated, his eyes widening.

He breathed, "You're gorgeous."

"Show me."

"With pleasure."

He reached up, both hands covering her breasts and rubbing slow, soft circles over her nipples, making them ache with desire.

Desperate to touch him, needing to feel him, Mia yanked his flirt free of his jeans before making quick work of the buttons. Oh, his skin. Hot, hard and dusted with silky hair.

He felt amazing.

She couldn't stop touching him. Sliding her palms over his chest, across those shoulders, down his waist. When he changed angles, his tongue sliding down her throat and over the mounds of her breasts, her knees went wonky and weak. Needing to hang on to something, she hooked her fingers in his belt loops.

She gasped when his teeth scraped over her nipple. Hands frantic this time, she struggled with the buckle, ripped at his zipper and shoved until she freed the glorious length of his manhood. She wrapped her fingers around the velvety steel rod and moaned. He was so hard. So big.

She was vaguely aware of him shedding his pants, most of her attention on his lips as he blew cool air over her wet nipple, then nipped, rolling the sensitized flesh between his teeth.

"Spence," she groaned. "More."

"Now?"

"Please."

He pushed her panties free, sending them sliding down her thighs. As soon as they hit the floor, he swept her off her feet and onto the bed. Mia stretched out, the cool satin at her back an erotic contrast to the hot silk of his body over hers.

Mia whimpered at the feel of his body, rough and smooth and hard. His muscles bunched as he angled to one side to sheath himself.

Then he plunged.

She gasped. Oh, man, he felt good.

Mia threw her head back, her neck arched and her breasts lifted for his teasing tongue, and met him thrust for thrust.

Each plunge sent her higher; each undulation made her whimper with delight. Her body was on fire, passion burning hotter than she'd ever imagined. He reached down, his fingers sliding between her thighs, teasing and tempting.

She exploded, rays of pleasure shooting through her like stars, leaving trails of sensations in their wake.

Spence continued to slide in and out, each time penetrating deeper, harder.

She wrapped her legs around his waist, locking her

ankles at the small of his back and angling herself higher to meet each thrust.

His moves quickened. His breath grew labored. A light sheen of sweat slicked over his body as her hands caressed and fingers teased.

"Come," he demanded, his eyes locked on hers with an intensity that made her shudder.

She came again. And again. And twice more before his body stiffened, his back arching and arms taut.

He let out a guttural moan as the force of his orgasm shot through her body, making her shudder and gasp. Mia pressed tighter against him, her body gripping him to prolong his release.

It was like floating on a cloud of sensation, every cell of her being tingling with pleasure. Mia could only whimper as he pulled away for a moment before stretching to grab a blanket from the floor. She felt it glide over her, a silky-soft contrast to the hard muscles of his chest as he wrapped her in his arms.

As if unable to stop touching her, his fingers skimmed gently down her spine, then back up again. Thrilled at his touch, she nestled into him, her legs trapped between his hair-roughened thighs, and her body sliding into oblivion.

Her last thought before she drifted off to sleep was that whatever silly regret Spence was anticipating, this was definitely worth it.

Chapter 9

Here he was, at oh-five-hundred on a Friday morning, leaning against the second-floor wrought-iron bannister of a Spanish villa, drinking coffee rich enough to own its own country, while the heady scent wafting from huge vases of pink-and-orange tropical flowers filled the air.

He watched the first floor below, where an army of worker bees scurried through the open floor plan, their feet silent on the painted terra-cotta tiles as each one eagerly hurried to do Mia's bidding.

He couldn't blame them. He'd quickly come to realize that he was just as eager. He jumped to do whatever he could to make her happy. Whether it was helping her with an event, picking up her favorite Thai food as an after-work treat or giving her a foot rub.

And then there was two weeks of sex.

Mind-blowing, earthshaking, heart-stopping sex.

Maybe part of the reason he was so eager to please, in and out of bed, was because their relationship was almost at its end. If asked, Spence would have said that, to date, he'd had a pretty awesome sex life. Like his career, it'd been filled with adventure, enjoyment and just enough danger to keep it interesting.

So he'd never given much thought to romance or happiness. But these last two weeks with Mia had made him realize just how limited his previous experience had been.

With Mia, the sex was hot. Blinding hot, he thought, remembering the feel of her body sliding against him as she'd wrapped her legs around his hips to anchor herself as he took her against the back door of a club with a desperation he'd never felt for anything before.

Sometimes it was sweet. Sleepy morning lovemaking while the sunrise washed them in misty rainbow light. Remembering the laughs they'd shared when the chocolate Mia had been licking off his body had given her a goatee, he realized that it could even be fun.

What he hadn't realized—and should have—was that sex with Mia would be addicting. So addicting that he'd do damn near anything to keep having it. It, and her.

With a twitch of his head, Spence shook off the fantasy.

There was no point obsessing. He'd have it while he had it, and when they were done, it'd be finished.

Yet here he was.

Obsessing.

Again.

What the hell had happened to his life?

And what the hell was he going to do with it after he parted ways with Mia?

Put it away, he ordered himself. He had work to do. That'd always been enough for him before, and he'd make sure it was enough now. And until the job was done, he still had Mia.

Mia and Alcosta.

He scowled at the banner hanging from the opposite railing, the rich maroon-and-gold fabric woven around a depiction of haughty Alcosta's face.

He might owe the jerk credit for bringing Mia into his life, but that didn't mean he had to like the guy in any way, shape or form. Good thing, since the more Spence saw of Alcosta, the more he despised him.

As if drawn by Spence's thoughts, the man himself strode into the villa, surrounded by his cadre of toadies. The man never arrived without at least a dozen people. You'd think they'd be there to help, but as far as Spence had seen, they all scattered as soon as there was work to be done.

One good thing about starting so early in the day was that Alcosta usually never dragged himself into view until at least noon. Looked like today was the exception.

"Ah, Mia," he heard Alcosta call out. "Today is the big day. I hope you are prepared to make me a very, very happy man."

"Everything is coming together perfectly," Mia assured him, coming into view.

Having watched her dress that morning, Spence knew she'd chosen the draped emerald blouse, leggings and flat boots for ease since she'd be running from one end of the villa to the other, carting and arranging everything from flowers to photos to gift bags. But damn, she looked good.

From his body language, Alcosta thought so, too. He

grabbed her hand and pulled her to his side, hauling her with him as they went from one side of the ballroom to the other, Mia filling him in on their progress every step of the way.

His toadies trailed behind, their faces buried in their devices as they walked. Spence surveyed the group, noting two new additions he hadn't yet identified. Subtly angling his cell phone toward the group, he took a photo.

"These flowers, they are pretty enough. But the scent is overpowering, yes? Perhaps too much so."

Arrogant, obnoxious and irritating, the man had spent the last week and a half micromanaging unimportant details while trying to change the bigger elements he'd previously agreed to.

Figuring it was time to make an appearance before Alcosta got his hopes up, he went down the back staircase so he could make his way into the ballroom through the kitchen. The caterers were already hard at work, filling most of the twenty-foot-long room with ingredients, noise and frantic energy.

As he strode through the room, Spence matched faces with the names in his files, ensuring that he'd had Smidge run a background check on everyone Mia employed.

Halfway down the homage to stainless steel, he saw one face he'd been wanting to chat with. After a second's debate, he decided Mia should be fine for a few more minutes. He shouldered his way through a group of piping-bag-wielding decorators to a small, nook-style desk stacked chest-high with wrapped gift boxes.

"How's it going, Clair?"

"Hey, Hottie," the blonde greeted, pausing in the act of tying a personalized tag on each package to give him a smile way too predatory for this early in the morning. "I didn't realized I'd see you here."

"I'm assisting Mia. Where else would I be?"

"At the rate she goes through assistants? You could be in Brazil by now." Clair laughed. "Or in the hospital. You know, with Mia and the curse of the accidents."

"Yeah. Those accidents. Crazy how there haven't been any lately."

"I guess it helps to have a security guy lurking at fund-raisers and parties," Clair murmured, suddenly getting really interested in tying the tag on just right.

"That it does. Good thing I'm covering things at the fund-raiser weekend. An accident happens at huge party like this, Mia could easily be ruined." He waited for Clair to look up from the package she was tagging, but the bow seemed to take all of her attention. "I'll bet you're excited to work this event now, huh?"

"Excited? About putting names on gifts to give people for no reason?" She looked around the kitchen with a polite sneer. "I guess it's always good to have work."

"Don't you keep pretty busy with, what is that called? Forever Families?" He already knew the answer, but wanted to hear her response.

"I'm never too busy to help Mia out," Clair said with a toothy smile. "And if this event is a huge success, she'll be a huge success."

"Too successful to consider any other job offers, I suppose." He waited a beat while Clair's eyes widened. "Offers like the one I hear your boss was considering."

"What are you talking about?"

"From what I understand, Lorraine Perkins is crazy about the work Mia does. Crazy enough that she wants to hire her full-time. Bringing in a permanent event coordinator would probably cut into your workload, wouldn't it?"

"I'm a valued member of the Forever Families team," Clair snapped, a hint of angry color dotting her cheeks. "I can't be replaced by a party planner."

"I'm sure you couldn't. Unless Lorraine decided to revamp the fund-raising arm of her company and needed a coordinator to run it all. That'd probably cut into your hours."

"What's your point? If you're accusing me of something, just spit it out."

"No accusations," Spence assured her. "Just conversation."

"And is there a point to your conversation?"

"No point, either." Spence smiled. "It was good talking with you, though. I'm off to take care of that security stuff. You know, to make sure there are no accidents."

He left her shaken enough to ensure that there would be no accidents/sabotage screwing with this event.

He strode into the ballroom just as Mia and Alcosta, with his entourage in tow, came out of the dining room.

"Spence," Mia greeted, her voice as tranquil as a the sea and her eyes as turbulent as a winter ocean. "I'm glad you've joined us. We're just going over some last-minute details."

Alcosta looked anything but glad to see him.

"We have much still to discuss," the man said, waving his leather notepad between them as if he could shoo Spence away. "Mia, my dear, let's continue. Meanwhile, my assistant needs the details of security from your helper here."

And just like that, the man scooped Mia up by the arm and moved her to the other side of the room. As long as they stayed in view, Spence figured he'd let him get away with it.

"So you're the helper." The blonde smiled, her teeth gleaming white against her tanned face. "I can't believe we haven't met already. I'm Jessica."

Pulling off the femme-fatale look that Clair obviously aspired to, Jessica graciously held out her hand for him to either shake or kiss.

"Mia's roommate, right?"

"And you're what? Mia's boyfriend?" With a flutter of her lashes, Jessica dismissed that relationship as if it were nothing. "If you'll give me all the details of your security arrangements for the events, I'll go through them to make sure they meet Señor Alcosta's requirements. I need information on everything that you're planning to do, of course."

Everything?

That'd be a *no*, in all caps. She worked for the man Spence had deemed the enemy. No way was he handing the real details of his security plan to Alcosta's team.

Still, he knew the value of playing nice and keeping the enemy complacent.

"Mia already okayed the specifics, but I'll give you a rundown," he said. As he gave her a generic overview, the woman made copious notes with a slightly trembling hand.

"Are you okay?"

She glanced up from her notes, her perfectly enhanced eyes glittering like sapphires, hard and cold. "I'm fine. Excited about this weekend, of course. There's been a lot of work and time put into making this happen. It'll be gratifying to see it all finally happen."

An innocuous enough answer. So why did it make the hairs on the back of his neck stand up in warning?

"And since tonight's the big kick-off event, I've got a lot still to do," she said, her smile as friendly as her tone was dismissive. "It was nice to finally meet you."

"Yeah. I'll definitely see you around."

He dug his cell phone out as he watched her cross the room, and then he texted Smidge. Time to dig a little deeper into Ms. Jessica Alexander.

"Whew, I'm glad we came in at five," Mia said, hurrying up to take his coffee cup. She drank it down, handed him back the empty cup and gave a huge sigh. "I've already added an hour's worth of tasks to the day and we're just getting started."

"What do you need me to do?" he asked, skimming his fingers along the back of her neck as he checked Alcosta's position. Ten yards away from Mia, surrounded by cronies, the man waved his arms from here to there, directing his minions while he barked orders into his cell phone in Spanish.

"I've got it covered, but thanks." Mia leaned into him for a brief second, as if absorbing a little comfort from his presence before she dove back into the craziness. "Are you on schedule? Do you need any help from me?"

"I'm good." He glanced down, prepared to give her a grateful smile, and got lost in her. Just looking at her. The perfect glow of her skin, the confident tilt of her head, the assurance vibrating from every gorgeous inch of her. "Actually, I should be saying that you're good."

"Are you talking about last night?" Lowering her voice to a husky tease, she leaned closer to say, "I told you I could bend in ways you couldn't imagine. You shouldn't have bet on it."

"Losing never felt so good," he admitted with a laugh before shifting his stance, angling his weight back on his heels to take pressure off his suddenly tight zipper. "But I meant all of this. You're good at all of this."

Surprise showed in her eyes, and gratitude in her slowly widening smile.

"I appreciate that," she said softly. "It's not often that I hear that kind of support."

"Believe me, I have complete faith that you can do anything. Absolutely anything at all." Including, he realized in a moment of stunned awareness, make him fall in love with her. And that without even trying.

His stomach plunged into his feet, along with most of the blood in his body. Sweat beaded his brow. He felt as if he'd just jumped from a storm-tossed airplane into the raging sea without a parachute. Helpless, terrified and completely out of his depths.

"Spence?" Wide-eyed, Mia surveyed his expression. "Yo, Spence? Are you okay?"

"Sure."

"You're not. Something's wrong. Let's go upstairs. You can rest for a little while. If you don't feel better, I'll run you over to the health clinic."

Just like that, she'd walk out on the biggest event of her life because he was sick. Because she always put others first. That's the kind of woman she was. Right down to her career, she always focused on helping others.

Frowning now, she gave his arm a quick rub before subtly skimming the back of that same hand over his forehead. Checking for fever, he realized, falling even deeper. Who did that? Who cared that much?

Mia. Only Mia.

"I'm fine," he said before she tried to take his racing pulse and realized that something really was wrong with him. "I just got distracted by one of those crazy thoughts. You know how it is."

"Okay," she said, her tone making it clear she didn't know but was willing to humor him. "But maybe you should take a break anyhow. We were up really early, and we barely got any sleep last night."

He'd led successful missions into war zones while averaging only two hours of sleep in a sixty-hour period. But he couldn't tell her that. Because she didn't know who he was. Not really.

"I'm fine. Really," he lied. "I just realized there is a scenario I hadn't prepared for."

As he'd intended, she thought he was talking about event security, because Mia cast a worried look around the ballroom until she found Alcosta.

"I can't imagine any scenario that you haven't already covered," she murmured. "But now that you've thought of it, you can take steps, right?"

Steps. Right.

"I'll handle it," he vowed. "You won't even know it was an issue."

Part of handling it meant focusing on the here and now. Securing this event and doing his job. With the same determination that'd served him for years, Spence yanked all of his attention back to the matter at hand.

Alcosta.

He knew the man was dirty.

His unjustified travel to questionable locations and uncut, lifelong relationships with criminals proved that. But dammit, there was no credible threat. No actual suspicious activity. Nothing to tie Alcosta to any crime. But

Spence couldn't shake the feeling of impending trouble. Trouble that'd hit this weekend.

So Spence would do as he always did.

Take the op steps.

First, locate the target. His gaze narrowed on Alcosta, who'd commandeered the one table that'd been dressed for the evening, shoving aside the centerpiece and wrinkling the blue damask cloth as he spread paperwork over the surface.

Target located.

Second, assess any credible threats. Then third, secure the perimeter.

As far as Spence had been able to assess so far, an actual threat was nonexistent unless he counted Alcosta trying to hit on Mia. He had to admit that when he'd relayed that lack of apparent threat to the Admiral he hadn't been too frustrated to be told to stay on the job. Not when that order gave him more time with Mia.

Still, threat or not, it was a job.

Which put him right back to op step number two, determining if there any threats. Before he could start his rounds, though, Mia wrapped her hands around his empty mug.

"More coffee?"

"Sure thing." He surveyed the ballroom, noting that Jessica had found a private corner and was having an intense conversation on her cell phone. "Tell me about your roommate."

"Jessica?" Handing him back the full mug, Mia looked around until she spotted the other woman, too. "What do you want to know."

"You've lived together for quite a while, right? How well do you know her?"

"Actually, we haven't lived together all that long. We ran into each other a few months back, and Jessica needed somewhere to stay while she was working here in San Francisco. Since Alcosta is only here temporarily, she thought it'd be fun if we lived together."

Interesting. The intel Cade had sent on Alcosta's team showed Jessica Alexander having lived at Mia's address for a year and a half. Not a handful of months. Something that could easily be chalked up to a clerical error, but Spence wasn't that gullible.

"Fun. Like reliving the good-ole-days type of thing?" he murmured absently.

"That's pretty much how she put it, too. I didn't think we were that close but I guess we impact people in ways we don't even realize." Mia shrugged. "We were both nominated for homecoming queen, ran for class president. That sort of thing. We weren't really friends, but I suppose we did spend a lot of time together."

"Who won?"

"What?"

"Who won?" He looked at Mia. "You or her?"

"I won sometimes. She won others. She was prom queen. I was homecoming queen. She was head cheerleader. I was class president. Why?"

"Just curious." Very curious. "Do you know how long Jessica's worked for Alcosta?"

"Years. She started with him right after college. She loves it. The travel, the excitement. She says working for a powerful man is almost as good as sex. Which she'd know," Mia added with a laugh. "From what she tells me about her and her man friend, their sex life is both wild and crazy."

"Have you met him? Her man friend?"

"No. She's supersecretive about him. I don't even know his name. I think that mystery adds another element to the wildness she likes so much," Mia said with a shrug before glancing at her watch. "That's it for my break time. I'd better get back to rocking this event."

"You rock your end. I'll get to rocking mine."

"You're the best," Mia said, stepping into him so that her body aligned perfectly with his. Ignoring their audience, she locked her gaze on his and, with so much emotion in her eyes that he felt like he'd been hit in the head, rubbed her lips over his. When she pulled away, he felt as if she were taking the very air he needed to live away with her. "See ya."

Unable to do otherwise, Spence watched her walk away. Might as well get used to it, he told himself.

Needing a little time to decompress after the emotional bombing he'd just survived, Spence took his coffee and headed for the second perimeter walk of the day, this time taking special note of the flow of the paths from the villa's patios through the gardens. He gauged the distance between each of the large glass doors, checking locks as he went.

Given that he was the entirety of Mia's security budget—and since Alcosta refused to pay for more—there was no option for putting guards on the doors. Mia had agreed to sensors on the doors and volunteers on the entrance to check in guests, but she'd put her foot down over cameras.

The special ops trained part of him wanted to insist on stronger security. On more personnel, stronger electronic surveillance.

But despite Alcosta's lousy rep, and Spence's own intense dislike for the guy, no amount of research had turned up an actual, credible threat. But Spence was still determined to complete the mission. Not only because the Admiral would insist, and because it was simply Spence's nature to finish what he started. That, and because he didn't want to leave Mia until he had to.

When he'd reached the back patio that she'd designated for outdoor dancing, he noted that the portable bar was already set up in the corner, and a dozen small tables were scattered among the tall flower arrangements.

He glanced overhead as he heard the hum of a low-flying plane as it glided through the blue sky, infinitesimally changing the trajectory of sunlight. It wasn't a gleam that caught Spence's eye. More a shift in the shadows. Frowning, he stepped around the chest-high vase overflowing with purple blooms and trailing greenery and reached into a manicured swirl of ivy, wrapping his fingers around the cold metal.

Someone had planted a gun.

Loaded, ready and waiting for murder.

"Mia, do you have a minute?"

She did not.

Not with the cocktail party that was going to launch her biggest career success in thirty minutes. Already dressed in an emerald silk sheath, five-inch Louboutins and her favorite hammered-brass jewelry, Mia had already done two rounds to ensure that everything was ready to rock.

It almost was.

She just had to finish adding her own personal touch to a few things. Like finish interspersing photos of children who'd be helped by the hospital in between the gaily wrapped packages on the gift table.

So Mia didn't have a second, let alone a minute.

Still, she shot Jessica a smile over her shoulder and asked, "How do you think this looks? I debated telling the florist to tone it down to two arrangements instead of three, but I'm glad I didn't. I think the profusion of lilacs and hydrangeas really makes a statement, don't you?"

Already frowning, Jessica looked at the bowls of flowers arranged between pyramids of colorful gifts decorating the round marble-and-wrought-iron table and shrugged.

"I guess it looks okay. I don't understand why we're giving gifts to the guests, though. Isn't the whole point to get as much money as we can, not to give it away?"

"The point is to make sure that our guests are so comfortable and grateful as they enjoy themselves that they are happy to donate as much money as possible." Mia defiantly adjusted the top package so the bright turquoise bow was at a sassier angle. "Gifts tend to make people feel a little more beholden than they might feel before the party, and seeing them next to these sweet faces will inspire and make people feel good about themselves."

"And the pictures? Who are those kids?"

"They're special-needs or chronically-ill children in the area who will be served by the hospital," Mia said, wondering why she was explaining. She glanced over her shoulder to frown at Jessica. "I'd think you'd know that. Aren't you the one who got the photos for me?"

"Oh. Oh, yeah." Peering at the images in their antiqued pewter frames, Jessica pulled a face. "I guess I didn't recognize them in such a fancy setting."

Wrinkling her nose at her roommate's tone, Mia pulled a tray of donation cards from the box she'd used to load everything, adding it to the very center of the table, then stood back.

"It looks good," she decided.

"I guess you're the expert."

About to snap back that *yes, I am*, Mia drew in a long breath through clenched teeth. Once she got a good look at Jessica's face, she added a sigh. She didn't have time for drama, dammit. But she made herself ask, "Is everything okay?"

"I think we have an issue." Scooping up one of the now-empty cardboard boxes, Jessica headed toward the back of the house.

An issue? Panic clawing in her gut, Mia grabbed the other box and hurried after Jessica, double-stepping through the kitchen. Her mind raced, cataloging every possible *issue* that could have come up. Since the vendors would all come to her, not Jessica, it had to be something to do with Señor Alcosta or his team. Had he changed his mind about something?

Mia yanked her cell phone out from where she'd tucked it in her jeweled belt as she hurried after Jessica into her staging area, a long room that spanned the back of the villa. A couple of the subcontractors were taking a break before the party started, chatting with each other over sandwiches.

"What's wrong?" Mia asked as soon as she crossed the threshold. Cell phone at the ready, she prepared to call, summon or bribe her way into fixing the issue. "Is there something Señor Alcosta wants changed? Is someone missing? What needs to be fixed?"

"Get out," Jessica snapped at the contractors, dropping the box. "We need the room."

"We're almost done."

"Now."

What the hell?

As shocked as the diners, Mia murmured her apology as the pair hurried past, sandwiches in hand and glares at the ready.

"There's no reason to be nasty," Mia said quietly. "Whatever the problem is, we can fix it. They weren't to blame."

"I don't have time to play nice with the help."

Whoa, flashback time. Images of Jessica browbeating a freshman who'd walked in front of her, of ruining the reputation of the girl who'd gone up against her as head cheerleader and even the rumor that she'd claimed sexual harassment to get a teacher fired after giving her a C. Eyes wide, Mia pursed her lips.

She'd told Spence that Jessica wasn't nasty, and she'd meant it. But she'd forgotten about that vindictive streak. Seeing Mia's expression, Jessica's face smoothed out, the angry furrows fading into a rueful smile.

"Sorry, I'm just so upset that I've lost my grip on civility. I don't mean to be rude."

And just like that, Mia remembered how often she'd heard of Jessica sidestepping the trouble she'd made with a smile and a flash of charm.

How had she forgotten all of that?

Well, this sucked, Mia thought, shoving her fingers through the spiky disarray of her hair. Her mom was right. She hated that.

"What do you need to talk with me about?"

Jessica's smile dimmed just a little at Mia's clipped tone.

"We need to discuss that man you're dating. Your assistant-slash-security expert. Spence Lloyd." Even though it was just the two of them in the room, Jessica leaned in and asked in a hushed voice, "Do you know where he is right now?"

"Spence? I'm sure he's around somewhere." She'd actually gone searching for him herself after she'd changed into the clothes stashed in her car, but he'd been nowhere to be seen. Roommate or not, she wasn't going to tell that to Señor Alcosta's assistant, though. "His security strategy has a lot of elements that he has to oversee himself."

"Security strategy? What strategy, Mia? The guy is way out of control. He's poking into places he shouldn't, asking about things that are none of his business."

"You don't like Spence?"

"I don't like Spence."

Mia glanced at her watch.

"The party starts in fifteen minutes, Jessica. Unless there's an actual problem that you need to discuss with me immediately, I need to get in there and make sure everything is ready."

"It's ready," Jessica said, flicking a dismissive wave toward the door. "You've done everything that has to be done, double- and triple-checked it, and nagged your staff until they can probably handle this in their sleep."

"Two minutes," Mia decided, figuring she could afford to lose 120 seconds in order to avoid the drama brewing in Jessica's eyes. But even as she agreed to hear Jessica out, her body poised to get back to work.

"This Spence guy. Like I said, he's going way overboard with the research. He's even digging into Santiago's past. That's ridiculous. Santiago is the one throwing this party," Jessica said, her words coming so fast that they almost fell over each other.

Spence had investigated Alcosta? Mia mulled on that for a heartbeat, then shrugged it off.

"Any research that's been done on anyone is for the good of the fund-raiser. Spence's job is to make sure these events are secure. That means looking into any potential threats."

"You just met the guy. How can you trust him? Other than sex, what do you really know about the guy?"

"Maybe I've only known him a month, but I'd trust Spence with my life," she said honestly. "I know he's a good man with strong convictions. He's hardworking and focused and, honestly, maybe even more driven than I am."

He was sweet, tender, passionate and intense, too. And unlike everyone else in her life, he believed in her 100 percent, having total faith that she could do anything she set her mind to. He filled her life with pleasure, in and out of bed. What more did she need to know?

"Jessica, I appreciate your concern, but it's misplaced. Now, the cocktail party is about to begin. I need to go."

"Fine, if the guy is that good in bed, keep him around. But I'm surprised that you'd put someone in charge of security that you haven't even done a thorough background check on. I'll bet Santiago would be, too."

Blackmail? Mia's fists clenched. Enough already.

"I did a check, Jessica. Spence is clear."

"You did a check?" The disbelief in Jessica's tone was so thick, it practically dripped on the floor. "Like what? You did a Google search?"

"I called my father," Mia snapped, irritated enough to confess, "I used his military connection to run a background check. Satisfied?"

The admission filled her with shame for giving into

Jessica's relentless litany of dire warnings. But she couldn't put it past the other woman to mention her concerns to Alcosta. So while Mia hadn't been willing to overtly poke into Spence's background, she had caved enough to ask her father to check and simply let her know if there were any issues. She'd gladly taken his lack of a response as a thumbs-up.

"Your father, the Navy Admiral, checked him out?" She looked like she still wanted to argue, but Jessica finally shrugged. "I guess that's thorough enough."

"Thank you. Now, if you don't mind, we have a party to host."

If there was one person she could trust most in the world, she knew it was Spence.

Chapter 10

Mia had never been so exhilarated, stressed and irritated at the same time. As she herded the last of the guests to the exit, she struggled to keep her chitchat as light and breezy as the cool night air wafting in through the wall of open doors at the opposite end of the villa.

Since the party had run an hour past schedule, the cleanup crew subtly moved through the ballroom, starting their sweep while she handed out the thank-you gifts, accepted end-of-the-night donations and networked her way into two more events.

"Darling, this party is absolutely wonderful. Elegance with a touch of fun," Lorraine Perkins stated as the attendant delivered her stole. She flipped the ends of the silver fur over the ruched bodice of her cocktail dress, her diamonds winking in the light. "The mariachi band added just the right touch of light entertainment to an elegant gathering honoring Mexico City and this fund-raiser."

"I'm so glad you enjoyed it. Did you have a chance to visit with Señor Alcosta?" If so, she'd have been one of the few who had.

"I did. I made a generous donation, and in fact have a lunch appointment with him next week to discuss possibilities for our foundations to work together. You'll coordinate, of course."

Hopefully Alcosta would show up, Mia thought with a mental grimace. Fund-raisers, commitments, parties—apparently none of them were critical enough to guarantee his presence. She didn't know what to make of that. For a man who'd insisted on putting his personal touch on every element of these events, he'd skipped out on a surprising number of planning sessions and meetings.

"And speaking of coordinating—" Lorraine continued, tucking her arm through Mia's "—let's do lunch to discuss something special."

"The Winter Ball?" Mia asked, trying to keep her tone enthusiastic but not desperate.

"Oh, darling, that's already yours. No, no, this is a different proposal."

Hers? She had the Winter Ball? Mia had to imagine her feet filled with lead to keep from jumping up and down. She wanted to add a shout to her happy jumping. Not because she necessarily wanted the job, but because the offer itself was a huge sign of success.

"Lunch would be great. Almost as great as tomorrow's sunrise breakfast and spa day," Mia said, doing her duty by dropping in the subtle reminder of the next day's event. "I've saved you a seat at the head table and made sure you're booked with Sven."

"Oooh, Sven?" Lorraine rounded her eyes as wide as her Botox would allow and gave Mia a breathy leer. "He sounds muscular."

"Blond, buff and brainy. He holds the most intriguing conversations while pummeling your body into putty."

By the time she and Lorraine reached the front door, the other woman had already promised to buy the deluxe spa package, to bring ten extra guests to Monte Carlo night and, if he was as good as Mia said, to hire Sven to give office massages twice a month.

She gave a relieved sigh as the heavy door shut, resisting the urge to prop her body against it, both for support and to make sure nobody came back in.

"All finished?"

This time Mia did jump, accompanied by a loud squeak of surprise.

"I didn't see you there," she gasped, one hand pressed against her chest to keep her heart from hitting the floor. "Where have you been?"

As he stood in the hallway leading to the kitchen, Spence's face was in shadows. Even so, she could see his body tense. She told herself not to feel like a clingy girlie girl for asking. The man worked for her; he was on duty this evening. Knowing his location was part of her business. It had nothing to do with missing him.

"I've been around." Stepping out of the hallway, he scanned the foyer, then the ballroom before meeting her eyes. "Securing the perimeter, ensuring the safety of your guests. That kind of thing. There were a few complications."

"What complications?" Mia thought she could hear her feet scream at the very thought of trooping over the grounds to check out the perimeter breach or camera glitch or security snafu. Ignoring them, she asked, "Is there something I need to take care of?"

"No," he said so decisively that she blinked. "I took care of everything."

"So, the evening went well? No break-ins, robberies or threats of bodily harm?" she asked slowly, searching his face for a hint of what was feeding that underlying intensity.

"None. Everything is fine."

"Why don't I believe you?"

"You don't?" He frowned. Then, with a twitch of his shoulders, he seemed as chill and friendly as ever. "Sorry, I'm always a little tense after an operation. Left-over adrenaline, I suppose."

"An operation?" she said, half laughing and half worried about the tingle running down her spine. "That sounds so military."

"Terminology is terminology." He shrugged before giving her that look. The slow, melt-her-insides-with-desire look. Then he smiled. And that desire was set aflame. "You look like you could use a glass of wine or one of those massages you were talking about."

"Are you offering? I'll bet Sven's got nothing on you." And oh, how amazing did a massage sound? Preferably a naked, set-to-music-and-candlelight massage. Suddenly, the heavy exhaustion she'd dragged around for the last hour disappeared. "I just need to do rounds."

At his blank look, she explained, "I need to check on the subcontractors, make sure we're on track for tomorrow, then go through the estate to check for stragglers."

"Stragglers?"

"Every once in a while, people have so much fun at an event that they forget to leave when it's over. No biggie if it's held at a hotel or public venue, but when it's private property, I like to double-check." Mia held up one hand before he could offer to do the rounds for her. "I won't be able to relax unless I do this part myself. But you're welcome to keep me company."

"My pleasure," he said, his tone so easy that she wondered if she'd imagined his hesitation.

She tucked her arm through his as they made their way through the first floor of the villa, as much to cuddle as to better support herself because her feet were killing her. Still, she decompressed a little with every painful step.

Everything was on schedule. The flowers and decorations had been cleared, the caterers had vacated the kitchen, and the cleaning crew was hard at work. As soon as the rooms were cleaned, they'd begin setting up for the next morning's sunrise breakfast.

"Let's check the grounds while the crew finishes the floors," she decided. That way she only had to climb the stairs once. As soon as they stepped out onto the tiled patio, Mia's feet screamed in protest. Gripping Spence's arm with one hand, she used the other to peel off her stilettos.

"I love these shoes, but five hours in them is torture. Between walking and dancing, I think I covered three miles, and that's not counting all the standing around, socializing."

"Can you finish the tour barefoot?"

"Believe me, it'll be a pleasure."

Spence gave her naked limbs a long, heated stare that had Mia leaning in for the kiss she knew would follow. But he didn't lean closer. Instead, he slipped the shoes from her fingers, letting them dangle by the straps from one hand while gesturing for her to lead the way. Mia blinked in hurt shock.

"I'll carry those and you can tell me about the launch of your fund-raising extravaganza. How'd everything go with the cocktail party? Why are you so stressed when it was clearly a huge success?"

His easy confidence in her abilities soothed Mia's feelings.

"All things considered, it went well."

"What went wrong?" At her frown, he shrugged. "You have that things-went-wrong crease between your brows."

"Nothing went seriously wrong," Mia claimed. Still, she rubbed her fingers over the furrow creasing her forehead, hoping it'd ease the stress evidenced there. "At least, nothing wrong on my end. The subs were great—everyone did a fabulous job. The guests enjoyed the food and drink, the entertainment and the music."

"But?"

But Spence had been so scarce during the event that she'd only caught a handful of glances of him from afar. The launch of the biggest triumph of her career, and she'd spent more time obsessing over where her crush was than doing her job.

But she couldn't say any of that. She'd only known the man a month. There was no way she was going to admit how much he meant to her.

"But there were a lot of glitches on the Alcosta side of things," she said instead. "You'd think tonight would rank really high on the priority list, wouldn't you? Considering the amount of money this fund-raiser is costing him, to say nothing of how important it is to solicit enough donations to pay for that hospital, I mean."

"So, why did Alcosta leave early?" Spence asked, voicing the same thing she'd been wondering for half the night.

"How'd you know he left?"

"I monitored the coming and going of everyone tonight, remember?"

Mia tried to tamp down her irritated curiosity. Alcosta was her client and his business was his own. He'd hired Mia so he didn't have to do all the work on this fund-raiser—including hosting duties—so what did it matter if he left them for her? After a few more seconds attempting lame excuses for the man's lousy behavior, she gave up.

"You saw him leave—did he seem okay? You know, like was he sick, or did he seem upset?" He'd hit on her again, but had seemed to take her refusal in stride. He wouldn't have left because of that, would he? Mia shoved her free hand through her hair as if that'd dislodge the tension pounding in her head.

"He didn't say a word about leaving early to me. He just disappeared. I didn't even know he was gone until after an eager donor and I searched the ballroom twice."

Talk about looking ineffective. Her stomach ached as lingering humiliation warmed her cheeks. Hopefully her fast-talking charm had offset the impression that she didn't know what she was doing.

"Alcosta was on the phone when he left. Judging by his body language and extensive cussing, he was pissed, but he looked healthy enough." She felt rather than saw Spence's shrug. "He did have your roommate with him."

"Jessica?" Surprised, Mia stopped to stare at him in the moonlight. "Really? I was irritated that she was gone, too. But I figured she'd ditched the party to have makeup sex with her lover."

"Not unless Alcosta is her lover." When Spence arched one brow, Mia shook her head. "Why'd you think she'd run off for sex? And what was she using it to make up for?"

"I feel like I'm gossiping," Mia realized, acknowledging the hint of shame in the back of her throat with a rough laugh. "Whispering salacious secrets and innuendos in the dark."

"You, the coordinator of a multimillion-dollar fundraising event, are giving me, the head of security for the same, a rundown on the evening. Every piece of information helps me to safeguard the rest of the events for the guests, for the charity and, most of all, for you."

Awww. For her? Mia's heart melted a little, as did the last of her reservations.

"About an hour into the party, Señor Alcosta was holding court with a lot of muckety-mucks, wowing them with stories about all the great things he's done over the years. At that point, I estimated that we had about 15 percent more drop-in guests than we'd estimated." She smiled when he gave her a congratulatory shoulder bump. "I wanted to make sure there were enough canapés, so I snuck back to the kitchen to talk to the caterer. That's when I heard Jessica on her cell phone, having an ugly argument. Like a cussing-and-insults-and-raging-tears argument."

Maybe it was the breeze—it was cooler here on the far side of the grounds, away from the house—but Mia swore she felt Spence stiffen.

"Did you overhear anything?"

"Just enough to figure she was fighting with her boyfriend. Accusations about not being there, saying he'd do things and he didn't—that sort of thing." Mia shrugged, not sure how that factored into security for the events.

"And Alcosta didn't say anything to you before he bailed?"

"He didn't say anything that gave me the impression that he was thinking about leaving, but I knew he was irked. With me, mostly," she admitted with a grimace. Since mentioning the pass would only irritate Spence, she explained Alcosta's other issue. "He wanted my uncle here for all of the events. Apparently, he talked his attendance up quite a bit and was even hoping for a private meeting or two. So he was pretty irked to find out that Uncle Luis won't be here until tomorrow, at the soonest. I suppose he thinks I didn't do enough to ensure my uncle would be here all weekend."

God knows how much the man would pout if Uncle Luis canceled altogether.

"Hell of a night," Spence murmured.

"It was, and mostly in a good way." Surprised at how good she felt after dumping her stress and irritations all over Spence, Mia was finally able to flip the coin and focus on the upside. "Everything else in the evening went really well, from the response to the mariachi band to the gourmet-margarita bar, the guests seemed to have a great time. The party did so well that we've already raised half of the target funding."

Her arm still tucked through Spence's, Mia paused next to the statuary garden, an expanse of weathered and cracked stone lions and conquistadors, to do a bare-footed, hip-wiggling happy dance.

"Half, baby," she crowed when he laughed. "That's millions of dollars. Added to that, we're completely booked for the morning's breakfast auction, we sold another forty tickets for tomorrow's golf tournament, and I've already had to call for two more croupiers and another bank of slot machines for Monte Carlo night."

"Damn." He breathed in evident admiration. "If a lover's tiff and the host bailing early are the worst things that happened, you should consider this a huge success."

"I think I will," Mia said with a laugh. Even as the idea of owning her success settled in, she shivered a little as the statues seemed to stare menacingly out at them in the dark. To avoid them, she took the next twist in the path, the one that led to a small, remote terrace.

"I'm proud of you," Spence murmured, stopping on the path between two rose hedges to take both of her hands in his. The moon glowed behind him, throwing his face into shadows. "You saw what you wanted, and you went after it. And despite all the nay-saying claims that it'd either be impossible or it'd be a mess, you worked your ass off and made this fund-raiser a success. No matter what comes next, you did that. You are a success."

"Thank you," she murmured, reveling in the feeling of someone's compete faith in her.

She waited, wanting him to kiss her. The memory of his lips on hers made her tingle with need.

But he only watched her. Staring with an intensity gleaming in his eyes that made her twitchy. What did he see? What did he want?

Pulling her hands free, Mia ran a self-conscious hand through her hair and wondered if stress had worn away all of her makeup.

"Why don't we finish our tour of the grounds, then see if the crew is finished," she suggested, wanting the anonymity of darkness. At least until she figured out what he saw when he looked at her like that.

He continued to stare for a long moment and then nodded. With a gesture that she choose their direction, he waited to move at her signal.

Mia let out a long, satisfied breath, the last dregs of lingering tension fading from her shoulders as they strolled along the cobbled paths.

"Will you use this terrace for the last event?" he asked as they approached the small enclosed patio on the far-thest side of the house. With its fountain and comfort-able chair groupings, it'd be nice for a small gathering. But the remote location and lack of doors inside made Mia shake her head.

"No. We'll keep the guests to the more easily acces-sible areas."

And with that, everything seemed back on an even keel. They discussed traffic patterns, the variety of menu options planned throughout the weekend and personal tastes in music as they wandered their way back to the main patio. By the time they stepped onto the covered tiles, Mia was relaxed again.

"It's nice out here," she sighed, leaning against the railing for just a moment as she breathed the jasmine-scented air. Even with the fairy lights twinkling through the trees and over the trellises, the stars still shone, bright and gleaming. "I think if I'd been a guest tonight, this is where I'd have spent all my time."

"Out here?" He shifted so he could once again stare at her with those soul-searching eyes. "What would you have done since most of the activity was inside?"

Music still played through the speakers, a delicate collision of flutes and drums. Mia reminded herself to shut down the sound system when they went inside. At least she'd turn it off out here. Maybe she'd let it play upstairs, since, as she usually did when she had a day-break event, she was sleeping on-site.

And she hoped Spence was sleeping with her.

"I'd have danced. Want to try it now?" she asked, gesturing to the softly lit tiled area she'd cordoned off for dancing.

"The party is over, and you're barefoot," he pointed out.

Since barefoot meant she was that much closer to being naked with him, Mia was okay with that.

"It was a busy night, but I'm sorry I missed being held by you," she said honestly. Then, because she desperately needed to confess at least some of what she was feeling, she drew in a bolstering breath and watched him through her lashes. "It was a triumphant night, but I missed being with you. I think it would have felt even better to experience all that success with you right there by my side."

After a long moment, he held out his hand for hers. "Let's make up for it."

With the music washing over them, and the night air wrapping intimately around them, she went into his arms. Cheek resting against the hardness of his chest, everything suddenly felt right.

So, so right.

Spence woke slowly, the heaviness in his heart at war with the delight of his flesh. He didn't have to open his eyes to know it was a couple of hours before dawn. He could feel the change in the air.

He wanted to grab this moment and hold it tightly. A

memory he could take out later for comfort, for pleasure, for assurance that life could be filled with blessings.

The scent of gutted candles mingled with the spicy roses, both a distant pleasure compared to Mia's perfume. He could smell it on him, just as he could feel her body, warm and lush, pressed against him.

Pure heaven.

He knew he shouldn't be here.

Not with Mia. Not like this.

After finding the gun hidden in the flower bed, he'd spent hours searching bushes, nooks and crannies. But other than that initial weapon, the location was clean.

Who'd leave a loaded gun in a flower bed? Not only was it a dangerous and unprofessional move, it seemed desperate. But desperate and dangerous sometimes worked, he mused. Planting a gun meant not worrying about getting it past any security he might add at the last minute, past any security Penz would bring on board.

He'd done due diligence on all of the guest lists, and while there were plenty of wealthy names, he was sure that Penz was the potential target. Unfortunately, other than his gut, he had no proof.

Still, he'd notified the admiral, leaving a coded message since the damned man hadn't been available.

Frustration had fueled the rest of his day, between waiting to hear back and trying to cover the location and the event, as well as protect Mia at the same time. Especially since his thoughts kept ricocheting between the memory of making love with her and her adamant statement about never getting involved with a military man.

About the fact that his feelings for her were intense and authentic and deep, and the truth that he was straight up lying to her about who he was, why he was there and what he was doing.

Reality and what he figured was best for Mia had won out over his own wants and needs. So he'd been determined to leave after the event. To go back to his hotel and grab some reality.

Instead, they'd ended up making love for hours.

Something about Mia simply short-circuited his good sense. When he was with her, he wanted to give her anything—everything—she wanted.

As if she'd reached into his thoughts and heard the offer, Mia stirred in his arms. One hand slid down his body in a tempting trail to snuggle between his thighs. Instantly aroused, he reciprocated with a groan.

As night drifted closer to day, he slid into the pleasure of Mia's body. Mouths slid, tongues tangled. Limbs twisted between the sheets as the heat built in a slow, steady swirl of passion, until he slid into the hot welcome of her body.

Twining their fingers together, he pulled her arms over her head so her back arched and her breasts rose. Lifting her chin, Mia arched her back and met him, thrust for thrust.

Desire built, climbing, winding, tightening. Until it was all he was, all he saw. All he had.

He stared into the velvety depths of Mia's eyes, watching them blur as her breath came faster, as her pulse raced and, finally, her body buckled beneath his. Watching her climax sent his own body flying, his orgasm rocking through him like an earthquake.

By the time Spence returned to earth, Mia had curled into him with a sleepy sigh. Wanting her to rest, he rubbed his palm in a soothing, sleepy rhythm over her back. He could feel her heartbeat slowing against his chest, her breath easing as she fell asleep.

This was good. Really damned good. He should probably try to figure out why, as amazing as it was to make love with Mia, somehow the holding her afterward made him feel just as good.

Actually, he probably shouldn't think about it too hard, he realized. Since there was no chance of a future for him and Mia, the answer would pretty much suck.

Deep in contemplation of how bad it was going to suck, he heard his cell phone buzz. With the same care he'd use dismantling an IED, he unwrapped himself from Mia's arms and reached over to snag his pants from the floor and retrieve his phone.

He glanced at the display.

Damn.

The bed of the woman he was protecting without her knowledge was hardly the place to receive intel, so Spence rolled off the mattress with nary a ripple. He waited until he was on the patio before toggling his phone to talk.

"Lloyd," he answered in lieu of a greeting.

"Yo, Improv. It's me, Smidge."

"What've you got?"

"How about the fact that once upon a time, Santiago Alcosta had a stepbrother? 'Step' went with the mom when the dad moved on to his fifth wife, but rumor is the brothers stayed in touch. Right up to the time that Step went boom in a military operation led by a certain US Army Captain to close down his hobby of trafficking pretty little girls over the border."

"Revenge," Spence realized quietly, all the pieces falling into place. "It's not blackmail—it's revenge for killing Alcosta's stepbrother."

"That'd be my take. According to the Army, the op was legit. Nothing hinky, nothing untoward. They didn't advertise that Penz led the op, but it's right there in the files. Anyone with a skills could pull it up." Smidge's tone changed from is usual jovial reporting to worry as he added, "Improv, this is serious. You okay to handle it on your own?"

Training, experience and, yeah, pure, cocky confidence had an affirmative teetering on the tip of his tongue. Then Spence glanced through the French doors, the filmy curtains casting his view of Mia in a dreamy haze.

He couldn't risk her safety on confidence alone.

"Did you check the other names I sent you last night? Alcosta's team?" he asked instead.

"I've worked straight through for three damned nights, sifting through a mountain of tiny hints of information—most of it in a foreign language—with a tweezer and a flashlight. I pieced it together one freaking word at a time to get you this intel. And instead of thanking me, you ask if I got more?"

Smidge's cussing washed over him. Spence waited until it ran dry.

"Get me those reports when you can," he said. "And thanks."

Hanging up, Spence absently shrugged into his shirt but didn't bother to button it against the morning chill. He stared out over the lush grounds surrounding the villa. After a moment's consideration, he placed a call. He punched in a series of numbers, then hung up.

Two minutes later, his phone rang again.

"Sir," he said by way of greeting. "News has come to my attention and I believe the situation is escalating. Permission to adjust protocols."

"Report."

Spence filled the admiral in on the new intel about Penz's role in Alcosta's stepbrother's death, and on the stashed gun. He emphasized the social nature of the weekend's gatherings and the challenge of keeping Mia safe.

"And you still believe that Penz is Alcosta's target." The words weren't a question, but simply Admiral Cade summing up the sitrep.

"Yes, sir, I do."

"Very well. Continue as before. I'll notify Penz and suggest he take proper measures."

"Will he cancel his appearance?" It was probably for the best, but Mia would be crushed.

"Doubtful. Prepare to secure each and every event, provide backup to Penz's own security team and, if necessary, eliminate the enemy."

"And Mia?"

"What about her?"

"Sir, if there's a skirmish, she'll be in the line of fire." And knowing Alcosta, being used as a human shield.

"Your first priority is to keep her safe, but under no circumstances are you to break your cover."

Relief surged through him, knowing that order meant he had a few more days with Mia before she hated him. Drawing in a long, painful breath, Spence reminded himself that Mia hating him was a small price to pay for her safety.

"Sir, she has to be told," Spence insisted. "There is a clear and credible threat. The target will be attending at her request. Added to that, she has a lot riding on this event. Not the least of which are her career and her reputation."

"Very well. I'll send in backup. Mia will be safe enough. As for the rest, she was warned not to have dealings with Alcosta, but she chose to do so anyway. Perhaps next time, she'll listen."

"You're using this threat to make a point?" Putting his daughter in danger so she'd listen next time he told her what to do?

"I'm doing as I think best, Lieutenant. You will do the same."

Spence knew when to shut up, and the *when* was now. The admiral's orders were clear.

"Admiral, with all due respect, she can't go into this blind. Not only is her business—something she values and has worked very hard at—in jeopardy, but so is her safety. Your daughter is an intelligent woman. If I don't appraise her of the situation, she's quite likely to figure it out for herself."

Spence didn't need to see the admiral to feel his rage at being challenged. The fury of it came through the phone line, loud and clear despite the silence. But Spence stood his ground.

Finally his commanding officer said in a tone that could peel the skin off a man at twenty paces, "You have your orders, Lieutenant. Failure to follow said orders will result in retaliatory measures being taken. And in case you are harboring any misbeliefs about your current status as a civilian, be assured that if you do not follow orders, I will personally ensure that you do not get a position with Aegis, or with any other entity that

I have influence with. And believe me, Lloyd, I have a great deal of influence."

Well. Spence clenched his teeth as the line went dead. That was clear enough.

He had his orders.

Lie to the woman he loved, quite possibly putting her in harm's way. Or throw away the rest of his career.

Destroy his own future.

Something he and Mia didn't have.

He didn't know how long he stared out at the bright green morning, watching the warming sun melt the dew off the grass before he returned to the bedroom.

Mia lay spent, her face flushed with sleep, her arm outstretched as if reaching for him.

That she was easily the most beautiful woman he'd ever seen, the sweetest he'd ever known, didn't matter. No matter how the rest of this weekend went down, he reminded himself, his work with Mia was finished come Monday. He knew it; she knew it. They both accepted it.

Was he going to throw away twelve years of training, a chance at the career of a lifetime and his reputation, to boot?

Cade was right.

He was a highly trained Special Operative. He could handle this mission, maintain its secrecy and keep Mia safe, all at the same time.

And if he felt like a lowlife, lying dirtbag doing it?

Well, that was his problem.

Chapter 11

This was his first time in a country club, Spence realized the next day. Leaning against the wainscoted wall, partially hidden by one of the pillars flanking the membership desk, he watched a gaggle of well-dressed, wealthy women giggle like a bunch of schoolgirls. Apparently a champagne-and-chocolate-themed spa day brought out giddiness, even in women wearing enough diamonds to buy a small country.

Amusement faded when he spotted Mia.

Instantly surrounded by the clamoring group of women, all he could see at first were a series of eye-popping lime-green straps holding her feet in mile-high stilettos. As great as heels made her legs look, he had a sudden craving to see her barefoot again.

The crowd parted as they walked toward the spa, giving him a great view of the rest of her. In sharp contrast to the off-shoulder, body-hugging bodice, the skirt of her dress flowed in deep pleats, from a tiny waist to full billows at her knees. The rich berry color made him think of raspberry ice cream. The kind he wanted to lick and suck and nibble.

He forced himself to tear his gaze from that body and focus on her face. Instead of the usual spiky disarray, her raven hair was slicked back from her face at the sides, rising high in a pompadour on top. The style seemed to accent those huge eyes and sharp cheekbones. He blew out a long, long breath, but it did nothing to cool his desire.

Damn.

She looked almost as good as she had that morning, naked and sleeping in a nest of silk sheets. It'd taken all of his willpower—and the fresh memory of her father's voice in his ear—to keep from climbing back in that bed and losing himself in her sweetness.

Instead, he'd snuck out of her bedroom like the liar he was. Tiptoeing, boots in hand and looking over his shoulder with each step to make sure she didn't wake. Then he'd silently eased the door shut. He'd felt like a jerk the entire way down the stairs and out the front door, but that hadn't stopped him from leaving.

Later, truthfully citing a ton to do for the weekend's events, he'd managed to keep all of their communications to text messages so far. Thankfully, between the auction, the spa gig and this afternoon's golf tournament, she'd stay hella busy all day.

Knowing he was indulging himself by acting like a lovesick idiot, Spence still shifted positions so he could watch Mia until she disappeared through the frosted doors of the day spa.

Indulgence over, he allowed himself another long breath, then told himself to get his ass to work. His job was a busy one today.

Brief Penz's team, liaise with Cade's backup team, bring down a criminal and break Mia's heart.

Given the option, he'd prefer to skip that last one.

But he was out of options.

As if life needed to emphasize that point, there was a commotion at the entrance. Six men in black suits, earbuds and dark glasses strode in, two taking position on either side of the door while the others approached the desk.

Showtime, Spence thought.

Where his staff and security teams went, Senator Penz was sure to follow.

With that in mind, he intercepted the leader, the senator's chief of staff, if Spence wasn't mistaken.

"Gentlemen, I'm Spence Lloyd. I've been instructed to brief you."

"Jon Bertram," the man said with a hearty shake. "The senator will arrive in two hours. Do you have an operations room ready?"

"This way." Without waiting to see if they followed, Spence led the way down a narrow hallway, past the sports center and, unlocking it with a key card, into the large conference room he'd designated their CIC, or combat information center.

"Secure the room," Bertram ordered his men. "Equipment-check first, surveillance systems next, followed by perimeter detail. We have press arriving in three hours and need to be ready."

At ease with his feet planted, hands clasped behind him, Spence observed from the door as the men got down to business. Geek business, Spence realized, a little intrigued by how cool their techie equipment was. Who knew politicians had better toys than the military?

He wondered how Aegis's toys stacked up.

And if he'd ever get to find out.

By the time they'd set up their computers, checked their cameras and two of them left to set up the press room, the security team arrived. If the first wave qualified as geeks, these guys were gorillas.

Built like a fleet of aircraft carriers, four men filed into the conference room. It was a big space, but these guys seemed to fill every niche of it. Spence rarely felt small, but next to them, he was a hundred-pound weakling.

"Well, well, look who it is," the burliest of the gorillas said when he caught sight of Spence. A grin splitting his face, he strode over. "The SEAL they call Improv."

"Michelson," Spence greeted, shaking his old friend's hand. "How've you been?"

After a few minutes of playing catch-up, Michelson asked, "What brings a SEAL to a charity golf tournament?"

"Former SEAL." A firm believer in full disclosure to anyone depending on him to cover their back—at least, when he was given that option—Spence briefly explained the accident that'd destroyed his night vision.

"Bummer, dude. So what? Now you're moonlighting as a golf pro?"

Spence glanced around the crowded room, then tilted his head. "Do you have a minute? I'd like to run something by you."

As he caught the tone, Michelson's easy grin faded. With a nod, he gestured to the empty corner of the room where Spence filled him in on the same information he'd given the Admiral.

He outlined the senator's role in Alcosta's stepbrother's death, detailing the steps required to access Penz's sealed military records. He described the unregistered gun he'd found stashed in the bushes and his steps to search and secure the property. He emphasized the social nature of the weekend's gatherings and the challenges of securing the senator's safety, ending with the assurance that Admiral Cade had given that he'd personally contact Penz.

Ten minutes later, Michelson called Penz's chief of staff over.

"Mr. Bertram, I think you've met Lieutenant Spencer Lloyd. We served together on SEAL Team One a few years back. Lloyd's covering security at this gig, and he's got a few things you need to hear."

Used to reporting his way up the chain of command, Spence started again from the beginning. He answered the same questions Michelson had asked, along with a dozen or so more.

"The senator hasn't told me any of this," Bertram said, the suspicion in his tone echoed on his face.

"As I said, Admiral Cade indicated that he'd personally contact the senator. He didn't fill me in on his timetable or plans beyond that."

"I'll be asking him about that," Bertram snapped.

Ignoring Michelson's eye roll, Spence simply nodded. He'd expect the guy to do no less.

"What's your role in this?" Bertram asked once he realized the nod was going to be Spence's only response.

"I'm here to assist in any way you deem necessary. When Aegis arrives at oh-ten-hundred, I'll liaise between your team and theirs to ensure that your task of keeping the senator safe and theirs of bringing down the assailant are successful, while also protecting the Admiral's daughter from all harm."

"The Admiral's daughter? That'd be Penz's niece, correct? Is she prepared to assist?"

"No, sir. Per Admiral Cade's orders, I'm to remain undercover," he said, bitterness coating his tongue. "As she's not on his NTK list, she is to be kept oblivious."

"I agree that Ms. Cade doesn't need to know. But you don't like that order." Bertram realized with a quirk of his lips.

"I don't have to like orders to follow them."

"My orders are to hand over the senator's security to a bunch of yahoos I've never met before on an unverified rumor. So believe me, I know all about not liking orders."

Unoffended, Spence relaxed enough to arch his brow.

"Can you talk Penz into canceling?"

"No chance. The senator never backs down from a threat."

Before Spence could respond, one of the techies handed the chief of staff a phone. Bertram's eyes went blank, his head tilting just a little as he listened. His jaw tightened as he announced to the room, "Aegis is in house."

"Now things are about to get serious," Michelson told Spence in a hushed tone.

Mia's world was damn near perfect.

Part of the perfection came from falling to sleep with an orgasm still trembling through her, then waking to revel in another one.

Part of it was the way Spence's words kept echoing through her head. He was proud of her. She was a success. A freaking success.

She bounced a little in the cushy chair of her temporary office. While the ladies—and two gentlemen—luxuriated in their spa experience, she'd settled in to work at one of the small outdoor tables, with her tablet, her notepad and her iced tea. With most everyone inside, enjoying the country club's varied amenities, she worked in silence broken only by the trickling water from a nearby wall fountain.

Woo, yeah. On every level, the auction breakfast was just as successful as the previous night's cocktail party. Generous bids continued to pour in, pushing the fundraiser's net contributions well over the three-quarters mark toward their goal. And that was net.

Net, baby.

Mia was actively dancing in her seat when her cell phone buzzed.

"Mia Cade," she answered, her voice chiming with joy. That happiness dimmed when she realized it was the bank calling about a problem with the last two checks she'd issued.

"There shouldn't be a problem. I verified funds myself—the account is more than solvent enough to cover all of these expenses," she insisted.

It took her another ten minutes and a discussion with the head of the bank before the man was satisfied. Mia, however, wasn't. Frowning, she stared at her notes as she absently hit the off button on her phone.

What was going on?

Before she could start delving into it—before she

could even figure out how—footsteps ricocheted like bullets on the concert.

"Where's Spence?"

"Hmm?" Mia looked up from her notes to give Jessica a questioning look. "Sorry, what'd you say?"

Undoubtedly it hadn't been an apology or explanation for running out on the cocktail party, let alone the screaming fit she'd had there. Which, the more she thought about it, the more annoyed Mia became.

Jessica was not only employed by the company raising the damned funds, but technically she'd also been one of the hostesses in charge of socializing, soliciting and schmoozing last night. To say nothing of the fact that she'd spent months begging Mia to let her work with her, then ignored that work to run after her boyfriend, a man Mia still hadn't met.

Jaw tight with irritation, Mia was about to point that out when she finally took in Jessica's appearance.

It wasn't the blonde's furious expression that made her eyes widen. It was the woman's bare face. In all the months they'd lived together, she'd never seen Jessica makeup-free.

"Spence," Jessica spat. "Where is he?"

Biting back the flurry of questions over Jessica's appearance, Mia glanced at her watch, then tapped the laminated print copy of the day's schedule sitting on the table in front of her. "It's 11:00 a.m., so he's here at the country club, preparing security for this afternoon's golf tournament."

"You need to fire him, Mia. He has to go."

This again?

"You need to stop whining about Spence. Look, I know what your issue is with him, but get over it. It's not like the two of you have to actually spend time to-gether," Mia pointed out impatiently. "He's great at his job and he's made my work a million times easier. Even if he wasn't, we're in the middle of the biggest event of my career. There is no way I'm dealing with drama or making staff changes now."

Besides, Spence was leaving the job next week.

Swallowing against the ache in her throat, Mia told herself that was no big deal. He wouldn't work with her anymore, but even though they hadn't actually talked about it, she was sure they'd still be together.

"He lied to you." The words were tossed between them with the force of a gauntlet, their challenge de-manding a response. "Spence Lloyd has been lying to you from day one."

What the hell? Mia shook her head as irritation faded into confusion. Her chair scraped jarringly against the concrete as Mia pushed away from the table. She had a feeling she was going to want to be standing for this.

"He's a lieutenant in the freaking Navy. And if that's not bad enough, he's a SEAL. A freaking SEAL, Mia." Jessica spat the words like they were covered in filth in-stead of being one of the most prestigious professions in the country.

"A SEAL?" Mia breathed, gripping the table to keep from swaying as her heart sank to her toes in a long, heavy slide. Military? "Spence is in the Navy?"

Mia bit her lip, trying to remember if he'd ever actu-ally said what he'd done before coming to work for her. He hadn't. He'd told her how much he loved his career, how hurt he'd been when an injury had ended it.

Was that a lie, too?

"Why?" she breathed.

"Who cares why? The bottom line is that he lied to you," Jessica said again, this time with enough satisfied relish to cut through Mia's shock.

"Where did you get your information?" She didn't bother asking why she'd gotten it. Jessica had obviously done a background check.

Of course Mia had done one, too. Apparently her source was suspect.

"I asked my lover to find out everything he could. Roberto has connections." She tossed her hair. "Good connections, too, because the truth was buried under a layer of lies. Roberto said there were many careful layers. The kind that take military or government skill to create."

Jessica must be seriously pissed. No makeup *and* she'd finally admitted the name of her lover? And that he knew how scammers worked?

Mia's head throbbed as if that last bit of information was just one piece too many for her to process. Needing to move, desperate to pull all her thoughts into a clean, manageable line that she could actually follow, she started pacing.

Spence was in the military.

Mia stormed to one side of the patio, staring out at the acres and acres of rich green grass.

That much had to be fact, since no matter how much Jessica hated him, she wouldn't claim something that couldn't be confirmed.

She stomped to the other side of the patio, the sound of her grinding teeth drowning out the delicate trickle of the fountain.

He'd deliberately hidden his career, his position, his

livelihood from her. It had to be deliberate, since he'd done some trick to conceal his background.

Fists clenched at her sides, she spun around to pace the other way.

Was her father involved in the lie?

He might not be. A cursory check probably wouldn't pull up anything Spence was trying to hide, and her father was more the cursory-favor type when it came to her.

But, she realized as she continued to pace, her father wasn't just in the Navy, he was in charge of a lot of it. The SEAL teams, for instance, were under his command.

So how was it possible that he hadn't known?

Her eyes burned.

If he had, was it possible that he'd taken part in deceiving her?

It wasn't until she felt the bite of the twisted metal railing digging into her hands that she realized she'd stopped pacing to grab ahold and stare blindly at the tree-framed golf course.

Why had Spence lied to her? What did he have to gain?

Did it even matter?

Whatever his reasons for hiding his career, he knew how she felt. She'd told him the exact reasons why she'd never be in a relationship with a military man.

Fury swirled, building and intensifying with every breath.

Because she'd told him *before* they'd slept together.

He'd known they had no future. That they'd never have more than a month and a lie.

So many questions slammed through her brain, one

after the other, until she wanted to scream. She wanted answers. And she knew exactly where to get them.

Turning on one heel, she marched toward the club door. Fury blurred her vision so much, she almost rammed her hip into a table on her way. The near miss only added to her ire.

"Where are you going?" Jessica snapped, clearly annoyed at not getting the nasty meltdown reaction she'd hoped for.

"To get answers."

"How?"

How else?

She was going to confront Spence and find out what the hell he thought he was doing, breaking her heart.

All his life, Spence had wanted one thing. To be a Navy SEAL. Before and after he'd earned his trident, he'd pushed, aimed and strived to be the best.

When Cade had offered him a shot at joining Aegis, he'd jumped at the opportunity because, hell, he had nothing else worthwhile going on. But even though he'd accepted the assignment, even while he given it his all, the skeptical voice in his head figured it wasn't going to happen.

After all, why should he be rewarded for deceiving Mia?

But now, watching two Aegis operatives walk into the room, he wanted that shot more than he wanted his next breath.

These were men of power.

A power so sharp, it practically radiated off them.

Even the air changed. Electrified.

A sharp contrast to Penz's security suits, with their

guns bulging under their jackets, these guys were dressed simply in jeans and tees. They moved like warriors, each carrying a metal case, and instead of guns, they both wore satellite phones on their belts. Echoing Spence's impression, everyone in the room subtly came to attention.

"Yo," the taller of the two said, greeting the room in general. "Anywhere in particular you'd like us to set up?"

"I'd prefer that you find a corner and wait until we deem this event an actual security risk before you start grandstanding," Bertram said, clearly put out that he hadn't been able to rescind Spence's order to bring in Aegis.

Unoffended, the two men just grinned. They obviously had nothing to prove and were used to crap attitudes like Bertram's.

Spence admired that. If he played his cards right, this could be it. His future.

Before Spence could go over and introduce himself, Bertram got in his face.

"Lloyd, this intel you offered is useless. Useless and wrong."

Well. So much for his future. Spence's gaze didn't cut over to the Aegis men. Instead, he handled the situation in the same way he'd always done when confronted by a superior officer/inferior human being. He kept his cool, his tone and his demeanor in line.

"How so, sir?"

"We've looked into your claims and while the hidden weapon is a concern, our intel indicates a strong possibility that Alcosta might try to put a PR spin on the senator's past in a blackmail attempt. The events that lead to that possibility are verifiable. What is your source for this new claim of assault?" Bertram asked impatiently.

"What intel indicates that the senator has committed a blackmailable offense?" Spence countered, meeting Bertram's cold stare with a chilly arch of his brow. It took the other man all of five seconds to jerk his chin in surrender.

"Nothing specific. Our best guess is that it will relate to his military service. Many of his missions are still under classified seal. Any one of them could be exploited, exaggerated or used in some way to create a semblance of wrongdoing."

"And your reaction will be?"

"We'll follow standard protocol, of course. All safety measures will be in place, but the senator does not bow to threats, including blackmail."

Even as Spence nodded his understanding, Bertram gave an impatient gesture. "Now, if you please, what is your source for claiming that the senator's life is in danger?"

How did he explain his hacker friend had cobbled together a slew of rumors and innuendo as a launching point for his conclusion jumping?

Spence's hesitation was all Bertram needed. Shaking his head, he waved his hand in the air.

"The senator is not curtailing any of his activities at this event. I'm green-lighting all press, interviews and event activities without restrictions."

"Sir, I strongly disagree with your assessment that blackmail is the issue at hand. It's my belief that the senator's role in the death of Alberto Alcosta, stepbrother to Santiago Alcosta, has triggered this threat. Given the discovery of a loaded weapon, I deem that threat to be life threatening."

"Disagree all you want," Bertram said, returning to his geek squad to get back to work. "But you and Cade's security squad can take it somewhere else."

Spence barely bit back his curse. Before he could re-group or think of a reasonable way to tell the man he was being a major asshole without insulting him, another man stepped over and held out his hand.

"Lloyd? I'm Lucas Adrian. Good to meet you."

"My pleasure," Spence said, taking the head of Aegis's hand. Despite the voice in his head cautioning him to tread lightly, he had to admit, "I'm sorry if I've brought you here on a goose chase."

"I've met Penz from time to time through his work on the Intelligence Committee. He's a good man. His team is thorough and efficient, but that's about it."

"Well, they thoroughly and efficiently dismissed this threat," Spence muttered.

"What's your gut say?"

"My gut says this is bigger than some petty extortion scheme. There is too much going on for it to be that sim-ple." As he had to Michelson and then Bertram, Spence described all of the events, including the gun and his sus-picions about Alcosta's staff. Unlike with his report to Bertram, he divulged the source of his rumors to Adrian.

"I've heard of Smidge. The man's got skills," Adrian admitted with a nod. "Very few morals, but his skills can't be beat."

"You believe me?"

"Your gut over a politician's suspicions? Any day and every day." He jerked his head to the man joining them, introducing him as Cal Samson before returning to the threat topic. "This guy you've seen—can you identify him?"

"I haven't been successful yet," Spence admitted.

"We've got a solid facial-recognition program. If you can describe him, we can find him." Cal glanced around the room, then suggested, "I'll go find us a different hole, though. Something with fewer negative vibes."

Even as his lips twitched, Spence nodded. While the other man scooped up his metal briefcase and headed out, Spence and Adrian turned toward Bertram to say their goodbyes.

Before he could, though, Mia stormed through the doorway.

And everything inside of him froze. He knew that face. He knew her voice, her body language and, hell, he knew every damned thing about her.

And apparently she knew about him, now, too.

"Spence," she said in a tone clipped with ice. "We need to talk."

Damn.

More to buy time and hopefully figure out a way to salvage the op, Spence gestured to the man next to him.

"Lucas Adrian, please meet Mia Cade. The admiral's daughter is coordinating this weekend's series of events."

"Ma'am."

Mia spared Adrian a brief glance. "Please excuse us."

Seeing no way out, Spence gestured toward the exit. When Mia stood her ground, he wrapped his hand around her arm and led her from the room. He'd already taken one slam in front of Aegis. He didn't need another.

They didn't make it farther than the hallway outside the door before she dug in her heels and glared.

"Is something wrong?" he asked, still holding the

vague hope she was pissed about a personal issue. Maybe lack of sufficient foreplay or morning breath.

"You'd know that better than I would. After all, you're paid to make sure nothing is wrong, aren't you? At least, nothing to do with me," Mia spat out. "Aren't those your orders? To babysit me?"

Damn it all to hell. She didn't just know something; she knew everything.

"Jessica recognized you," she said when he stayed silent.

"As what? Your lover?"

"Former lover," Mia corrected, biting off the words. "And former Navy SEAL."

And *boom*, there went the dynamite.

Along with any ridiculous fantasy he might have harbored deep in his heart about a future with Mia.

It was all Mia could do to keep from screaming.

She watched Spence's jaw clench, his gaze narrowing as if he were calculating the various means of escape from, what? The truth? She wanted to kick him in the shins. Or somewhere about three feet higher.

"Why would Jessica think I was a Navy SEAL?" he finally asked.

Mia's leg muscles actually bunched before she forced herself to relax them. He wasn't worth the damage to her shoes, she told herself.

"Don't bother to deny it. I called and confronted my father. He admitted that you're here under his orders." She had to stop for a second and clench her teeth to keep the tears at bay. "Aren't you the good little sailor, following those orders to the letter? Does he know how far you went to keep me in line? How about those between-the-sheets maneuvers? Were those your idea?"

"It wasn't like that. It isn't like that," he corrected swiftly, grabbing her arm before she could storm past him. "Let me explain."

"No." She wrenched her arm away. "Nothing I want to hear starts with the words *let me explain*. Why would I believe anything you say aren't words ordered by my father?"

As if on cue, she heard the buzz of his cell phone at his hip.

"You'd better get that." Mia pointed. "I'm sure it's him, calling to coordinate your new cover story."

She didn't consider it points to his credit that he ignored the phone.

"You have every right to be furious with me. But you need to understand the reasons I'm here. You have to listen to the threat at hand."

"Actually, I don't have to do anything you tell me. I want you to leave." Now. Before she started crying.

"I'm sorry but I can't do that."

"Orders, again?" she asked, the words bitter on her tongue.

"Common sense. Mia, I was sent here for your protection. I won't leave until I'm sure nothing is going to happen that will hurt you."

He'd already hurt her. But seeing no point in voicing the obvious, she sneered instead.

"Right. For my protection." Grateful that the anger was searing away her misery like the sun melted fog, Mia sneered. "The only thing I need protection from is my parents' paranoia."

And Spence. Her fists clenched at her sides as Mia

admitted to herself that her heart could have used protecting from him.

Now it was too late.

"Look, Alcosta's dirty. I can't prove it yet, but I know something bad is going to go down this weekend." Seeing the disbelief on her face, he said, "I found a gun planted in the garden last night. Planted there, I'm sure, to avoid the metal detectors that'll be at every entrance tomorrow night."

"A gun?" she repeated skeptically.

"Alcosta's family has a personal issue with your uncle dating back to his time in the military," Spence continued in a quieter tone, shifting his body so his words reached her and her alone. "I haven't firmly identified that man we keep seeing, but my suspicion is that he's involved. And he's dangerous."

Her anger took a sideline as Mia tried to process all of that. Her father was undoubtedly overprotective and unquestionably interfering. But he wasn't one to waste resources. If he deemed this situation a security risk, there was probably some truth to it. Some.

So while she'd never excuse what Spence had done, for her uncle's sake, she had to listen.

Clearly reading that decision on her face, Spence launched into his findings. She could tell that he was censoring the information and probably saying more than she was authorized to know. Before he finished, Jon Bertram, whom Mia recognized as her uncle's chief of staff, joined them in the hallway.

"The senator is on his way in," he murmured, his expression making it clear he wanted them to take their spat and get the hell out of the way. Ignoring that, Mia gave the man a hard look.

"What is your opinion of Lieutenant Lloyd's suspicions?"

"They're being taken under consideration," the man said absently before giving them an impatient wave of his hand.

Oh yeah, he wanted them out of the way. As soon as Mia glanced down the hall, she saw why.

"Uncle Luis," Mia called halfway across the hallway before she even realized she was running. "I'm so glad you're here."

His security team parted like warm butter so, just as he had since she was a toddler, the burly man could take her up in his arms and swung her around in a dizzying circle.

"Mia, my girl, look at you," Luis said, stepping back to hold her at arm's length. "Gorgeous. Just gorgeous. You obviously get those good looks from your mother."

His smile faded when he saw the distress in her eyes.

"What's the matter?"

"Sir, we have matters that need your attention."

"One minute, Bertram."

"Go ahead," Mia murmured. "I'm sure you need to hear this."

Swept into the room with her uncle, Mia listened to Spence's report. Her body tensed, stomach tight as the men she recognized as being part of Aegis Security supported his findings. It wasn't until the senator's own security team shot down the findings, deeming them highly implausible, that she could unclench her fingers.

"And the gun?" Spence shot back at the chief of staff. "How do you dismiss that?"

"Did you forget to mention that the bullets in the loaded, unregistered gun were addressed to Senator

Penz?" Bertram shot right back, his expression pure disdain. "You have no proof that weapon was planted there in anticipation of the senator's visit. For all you know, the property owners kept it there for security."

Mia didn't have to watch the expressions of disbelief on the faces of half the men in the room to know that was a ridiculous claim. She heard the stupidity of it with her own ears. Apparently, so did her uncle.

"Do you at this time have proof of anything more incendiary than a possible blackmail scheme based on a twisted retelling of information found in sealed military records and as-yet-confidential operations I served on as a threat?" her uncle finally asked.

His face remained impassive, but she could see the battle in Spence's eyes. After a long moment of consideration, he offered a reluctant shake of his head.

"Uncle Luis?" Mia prodded, knowing he'd tell her the truth. "Do you believe there's a danger here?"

With his usual care, her uncle considered the question before inclining his head. "While I do believe that the intelligence these men have gathered merits caution, no actual threats have been made. In addition, I made a commitment to be at this event and to support the cause."

"Sir—"

Uncle Luis raised his hand to stop Spence's protest.

"I'll take every precaution. I'll personally instruct my team to coordinate with you as you arrange the necessary security, Lieutenant."

"But you won't leave."

"But I won't leave." The older man reached out, wrapping his arm around Mia's shoulder to give her a hug. He smelled like pine and comfort, reminding her of her childhood. "In addition to promising Mia that I'd be here, my people informed the press and put word out of my attendance. They've arranged numerous meetings already, a number of photo ops and a press conference. Walking away from any of that in an election year would be the height of stupidity."

Mia wanted to protest. If her uncle was in danger, sauntering around a golf course or playing blackjack seemed like really stupid things to do. But she knew her protest would fall on deaf ears. Uncle Luis had formed his career out of forging through, regardless of the danger. Knowing there was a possible threat would only make him more determined to stick around.

"I will take every precaution, but I do need your cooperation, Mia," her uncle said. "Can I count on you?"

"Of course," she murmured. Then, because she couldn't stand it any longer, she said, "If you'll excuse me, I have work to do."

She made it two steps into the hallway when Spence joined her. Mia didn't bother slowing her pace.

"You're going to keep this to yourself, right? You won't mention it to Jessica or Alcosta or anyone?"

Jaw clenched, Mia gave a sharp nod.

"I'll help. I'll keep your secret and I'll do whatever I'm instructed in order to ensure my uncle's safety," she said, her words low and vicious. "But I'm telling you the same thing I told my father. We're finished. Through, done, over. Once this weekend's farce is finished, you get out of my life and stay out. For good."

Chapter 12

Mia stood poised on the edge of the most important event of her career, staring at the villa's ballroom, which was filled with some of the most influential people not only in the country, but in the world. They were all ready to hand her money for a cause she'd made sound irresistibly appealing.

The ballroom's rich tiles and lush plants were accented by beautifully lacquered card tables inlaid with green felt, the brass of the roulette wheel glistening under chandelier lights and the chiming ring of slot machines. The red-and-black-clad servers wove among guests wearing more designer labels than appeared on the runways at New York Fashion Week and sparkling with enough diamonds to build three hospitals.

She nervously fingered the glistening crystal beads of her waist-length necklace as she eyed the handful of security personnel not so subtly sprinkled through the crowd for a dash of contrast. She didn't see Spence, but she knew he was there. Not just because he'd said he would be, but because she could sense him. Like lurking evil, she thought with a sneer. Just waiting in the wings to ruin her evening.

Thankfully her client didn't know that. In the center of the room, Señor Alcosta gloated. Not so much out of pride at hosting a hugely successful fund-raiser benefiting his pet cause, but because his guest of honor was an influential US Senator.

With Uncle Luis in tow, Alcosta socialized and gladhanded his way through the guests with hearty good cheer and a clear determination that every single person in the room see him buddied up with the senator. She could see the edgy nerves peeking through his usual charisma, hopefully due to excitement, not guilt over criminal intentions, as Spence would claim.

Her gaze shifted to Alcosta's companions. Having finally given up on getting her into bed, Alcosta had brought a more amenable date. Her ample curves highlighted by black sequins, the sultry redhead clung to his arm, smiled vapidly and guzzled champagne like a champ.

And then there was Uncle Luis, looking like a sea of calm in a wild storm of decadence as he greeted constituents, networked with influencers and generally contrasted Alcosta's frenzied cheer with amiable serenity. She didn't totally believe Spence's claim of danger, but she still wished her uncle had foregone making an impression on voters by staying away.

Mia sighed.

Sex, gambling and politics.

Monte Carlo had nothing on this, she decided, knotting and unknotting her necklace around her fingers. Except, of course, being a long, long way from Spence. Which made it about the most appealing place she could think of right now, outside of curling into her own bed in her sick-day jammies.

As if drawn by her thoughts, Spence stepped through the open glass doors into the ballroom. Like the other men in the room, he wore a tux. But he wore it unlike anyone else. Evening wear couldn't hide the coiled power in his movements or the implicit threat of his stance.

Damn the man.

She wished, with every fiber of her being, that this night was over. Or better yet, that it'd been canceled. But despite her fury with the situation, Mia had been weaned on the theme of duty before pleasure. So, as much pleasure as she'd take by ignoring Spence's request, her father's orders and her own responsibilities, she'd do her job as hostess.

With that in mind, after checking in with the caterer, she started another round of networking. To distract herself from the pain of seeing Spence, she set a personal goal of greeting twenty people and soliciting three more donations before the call for dinner.

She made it two steps before her view was blocked by a glistening cloud of hot pink.

"Mia, sweetheart." With that, Mia was engulfed in Lorraine's Chanel and feathers. "You've done such a wonderful job. This evening is a huge smash. The entire weekend has been simply divine. You're the queen, darling. The absolute queen."

Gratitude infused Mia. She truly appreciated the woman's praise. With everything that'd happened with

Spence—the heartbreak and lies and suspicions—she'd spent a sleepless night worrying that her judgment was pure crap. How could she throw a successful, engaging event without it?

A part of her—the nagging, desperate part—wanted to ask if Lorraine still wanted to hire her, and if so, could she do it now. That way, in the event that Spence was right, Mia might still have a career at the end of the night.

Instead, she picked a bright pink feather off her dress and gave the other woman a bright smile.

"I'm so glad you're enjoying yourself," she said, turning with Lorraine to survey the room. "I know you were interested in meeting Senator Penz. Would you like to speak with him before we go in to dinner?"

At Lorraine's enthusiastic agreement, Mia led her to the grouping of small sofas on a raised dais at one end of the room, where Alcosta was monopolizing her uncle. After introductions and enough chitchat to put everyone at ease, she excused herself to work the room. Experience and skill meant it only took her thirty minutes to work her way around the room, making small talk and offering gentle nudges to a hundred or so people before signaling to the band to prepare for the shift to dinner music.

Five gourmet courses served on the finest china, accompanied by the best California wines in delicate crystal, were set against a backdrop of white linen, gilt-edged roses and the gentle melody of a harp's song, ending the highlight of the evening, the culmination of the fundraising weekend: the bidding war over hospital-wing naming rights. Up for auction were six wings, two gardens and a playroom, all waiting to be named after generous benefactors.

She tried not to groan when she surreptitiously checked her watch. Still ten minutes until dinner. God. This evening was lasting forever. She didn't care how much money they raised, she didn't care how many clients she wooed. She simply wanted this event to be over.

Everything would be over.

Heart aching, her eyes automatically sought out and found Spence. Standing only a few feet behind Alcosta, he watched the other man as if expecting him to set off a bomb or something. Apparently sensing her gaze, he glanced over to stare at Mia.

Not wanting even that much connection with him, she turned away. She could get the hell away from him. Check the foyer, maybe the terraces, look for guests to shoo inside for dinner. But as furious as she was with Spence, she couldn't completely dismiss his warning. Which meant there was no way she was leaving her uncle's vicinity. She'd check the serving staff instead. Maybe see if the musicians or the bartenders needed anything.

She'd barely managed one step when Jessica swept in. It was the first Mia had seen of her since the barefaced bomb drop the previous day. Mia couldn't hold the truth against the other woman, but she wasn't quite over how nasty Jessica had been about her delivery. So it took a lot of willpower to make herself smile in greeting.

"Mia, sweetie, are you okay?" Jessica handed her a glass of champagne through a cloud of Opium perfume. In a garnet-hued dress that clung at the bodice until flaring out from her waist in a luxurious sweep and her hair perfectly coifed, she fit in perfectly with a room full of the rich and famous. "I'm here for you, anything you need."

"I'm fine."

"Of course you're not. I waited up for you last night but you didn't come home," Jessica chastised with a chiding shake of her head. "And look at you, poor thing. I'm sure you did the best you could, but there's no hiding that devastation. It must be so hard to enjoy a party when your heart is broken."

"My heart is fine," Mia lied. Her head was starting to hurt, though. Hoping to encourage the other woman to leave, she started moving through the perimeter of the room. Much to her frustration, Jessica strolled right along with her.

"Let's go out on the terrace for a little fresh air. A few minutes out there and you'll feel much better."

"Thanks, but I've got a lot to see to in here." And she wasn't letting her uncle out of her sight. "You should go mingle, have fun. Didn't you say that your boyfriend was going to be here tonight? I've been looking forward to meeting him."

"He'll be here and believe me, I'll make sure that you meet him." For a second, Mia thought there was something predatory in her eyes, but then the light changed. "That's for later, though. Right now our priority is to make sure you're okay, and to keep everything running smooth in here."

"I'm fine."

"How can you be fine if you're clenching your teeth?"

"I'm smiling. See." Mia stretched her mouth as wide as she could. "Like I said, I'm fine."

"Why is he here?" Jessica gasped, her fingernails digging into Mia's arm to make her stop walking. "I thought you got rid of him."

Mia didn't need to—didn't want to—look around to see who Jessica was talking about. She simply knew.

"He's in charge of security," Mia reminded her, prying herself free before the other woman drew blood.

"You let him stay? He lied to you." So outraged that she looked like she was going to dive through the fancy crowd and claw his eyes out, Jessica planted her feet and glared across the room at Spence. "I can't believe you didn't break up with him."

Sworn to silence, Mia was unable to correct her so she just shrugged.

"We can talk about it later," Mia insisted. Seeing the argument forming on the other woman's lips, she added, "I don't have time right now, Jessica."

"I tried to help you," the blonde spat, outraged. "I'm trying to be here for you. And you don't have time for me?"

On the edge of jumping into automatic placating mode, Mia realized how much time she'd spent over the last few months trying to calm the woman down. Maybe it was that knowledge, or maybe it was simply being finished caving to other people's demands or being manipulated into things she didn't want to do.

But Mia was through.

To hell with trying to calm her down. Instead, Mia leaned in with her sweetest smile and said, "No. I don't have time. This fund-raiser might not mean anything to you, or to your boss, but it does to me. So if you don't mind, I have work to do."

Mia could see the thoughts race through the other woman's head as easily as if she were reading an electronic translator. Irritation, frustration and hints of something nasty. Then, in a blink, calculation.

"I thought we were friends," Jessica said, actually pulling off the woebegone-waif effect between the betrayed tone and teary eyes. "I don't understand why you're so angry with me."

Yes, she did. Mia sighed, but since she didn't have the time or, more important, the energy to deal with the ensuing argument, she let it go.

"If it means that much to you, we can discuss this later. But not here and not now," Mia insisted, steel infusing her otherwise calm tone.

"You're going to regret this," Jessica hissed, her expression a study in fury. With that, she turned with a flounce and stormed off, her shoulders ramming into people as she shoved through the guests and headed for the exit. Mia didn't know if she was gone for now or gone for good. She was just glad she was gone.

Mia offered an embarrassed smile to the staring crowd and tried to shake off the humiliation. But then her gaze landed on Spence. Staring at her as if he could see all the way into her soul, he gave her a sympathetic grimace.

Enough.

She'd had enough from Spence.

Deception, lies, heartache.

The last thing she wanted was his sympathy, on top of it all.

Her eyes burning, Mia swept out through the glass doors, onto the terrace. Guests spilled out here, too. Laughing, chatting, enjoying themselves. Damn them.

Desperate for a moment's respite, Mia remembered the other terrace. Located on the opposite side of the villa, it was too small and too far from the ballroom for this event. So, please, oh please, let it be private enough.

Stopping only long enough to tell the bartender she'd be on the far terrace if anyone needed her—see, she wasn't completely ignoring her obligations—Mia hurried down the tiled path, dimly lit to discourage guests from wandering the grounds; she could still make out the pathway well enough to avoid getting her heels stuck.

Rounding the copse of trees, she averted her eyes so she didn't have to look at the creepy shadows thrown off by the statuary garden. It still felt like the statues were staring, though, so she sped up her steps, risking a fall as a shiver skittered down her spine.

She climbed the wide steps, moving through the ivy-covered arch, onto the terrace. Motion-sensor lights triggered, washing the colorful Talavera tiles with a golden glow. Instead of water pouring from the central fountain, flowers poured in a carefully sculpted profusion of blooms, their color muted by the moonlight.

Glad chiffon was forgiving, Mia sank into one of the cushioned couches and blew out a long breath. Her heart jumped into her throat at the sound of footsteps on the tiles. She just wanted ten minutes alone to pull herself together instead of playing hostess.

But since she was the hostess, she got to her feet and mustered up a friendly smile. Okay, friendly-ish, she corrected when she realized she was clenching her teeth.

"Uncle Luis," she said, relief making her knees weak. She even managed a smile for his bodyguard. "What're you doing out here?"

"Following you," he said with a wink, joining her on the couch as Michelson took his position in front of the archway. "You looked like you could use a shoulder, so I brought mine with me."

"You should've stayed at the party," she murmured,

suddenly feeling even worse. "You came to get media coverage, to meet and greet and drum up support."

"I came to see you," he corrected. "To support your efforts and, yes, to garner some media attention while I'm at it."

He sighed when that last bit didn't get him a smile.

"Okay, let's talk about this mess you're in with Spence. And before you try to brush it off as nothing, remember that I have eyes. It's clear that the two of you have a relationship. Know, too, that your father called and filled me in."

"Did he?" Mia clenched her teeth against the humiliation heating her cheeks.

"My security team needed all of the details, Mia. So of course he did. But that isn't the point right now. The point is the issue between you and Spencer Lloyd," her uncle said in that chiding tone of reason he'd perfected on the senate floor. "First, clarify for me if you have feelings for the man or if it was just sex."

"Uncle Luis," Mia protested, shooting a mortified look at the bodyguard. Thankfully he didn't appear to be paying them any attention. Hands clasped behind his back, the hulking man seemed to be listening to something through his earbud as he stared at the villa's darkened windows.

"What difference does it make? He lied to me, he pretended to be something he wasn't and he used me to get close to my client." All it took was listing her top three issues to bury her heartbreak in fury. "He's a horrible, rotten, lying jerk."

"Why? Mia, he followed your father's orders. Their methods might be questionable, but they were motivated out of concern for your safety."

"Orders, orders, orders," Mia muttered. "What a good little soldier, always following orders. No, no, he's not a soldier. He's a sailor. A SEAL."

A man who put his career ahead of everyone and everything else in his life.

"Ahh, he served in the military. He's a strong man, a dedicated one who spent his career protecting our country. That he's a SEAL speaks to his determination and strength. That he tried to fulfill your father's request—a request made out of love and parental concern—speaks to his loyalty. And based on what I've seen, this is a man who despite the uncomfortable position he was put in by duty, does care deeply for you. Very deeply. How does any of that make him a bad man?"

Mia hated that she couldn't think of a reasonable argument. So she went back to basics.

"They manipulated me. My business, my emotions, my life. What's wrong with not wanting to be manipulated and pushed around?"

"Nothing. There's nothing wrong with wanting to live your own life and make your own choices. But, Mia, everyone manipulates. Everyone. Parents. Politicians. Even you."

Her back stiff with insult, Mia opened her mouth, but before she could argue, her uncle waved his hand toward the villa.

"You coordinate events focused on romancing the wealthy, on tugging heartstrings and manipulating donations. Boiled down to the very basics, your entire job is based on manipulation."

Mia started to argue, but then realized she couldn't deny those very basics.

"It's not the same," she finally murmured. "I'm raising money for good causes. My oh-so-perfect family is always interfering because they think I'm not good enough, or my job isn't big enough or that my choices aren't right enough."

"Mia, sweetheart, you're so afraid of not measuring up to this imagined standard, you're using this as an excuse to run away."

"I am not."

"But you are. You're so determined to stand on your own that you push away anyone you perceive as strong enough to be your match, and you see efforts made on your behalf as manipulation instead of simple concern." He gave her the same brow-arching stare her mother did. "Which, if this situation with Spence was just sex, is fine. But if it was more, if you cared for the man, those are sad reasons to throw away a shot at happiness."

It wasn't until he handed her his handkerchief that she realized she was crying.

"You need a drink of water," her uncle murmured, giving her shoulder another pat before looking around. "It'll just take me a moment to get it from the bar on the other patio."

Since her throat was on fire, Mia nodded. As the sound of her uncle's footsteps faded on tiles, she drew in a shaky breath, attempting to calm herself down.

"God, you're pathetic."

Mia peered through swollen eyes toward the night-drenched arch at the far end of the patio. She could barely make out a shadowed figure.

"Jessica?"

"I knew you had issues, Mia. But I had no clue just how many," Jessica said, moving through the archway and into the light. "That's a bummer, since I could have used them, too."

"What?" Mia shook her head in confusion. "I don't understand what you're talking about."

Before Jessica could explain, Uncle Luis's bodyguard left his position next to the archway. Mia cringed, embarrassment washing over her. She'd been so involved in her meltdown, she'd forgotten that he was still there.

"You'll need to go inside, ma'am," Michelson said, crossing to Jessica's side and gesturing her forward. "I'll escort you."

"No, thanks," Jessica said, all friendly good cheer as she reached into the folds of her evening dress and pulled out a gun. Still smiling, she aimed it directly at Michelson's head.

"How about you move instead?" she suggested, gesturing the man closer to the archway with her gun.

Hands raised in a gesture of peace and his eyes locked on the weapon, Michelson took two steps backward. As he did, a shadow moved in the dark.

Before Mia could yell a warning, the shadow swung a large object.

Michelson crumbled to the ground, a huge rock crashing on the tile next to him. As it shattered, Mia realized it wasn't a rock; it was the head of one of the lion statues.

"Mia?"

Mia sucked in air but before she could yell to her uncle to stay away, Jessica swung the gun barrel toward her.

"Stop right there," Jessica warned Luis when he stepped through the archway, a glass of water in hand.

"Well, this is unfortunate," her uncle said, one hand

in the air as he slowly set the glass on a table. "Ms. Alexander, is it? What seems to be the problem here? Did Mia raise your share of the rent?"

"One peep and I'll shoot," the blonde promised, including Uncle Luis in her smile.

Why hadn't she listened to Spence? As furious with herself as she was terrified, Mia wanted to shriek.

"Why?" she asked instead, the words a barely discernible whisper.

"Why what? Why that?" Jessica gestured with the gun toward the man bleeding on the ground. "I'm leaving town tonight and really wanted to tell you a few things before I went. He was trying to stop me, so I stopped him."

She glanced over her shoulder and gave a little laugh. "Or maybe I should say my lover stopped him."

"What do you want to tell me?"

"Oh, you know, just a few little things. Like how much I hate you. Little Miss Perfect, do-gooder and homecoming queen."

"This is about high school?" Mia asked, more shocked by that than the gun.

"You ruined my streak. Three years running, I won every single award, every damned prize. Then you come along—all cutesy and quiet and perky—and screwed me over." Jessica kept the rant going, accusing Mia of everything from cheating on her SATs to screwing the principal for the homecoming crown. While she bitched and whined and complained, Mia tried to sidle closer to the bushes while her uncle, one hand still in the air, checked Michelson's pulse.

"Remember when you said that you wanted to meet

my lover. Well, here he is," Jessica purred as her rant wound down. She gestured toward the arch with glee. "Roberto Alcosta, this is my dear old friend, Mia Cade, and our special guest this evening, Senator Penz. Shoot them."

Shoot them?

Oh, God.

Mia gave a silent moan as the man stepped out of the shadows, another gun at the ready and aimed directly at her uncle.

"Alcosta? You're related to Santiago?"

"Ahh, you know my uncle."

"You're crazy. You won't get away with this," Luis claimed. "This place is crawling with security."

"They're a little busy at the moment," Roberto said, his smile making Mia's skin crawl. "The security personnel, they just received the blackmail notice explaining that this lovely party would go up in flames if the good senator didn't transfer three million US dollars to a numbered account traceable to my uncle."

"He really is blackmailing Uncle Luis?"

"You are so damned gullible." Jessica's laugh was razor sharp. "How are we supposed to blackmail a man who is lily white?"

"You set your own uncle up," Uncle Luis realized, "You created a fake threat in order to distract my security team so you could get me alone?"

"You and Mia," Jessica confirmed.

"*Si*," Roberto agreed. "By the time those security fools finish dealing with *Tío* Santiago, I'll be finished, too."

Finished? Mia shivered. That sounded horribly ominous.

* * *

Spence watched Bertram instruct his team to man the exits, his expression a study of determination as he strode across the ballroom to where Alcosta held court with his crowd of rich friends.

"Is it wise to haul this guy out of his own benefit?" Spence shook his head. "The fallout is going to be a PR nightmare."

To say nothing of what it was going to do to Mia.

"Nightmare or a grandstanding platform?" Adrian muttered, shaking his head. Spence figured that's about as close as Lucas Adrian got to sneering.

While Alcosta shook off Bertram's hand, Spence watched the man's face. Shock and confusion were clear under the indignation. After a few moments of argument, he shoved his way through the avid and ever-growing crowd, Bertram hot on his heels. Since Alcosta headed for what he probably figured was a relatively private corner, there was clearly no concern about an escape attempt.

"It's not him," he murmured to Adrian. When the other man arched a brow, he shook his head. "A tidy note with an easily traced account number delivered here? Now? It just doesn't feel right."

"Not even a little right," Adrian agreed. But instead of taking charge, the man stood back and watched Spence with an eagle eye.

Fine.

Figuring the moves were his own, Spence strode across the room to get between Bertram and Alcosta. While the real-estate tycoon ranted at his back, he kept his voice low while addressing the chief of staff.

"Where's Penz?" When Bertram hesitated, he shoved

his face into the other man's and asked louder this time, "Where is Penz?"

"It'd be easier to control the narrative if he wasn't present when this went down, so I suggested he join his niece. Michelson said they're talking on the east terrace," Bertram finally said, resentment clear in his voice.

Sonuova bitch.

Shoving people out of his way, Spence ran through the terrace doors and into the dark. He flew down the path, through the night and toward the remote terrace. Halfway there, he heard voices and poured on more speed. His lungs burned as he aimed for the light. His brain registered the occupants, his mind noting two guns, both aimed at Mia. Both were on the far side of the patio, the patio between him and them.

"I think it'll bother your uncle more to watch you bleed out, so you'll go first. Time to say goodbye, señorita."

Charged with terror-fueled adrenaline, Spence dove across the patio, aiming for Mia instead of the shooter. He had to protect her.

He heard the snick of the silencer, imagined he could see the trajectory of the bullet shimmer its way across the patio. Beat the shimmer, he ordered himself. Get there first.

Save Mia.

She gasped when he hit her body. Wrapping her in the protective shield of his arms, he curled himself around her and took them both to the ground.

Through the roaring in his head, he heard a loud crash.

The senator's yell and Adrian's calm words washed over the top of someone cussing in Spanish.

Spence ignored them.

"Mia," he gasped, running frantic hands over her body, looking and feeling for the injury. Those velvet eyes were wide with shock, her breath coming in gasps. But he couldn't find an injury.

But there was blood.

There was so much blood.

She was alive.

She'd be okay.

She had to be.

Mia still in his arms, he straightened into a sitting position. He shifted to pull her into his lap, determined to hold her tightly until he was sure the scene was secure.

But as he tried to lift her, his head did a fast 360, sending fire shooting through his veins to explode in his side.

He looked down.

Damn.

All that blood was his.

Mia paled when she saw his side. She sucked in a breath as if to scream, and then her gaze met his. He watched as, with that strength he loved so much, she chained down the hysteria, blew her breath back out and pressed a gentle hand against his shoulder.

"Lie back," she murmured, gathering a few yards of her filmy skirt into a bundle. She bit her lip and then, with another deep breath, pressed the evening gown against his side.

"Harder," he murmured. Things were going to get iffy if he lost much more blood. Her lips closed so tightly, they went white, and she pressed harder. As much to distract her as because he needed to know, Spence asked, "Is the scene secured?"

"Aegis is here," Mia told him, her terrified gaze not leaving his face. "They've got it handled."

Good. Spence tried to nod, but couldn't move his head. Everything went hazy except Mia's face.

"Stay with me," she whispered, those huge eyes begging. Her breath wafted over his cheek, offering the only warmth he could feel. "Everything is going to be okay. Just stay with me."

She continued talking, murmuring encouragement and nonsense until her words all blended together. Spence stopped trying to understand them and just drew comfort.

It might have been seconds, or maybe it was years, before someone besides Mia dropped down beside him. Spence tensed, forcing his eyes open. Despite Mia's assurance, he had to make sure they were safe. Seeing the head of Aegis's calm expression, he knew he could let go.

"Get an ambulance here, fast," Adrian ordered, replacing Mia's skirt with his wadded-up jacket to stanch the flow of blood. "Hang in there, Lloyd. We've got you."

He didn't know how long he lay there, the tiles turning to ice beneath him. He was dimly aware of voices, but the only one that registered was Mia's.

"Lift," two voices said in unison.

Then the world tilted.

He bit back a scream when a hideously vicious pain ripped through him.

The ground rattled like he was being dragged over gravel.

As the sky faded in and out, stars spinning in the distance, Spence heard someone say, "The man's a freaking hero. He took that bullet for Senator Penz. Saved his life."

Spence wasn't sure if he said it or thought it, but his only response was, "Didn't do it for Penz."

Chapter 13

"Why is it taking so long? When will they let us know something?"

Something. Anything. Mia was desperate enough not to care which. In borrowed scrubs and her favorite Giuseppe Zanotti stilettos, she paced the ER's worn linoleum, her soles sticky from wading in blood.

Spence's blood.

Mia's breath shuddered, lodging like shattered glass in her chest. She clenched her fists and then stared at her open palms, remembering the feel of Spence's life pouring over them.

Because he'd saved *her* life.

He'd warned her. He'd been so sure an attack was imminent. She should have listened to him. But she'd been too busy wallowing in her own issues.

Now he was paying the price for her immaturity.

"Mia, sit," her uncle urged, watching her with concerned eyes from the waiting area. "You're going to wear yourself out."

"I can't sit." She couldn't stay still. She knew it was ridiculous, but she was sure that Spence wouldn't be okay unless she kept moving. So she continued to pace.

She knew the others were there. She was dimly aware of them talking on the phone, of texting or conversing. Words like *media frenzy*, *arrest* and *interviews* filtered through the haze but didn't slow her steps.

Every person in scrubs did, though.

But none of them stopped.

When Michelson joined them, his head bandaged and his expression sheepish, Mia offered a hug and sympathy, then went right back to her pacing.

After an hour, she was desperate to know something. Anything.

Edgy and tearfully desperate.

"Uncle Luis," she pleaded, still pacing.

Instantly understanding, he rose and, stopping only to pat Mia on the shoulder, strode to the nurse's station. A few minutes later, the surgery doors swung open. A woman so young that her scrubs looked like a Halloween costume on her stepped out, wearily lowering her mask while she spoke to the senator.

Mia wanted to run over, to hear what was going on for herself. But her legs froze. All she could do was stare, terror whispering in her ear, until her uncle returned. "They're still operating. He lost a great deal of blood, and while there is damage to several internal organs, they are relatively confident the bullet missed the spinal cord," he said, taking both of her hands in his, gripping tighter when she swayed. Looking into her eyes with his patented confidence and encouragement, he continued, "They are guardedly optimistic. He's young, strong and because of his military training, he has a powerful constitution. He was brought in quickly, and he's with an excellent surgeon."

Guardedly optimistic? Damaged organs? That was it? Mia searched her uncle's face for hints that there was more, but she could see he'd told her everything.

The weight of the night hit her with a resounding crash, sending little black dots spinning in front of her eyes and buckling her knees.

Moving fast, her uncle grabbed her around the waist before she went down.

"Sit, sweetheart." He called for cold water as he led her to the row of chairs. Cheeks on fire, eyes burning, Mia let him guide her into the seat, then curled into a ball with her arms around her legs so she could rest her face on her knees.

She couldn't stop the tears.

"Drink this so you don't dehydrate."

Not bothering to lift her head, she simply shifted it to one side. A large hand held out a bottle of water that was so chilled, she could see condensation beading the sides. It was only the rough scratchiness of her throat that motivated her to dig deep enough for the energy to straighten and take the bottle.

She studied the man next to her as she gulped down water. Like her, Lucas had arrived at the hospital splattered with blood. Apparently he'd actually found real clothes, though, since his shirt was once again a pristine white and his jeans spotless.

"He's going to be fine," Lucas said, once she'd lowered the bottle. "The wound will slow him down, but I know men like Lloyd. Nothing will stop him for long."

Mia tried a smile. It wobbled at the edges, but it was the best she could do.

"Did you serve with Spence when you were a SEAL?"

"We didn't serve together, but I know him by reputation. He's a good man. One I'd be proud to work with."

It seemed like there was some significance in those words, but before Mia could ask, the far doors were flung open with hurricane force. Orderlies and nurses scattered, getting out of the way of the man rolling into the ER.

Six-four with a burly build and a steel-gray hair, he looked like he could face down a storm and win. His creased features and overpowering personality said he made a habit of it.

In uniform or out, Admiral Theodore Cade made an impression.

"Daddy," she cried, leaping to her feet to rush so fast across the room that she almost fell into his arms.

The burly man enfolded her in her arms like a child would a teddy bear, wrapping her safe and tight. And held on so tightly that Mia lost her breath.

"You're okay," he decreed, the choked rumble in his voice telling her more than words how concerned he'd been. "I told your mother she was worrying for nothing."

Her face buried in his chest, Mia gave a choked laugh.

He was in uniform, so she knew he'd been on duty. Which meant that he must have dropped everything, called in a million favors and pulled a dozen strings, and traveled alone in order to make it here so quickly.

Yet according to him, her mother was the one who'd worried.

Suddenly, despite the fears and worries fighting for prime real estate in her brain, Mia felt better. There was no way Spence wasn't going to make it now, not with the admiral here to order him to get better.

After a long, reassuring hug, her father shifted his grip to her arms and set her back far enough to study her face. No green ensign, she'd had a lifetime facing that intense gaze, so Mia knew to keep her chin high and her own eyes steady as he peered into her soul.

Finally, satisfied that she really was okay and not about to crumble into girlie pieces, he gave a sharp nod. Then he glanced around the room. Those piercing dark eyes landed on the senator.

"Status?"

Her uncle repeated the same information he'd given Mia. Apparently just as unsatisfied with that as she'd been, her father gave her back an absent pat before turning her into Lucas's arms.

"Take care of her," he ordered before lumbering to the nurse's station. They all watched as the admiral's words got quieter and his gestures louder until three nurses scurried off. Within a minute, he was back with a full report on Spence's injuries, his condition and his recovery prognosis.

Right after that, one trembling nurse led them to a private waiting room closer to Spence.

"Impressive," Uncle Luis murmured, looking around the comfortable appointed room.

"Just goes to show you that the military gets a lot more done than politicians," the admiral barked, his tone serious but his expression friendly enough that Mia knew he was kidding. Kind of.

"Speaking of politics, I should be going." The senator

glanced at his watch, then over his shoulder at his waiting cadre of men. "I'm due at a press conference soon."

"Context?"

"After interviewing the arrested parties," Bertram began, "it's been determined that their motive was revenge. Thirty years ago, a United States Army mission led by Captain Penz resulted in the death of a human trafficker. Tonight at a charity benefit, that smuggler's son tried to kill the senator in an elaborate act of revenge against Penz. Roberto Alcosta timed his revenge this way in order to humiliate his uncle, who despite having raised him, he blames for not avenging the family's loss. Thanks to the security put in place by the event coordinator, the plot was foiled."

"What other details will you share?"

At the senator's gesture, Bertram swiped open his tablet and handed it over. Her father glanced through the notes, grunted out a couple of corrections and handed it back. Nobody was surprised to see the other man input those changes, hand it to the senator, who read it, then handed it back to the admiral for approval.

"Would you like any mention of Aegis's involvement?" Bertram asked in a subdued tone, his gaze shifting between the admiral and Lucas.

"Like the Navy, Aegis's presence was unofficial," Lucas pointed out. "If asked, we'll deny association to Alcosta International or this event."

Mia cringed a little at that last part, thinking about the potential effect of this entire debacle on her business for the first time.

While the men continued to debate which details to share with the public, she dropped into one of the chairs and pressed one hand against the nausea rolling in her belly.

It was all on her.

She wished she could blame someone else. She'd love to point a finger at Alcosta's grudge-holding nephew or her manipulative roommate, Jessica. But the boat had sailed on that option when she'd ignored Spence's warning.

Now what?

Talk about PR nightmares.

She rubbed her fingers over her forehead, trying to soothe the throbbing so she could organize her thoughts. But she didn't even know where to start getting everything that'd happened sorted enough that she could even find what was left of her business.

"You're not to blame."

Mia blinked at her father's words, looking over to see him wedge himself into the chair next to her. Even though everyone else had left, the room still felt crowded. Probably because her guilty conscience was sucking up all the air.

"Do not take responsibility for what happened, Mia," her father said again, scowling as if he could scare away any thoughts he hadn't approved. "You did nothing wrong."

"But it was my fault," she insisted, forcing herself to look her father in the eye. "Spence warned me that there was something going on with Señor Alcosta. Maybe Santiago had nothing to do with it, but that doesn't change that there was a threat against Uncle Luis and that someone was using my fund-raiser. A threat that I was warned about. But I didn't listen."

"You were used, Mia. That's never comfortable. But it doesn't put responsibility on your shoulders, either."

"Doesn't it? If I'd listened, tonight might not have happened. But I was so busy trying to prove you and Mom wrong that I refused to consider that the reasons you sent him might be right."

"Might be?" When Mia wrinkled her nose, his dark eyes warmed and he gave her hand a sympathetic pat. "I'm glad you are taking responsibility for your choices, Mia. It's a wise person who admits fault and understands their motivation."

Mia couldn't help but smile. As much as she bitched about it over the years, she did love her father's wise sayings. So often she'd hear them in her head, inspiring her to push harder, do better, be stronger. Her smile faded, because tonight was proof that she'd been none of those things.

Seeing her face fall, her father shook his head.

"Yours wasn't the only error in judgment," he said quietly. Puffing out his cheeks with consideration, he slowly blew out air and admitted, "I didn't listen, either. After his initial recon, Lloyd had reservations about the mission plan."

At Mia's questioning frown, he translated, "He didn't like deceiving you."

Mia bit her lip, remembering the look on Spence's face when she'd accused him of lying to her.

"As he'd been trained to do, rather than accepting my assessment and the intel provided, Lloyd evaluated the situation and, dissatisfied with the information we provided on Alcosta, tapped his own resources."

The admiral stopped talking when the door opened. Mia jerked her head around, but it was just Lucas bringing her father a cup of coffee. After a nod of thanks and a jerk of his head that apparently indicated the other man could stick around, her father continued his explanation.

"Lloyd convened a stronger, more comprehensive accounting than I'd been able to, with all my resources. He identified the actual threat, positioned himself not only to protect you as ordered, but to take any necessary action against the target."

As he paused, Mia realized this was the first time her father had actually discussed his work with her. She knew he wasn't revealing military secrets, but she still held her breath, not wanting to do anything to silence the moment.

"When Lloyd reported his findings, he wanted to inform you. Not only to ensure your safety, but because he strongly objected to the deception. So strongly that he was willing to throw away his incentive. I couldn't permit that, so to appease him, I called in Aegis."

"Incentive?" Mia interrupted. She knew how the rest turned out. Now she wanted to know why.

"Lloyd is being processed out of the Navy on a medical discharge. I used his lack of enthusiasm for the work available and his reluctance to waste his skills as leverage. In exchange for completing this mission, I said I'd use my influence to secure him a position with Aegis Security. That position would enable him to continue the work he'd trained for, to maintain his sense of self and to make his living in a way he'd enjoy."

In his corner, Lucas shifted as if to comment. Mia and her father ignored him.

"You blackmailed him into lying to me?" Mia summarized, her shock fighting with shame. Her callous dismissal of his warning had landed Spence in the hospital, but it turns out that her entire family had treated the man horribly. "How could you do that, Dad?"

The admiral seemed to sag in his chair and suddenly looked old. Old and frail. Mia was horrified to see her father shrink that way. But wasn't surprised at all to see him puff right back up with the next breath. That was the admiral. Always rallying.

"I'd prefer to refer to it as offering an incentive that'd mean as much to him as the job of protecting my daughter meant to me."

And that was the bottom line. Her father—her entire family—wanted the best for her. To make sure she was safe, to see her happy, to help her succeed.

Just like she'd wanted for her clients. She finagled, finessed and downright manipulated feelings, perceptions and heartstrings to solicit as much support for causes important to her clients. Sure, she always believed in the cause, but that just made her work harder. And her family believed in her.

Spence believed in her.

Uncle Luis was right.

Mia wanted to cry but she'd shed so many tears already that she was empty.

She jumped at the knock on the door, all of them turning when Uncle Luis walked through.

"The lieutenant is out of surgery. He came through better than expected and his prognosis is excellent," her uncle told her before turning his gaze to the rest of the room. "The doctor agreed to discuss the specifics of his procedure and injuries, but will only allow one person in to see the patient at this time."

"I'll speak with the doctor, then with the patient."

"No," Mia told her father. "You can talk with the surgeon. I'm sure he'll tell you more than he'd tell me. But I'm going to see Spence."

"You don't want to see him like this, Mia. More to the point, he wouldn't want you to see him in such a fragile state."

"He was on the table for quite a while and will appear very frail," the nurse agreed after a look from the admiral. "And as he's still sedated, he won't be aware of anything. If you don't mind waiting, he'll be moved to a regular room soon. Then you could stay with him as long as you like."

She didn't care.

Mia was determined to see Spence, to touch him, to assure herself that he really was okay. Nobody was going to stop her.

"I'll see him," she said again. She stood to follow the nurse, but paused to take her father's hand.

"I appreciate that you care enough to want to protect me," she told him quietly. "I honestly do. And I am almost resigned to the fact that you, and the rest of the family, will always try to do what's best for me."

"You mean interfere."

Mia laughed.

"I suppose it's all perspective. And here's mine." She paused to gather her nerve, then forced herself to continue. "It's okay to worry and to want to help. I'll even accept that you're going to help, whether I want you to or not. But you should have told me what was going on. You should have trusted me. If you had, instead of insisting on hiding it for my protection, Spence wouldn't be hurt."

Not waiting for a response, Mia gestured to the nurse

to follow and walked through the door. Forty minutes later, she was admitted to Spence's room.

"Five minutes," the nurse said before shutting the door.

It was like stepping into a spaceship. White tile and chrome gleamed. Tubes dripped and monitors beeped. One entire wall was a digital screen, flashing multicolored numbers with every heartbeat.

Despite the multitude of distractions, all Mia saw was the narrow bed in the center of the room, rails high and back lowered.

Spence.

She slowly approached the bed.

Her stomach lurched.

He looked so frail.

Chalky and gaunt and fragile.

The overhead lights reflected a russet glow in his hair, but left his skin tinged green. No hospital gown was in sight, probably because his chest was so covered with bandages that it'd be superfluous. Tubes ran to both arms, dripping comfort and life into his veins.

She pressed her fingers to her lips to keep from crying. She wasn't going to stand over him, sniveling like a baby. She was going to be grateful.

Because he was breathing. For a long, long moment, Mia stared at the rise and fall of his chest, taking comfort from the steady rhythm.

He was alive.

And suddenly her heart was sure that he would be fine.

Lucas was right. Men like Spence, they were too well trained to give in to this type of injury. Like the rest of him, his body was hardwired to follow orders. That training, those years as a SEAL, they'd save his life. Since she couldn't resent that, she had to be grateful for it.

Gently, oh so gently, she slid his hand into hers.

He didn't feel fragile.

He felt right. Strong and whole.

But as her gaze traced his features, she still held on. Then, because this might be her only chance, Mia leaned down to brush her lips over his cool cheek and whispered, "I love you."

Her eyes locked on his face, she released his hand and carefully smoothed the blankets over the bandages covering his chest. She was dimly aware of the door opening behind her, but ignored it until the nurse spoke.

"I'm sorry, Ms. Cade, but the five minutes are up." Despite her sympathetic expression, the nurse waved a determined hand to the exit. "You'll have to leave. You can visit again when he's in his room."

Mia nodded, but knew she wouldn't come back.

Not today.

Not until she'd sorted out her feelings, her beliefs and maybe even her life.

And then there was the shame to deal with.

So as much as she'd like to stay here by his hospital bed, holding his hand, and as desperate as she was to be the first face he saw when he opened his eyes, that wasn't fair to him. Too many of his choices had been manipulated or taken away from him. Whatever happened, she didn't want him to feel the same about their relationship.

"You're sure you want to do this?"

Spence looked up the flight of stairs leading to the landing outside of Mia's apartment, calculating how much pain he'd experience if she pushed him right over that railing and down the stairs.

About as much as he'd have if she told him to get the hell out of her life.

He was willing to risk both.

"I'm sure," he finally said, giving Adrian a nod. He ignored the question he could clearly see in the other man's eyes.

As grateful as he was to the guy for springing him early from that hospital prison and giving him a ride, he wasn't interested in an emotional confession.

"Then let's get it done," Adrian said, gesturing for Spence to go first.

Climbing those stairs took longer than he liked, each one a painful challenge. By the time he reached the top, he was actually glad that Adrian had insisted on escorting him to the door.

When he reached Mia's door, he had to take a minute to catch his breath and gather his thoughts. Then, prepared to battle for his future, he knocked.

It only took a few seconds for the door to open.

Mia.

He'd slept through her hospital visit, so it'd been a week since he'd seen her. It felt like forever, he realized as his eyes drank her in.

The ruffles of her flowing white shirt tucked into jeans and her feet bare but for the garnet-red toenail polish, she wore a black leather band around one wrist and earrings as big as Hula-Hoops.

Spence's barely recovered body started to hum.

She did look gorgeous.

She didn't look surprised to see him.

"Hello, gentlemen." Her greeting was for both of

them, but those dark eyes searched Spence's face as if she could read every detail of his recovery there. "What can I do for you?"

"Can we talk?"

Her lips twitching, Mia arched one brow, looking from one man to the other.

"All three of us?"

"Adrian drove me here." And had insisted on following him up the stairs in case he collapsed, but there was no point in mentioning that.

"Ahh." Studying his face again, Mia gave a slow nod and pulled the door open wider. "Please, come in."

"I'll head out," Adrian said as Spence started his slow trek across the threshold. "Give me a call when you're ready to go."

"I can take him wherever he needs to go," Mia offered as she walked Adrian to the door, surprising Spence so much that he almost missed his step.

Forcing himself to focus on keeping his balance instead of their conversation, he slowly made his way into the living room. A quick look assured him that nobody else was here, and a glance at emptiness through the open door of what had been Jessica's room assured him that she'd moved.

Or Mia had tossed all of her stuff out the door.

Grateful for the privacy, Spence gritted his teeth, steeled his muscles and slowly lowered himself onto the couch. It took him long enough that, by the time he was settled and swiping at the sweat on his forehead, he wondered what the hell Mia and Adrian were doing out there.

"Thanks, Lucas," he heard her murmur before the door closed.

"I'll get us something to drink," she said as soon as she came into the room. Not giving him a chance to say he wasn't thirsty, she swept right past him to the kitchen. Spence couldn't begrudge her taking however much time she needed before they talked.

"I see your roommate is gone," he said when she came back in. He figured he'd take his cue from her and work his way around all the externals before they got down to the point.

"Thank God." Grimacing at the empty room, Mia nodded as she set the tray if iced tea and cookies on the table. She handed him one of the glasses before taking her own seat next to him. "A moving crew showed up Tuesday to haul everything away. I doubt they were delivering it to her in jail, but I didn't ask."

"I was given some of the details," Spence said with a nod. "Jessica Alexander and Roberto Alcosta were arrested on multiple charges, not the least of which were aggravated assault and conspiracy to murder, right?"

"I think the prosecutor is trying to add a political angle in there since their target was a US senator. And even then, it won't be enough," Mia added, her eyes dark with anger. "They shot you. They could have killed you."

"Hence the aggravated assault." Seeing her expression, Spence added, "Their punishment will last a lot longer than the damage inflicted, I promise."

"Seeing as you're already out of the hospital and wandering the streets, I don't think that's nearly long enough."

"I meant damage in the bigger picture. To you, to the charity, even to Alcosta."

"Oh, he'll be too busy to worry about damage," Mia

said with a half laugh. "I guess you didn't hear that news?"

"Was he a part of the conspiracy?" Spence was surprised Adrian hadn't told him.

"Oh, no. He had no idea Jessica was even dating his nephew, let alone that they were planning to murder. Probably because he was so busy embezzling from the charity."

"Whoa."

"You said all along that he was dirty. You were right. I received a phone call during the golf tournament, one of those verification-of-funds things that concerned me enough to poke around."

"How much had he finagled?"

"Three million," she said, outraged. "Can you believe it? He was trying to steal money from sick children."

Actually, yeah. He could believe it. Alcosta was just that kind of guy.

But Spence had more important things on his mind than sleazy pseudotycoons.

"Your business? Your father mentioned that there was some concern about the impact this situation would have on everything."

"To be honest, I was concerned that it would destroy me." Before Spence could do more than wince at the guilt of that, she shrugged and went on. "But between you saving my uncle's life and me fingering Señor Alcosta for embezzlement, I'm in even bigger demand. I'm getting calls daily from people who figure I'm so smart and so well staffed that I run the best fund-raisers ever."

"And the people who donated to this one?"

"Alcosta was stopped before he could spend most of

the money, so I was able to pay the venders and bills incurred."

"And your fees?"

"I was warned about Alcosta by so many people and I ignored those warnings. That makes me responsible for giving him and his horrible nephew the opportunity they wanted." Before Spence could protest, before he could point out that she'd been a victim, too, Mia shook her head. "I didn't have to pay anything out of my own pocket, so I didn't take a loss on the job. But I don't feel right making a profit, either. Once all of the expenses were paid, I was able to negotiate an agreement for the rest of the donation to still go to the hospital fund."

"That's still going forward?"

"My uncle offered to handle the details of getting the hospital built." Her smile lit the room. "So little children are still going to get great medical help. Probably better than it would have been if Alcosta handled it, since my uncle's standards are a lot higher."

Relieved that she hadn't been hurt by it all, Spence laughed.

Returning his smile in a way that warmed his heart, Mia shrugged. "All things considered, I probably should have taken a bigger hit."

"No. You didn't do anything to deserve having your work or reputation damaged."

"Not even ignoring your warning?"

"Given the circumstances and the definite transparency issues, you can't be blamed for that, either."

"Can't I? Do you really believe that if I'd listened, you'd have been shot?"

"If I'd done the job I was assigned, do you really believe that woman would have pulled a gun on you?" he shot back, irritated that she was blaming herself for anything that'd happened.

"Apparently she'd been wanting to pull a gun on me since high school," Mia said with a horrified laugh. "Everything about her was a lie. She deliberately sought me out, pretending to need a place to live so she could use me to get to my uncle."

"She intended to kill you," he said quietly. "Penz might have been Roberto's goal, but you were her target all along."

Mia pressed her lips together, emotions swimming in those velvety eyes. Fear, regret and pain mixed, making him desperate to hold her. But he'd lost that privilege. Still, he didn't want those tears to fall, so he blurted out the first thing that came to mind.

"What about Forever Families? That Lorraine lady was pretty hot to get you working for her. So hot that her assistant was trying to sabotage you."

Mia's laugh was on the watery side, but her eyes cleared so he called it a victory.

"I had no idea so many women hated me," she said, shaking her head in dismay. "Between Jessica and Clair, I'm starting to get a complex."

"Don't. You're an amazing woman. Strong and gorgeous, ambitious and kind. Don't ever feel bad for being so fabulous that idiots get jealous."

"Thank you," she breathed with a shaky smile, laying her hand over his for a brief second.

Even that small a touch sent a thrill straight through him. This time he had to force himself not to reach out and grab her. Thankfully she distracted him by continuing her explanation.

"Lorraine did make the offer to hire me as her full-time coordinator and I seriously considered it. Less stress, less responsibility and less chance of a repeat of this last mess." Before he could protest, she shook her head. "But in the end, I couldn't do it. I love working for myself. I like being able to help a wide variety of charities, depending on what appeals to me, and to hold a lot of different types of events. After my father reminded me that I've never been the type to choose the safe route, I made Lorraine a counter offer."

Enjoying the hell out of how comfortable she looked in her own power, Spence relaxed enough to take a bite of a cookie.

"Instead of working for her full-time, I'll be her consultant. I'll plan her fund-raising strategy and design her events, but for all but the biggest ones, her own staff will handle them. That leaves me free to focus on helping more clients."

"That sounds perfect. It's a great use of your talents."

"Thanks." Mia's smile was just a little shy, confusing him a little since he knew she didn't have a shy bone in her body. She wet her lips, gave him another look from under her lashes, then, biting her lip, asked, "And you? You're going to work for Aegis Security?"

That wasn't what she'd been going to say. Still, it was a good question. And really, the core of the reason he was here.

"Maybe. I'm considering it."

Seriously considering it, since it was a dream career. But he'd had a lot of time lying in that hospital bed to consider his priorities.

"You'll do well there. From what I hear, Aegis is the best in the country. As it should be, being staffed with the best of the best in Special Ops," she said with a hint of a smile. "And Lucas is a great guy. I'm sure he'd be a really good boss."

"You know Adrian well enough to call him Lucas?" Spence had never experienced it personally before, but he was pretty sure the gnawing jab in his gut was jealousy.

"We spent a lot of time together while you were recovering from surgery."

"Is that so?" Somehow, Adrian had neglected to mention all that time together. "What'd you do in that time you spent together?"

"Actually, I spent most of that time asking him a lot of questions."

"What kind of questions?"

"Questions like what sort of jobs Aegis handles and what their security policies was. Since they're stationed in California but work all over the world, I wondered if you were working for them, if could you live in San Francisco. I was curious about things like traveling or long-term positions, and whether or not you'd ever be able to bring your significant other." She gave a delicate shrug. "That sort of thing."

All Spence heard was "significant other."

"You're going to give me a chance?"

"I'd be giving *us* a chance," she corrected. "But doing that depends."

"On what? Are you still hung up on my having been in the military?" God, he hoped not. He might be able to adjust his future to make her happy but there wasn't a damned thing he could do about his past.

"No. I finally realize that it's the man that matters, not the job." Her lips quirked in a teasing smile. "Besides, I've seen firsthand how just how handy all that training is."

"Then what? The idea of me working in a field where I might get shot at again? I'm not promising it won't happen, but I can promise that the odds are slim."

His frustration only mounted when Mia shook her head.

"Not at all. I think you'll be great with Aegis and I'd be proud if you worked there."

"Then what?"

"Us being together would only depend on one thing," she said quietly, sliding her hands into his. "I love you. And I'd do anything to know you love me back."

He knew there was relief in there somewhere, but Spence was so overwhelmed by other emotions that he barely recognized it.

"You love me?" When she nodded, he rested his forehead against hers and sighed. "I love you, too. Crazy love. Intense love. Forever love."

"Forever?"

"Yeah. Forever," he breathed against her lips. "I want to build a life with you. To embrace all of our tomorrows together."

Mia's breath trembled over his lips, a soft brush of the same excitement he could see in her eyes.

"I should warn you, my family will always interfere," she admitted. "They'll advise, they'll meddle, they'll pry."

"Their interference brought us together," he reminded her. "For that, I'll always be grateful."

He slid his mouth over hers in a soft promise before meeting her gaze again.

"I do love you," she breathed.

"Forever," he vowed. Just before he took her mouth in a deeper kiss, he challenged, "Let's get started."

* * * * *

Don't miss Navy SEAL to the Rescue,
the thrilling first volume in
the Aegis Security miniseries from
New York Times *bestselling author*
Tawny Weber, available now!

COMING NEXT MONTH FROM

HARLEQUIN®

ROMANTIC suspense

Available July 2, 2019

#2047 COLTON'S MISTAKEN IDENTITY
The Coltons of Roaring Springs • by Geri Krotow

Posing as her twin is easy for Phoebe Colton until she meets sexy Prescott Reynolds, whose dangerous action roles in films become too realistic when a stalker comes after Phoebe and forces them onto a dangerous cross-country road trip.

#2048 COLTON 911: COWBOY'S RESCUE
Colton 911 • by Marie Ferrarella

A sudden hurricane shakes up more than just the buildings in and around Whisperwood, Texas. A long-awaited wedding is put on hold, and as Jonah Colton rescues Maggie Reeves, the bad girl who's home to make amends, a devastating flood reveals a body—and a serial killer is on the loose!

#2049 SPECIAL FORCES: THE OPERATOR
Mission Medusa • by Cindy Dees

She's an American Special Forces soldier; he's an Israeli commando. On a covert mission in Australia, they have two weeks to stop a terror attack at the Olympics...and fall in love. Let the games begin!

#2050 RANCHER'S HOSTAGE RESCUE
The McCall Adventure Ranch • by Beth Cornelison

When Dave Giblan and Lilly Shaw are held hostage by an armed man, they must overcome personal heartaches and grudges to survive the ordeal...and claim the healing of true love.

HRSCNM0619

Get 4 FREE REWARDS!

We'll send you 2 FREE Books plus 2 FREE Mystery Gifts.

Harlequin® Romantic Suspense books feature heart-racing sensuality and the promise of a sweeping romance set against the backdrop of suspense.

FREE
Value Over
$20

Rebel asked more seriously, "How should a woman be treated, then?"

Avi smiled broadly. Now they were getting somewhere. "It would be my pleasure to show you."

She leaned back, staring openly at him. He was tempted to dare her to take him up on it. After all, no Special Forces operator he'd ever known could turn down a dare. But he was probably better served by backing off and letting her make the next move. Not to mention she deserved the decency on his part.

Waiting out her response was harder than he'd expected it to be. He wanted her to take him up on the offer more than he'd realized.

"What would showing me entail?" she finally asked.

He shrugged. "It would entail whatever you're comfortable with. Decent men don't force women to do anything they don't want to do or are uncomfortable with."

"Hmm."

Suppressing a smile at her hedging, he said quietly, "They do, however, insist on yes or no answers to questions of whether they should proceed. Consent must always be clearly given."

He waited her out while the SUV carrying Piper and Zane pulled up at the gate to the Olympic Village.

Gunnar delivered them to the back door of the building, and Avi watched the pair ride an elevator to their floor, walk down the hall and enter their room.

"Here comes Major Torsten now. He's going to spell me watching the cameras tonight."

"Excellent," Avi purred.

Alarm blossomed in Rebel's oh-so-expressive eyes. He liked making her a little nervous. If he didn't miss his guess, boredom would kill her interest in a man faster than just about anything else.

Avi moved his chair back to its position under the window. The hall door opened and he turned quickly. "Hey, Gun."

"Avi." A nod. "How's it going, Rebel?"

"All quiet on the western front."

"Great. You go get some sleep."

"Yes, sir," she said crisply.

"I'll walk you out," Avi said casually.

He followed Rebel into the hallway and closed the door behind her. They walked to the elevator in silence. Rebel was obviously as vividly aware as he was of the cameras Gunnar would be using to watch them.

"Walk with me?" he breathed without moving his lips as they reached the lobby. Gunnar no doubt read lips.

"Sure," Rebel uttered back, playing ventriloquist herself, and without so much as glancing in his direction.

It was a crisp Australian winter night under bright stars. The temperature was cool and bracing, perfect for a brisk walk. He matched his stride to Rebel's, relieved he didn't have to hold it back too much.

"So what's your answer, Rebel? Shall I show you how real men treat women? Yes or no?"

Don't miss
Special Forces: The Operator *by Cindy Dees,*
available July 2019 wherever
Harlequin® Romantic Suspense books
and ebooks are sold.

www.Harlequin.com